REMIND ME TO HATE YOU LATER

# REMIND ME TO HATE YOU LATER

## LIZZY MASON

BLOOMSBURY

NEW YORK  LONDON  OXFORD  NEW DELHI  SYDNEY

BLOOMSBURY YA
Bloomsbury Publishing Inc., part of Bloomsbury Publishing Plc
1385 Broadway, New York, NY 10018

BLOOMSBURY and the Diana logo are trademarks of Bloomsbury Publishing Plc

First published in the United States of America in February 2023 by Bloomsbury YA

Bloomsbury books may be purchased for business or promotional use.
For information on bulk purchases please contact Macmillan Corporate and
Premium Sales Department at specialmarkets@macmillan.com

Library of Congress Cataloging-in-Publication Data
Names: Mason, Lizzy, author.
Title: Remind me to hate you later / by Lizzy Mason.
Description: New York: Bloomsbury Children's Books, 2023.
Summary: Told in alternating timelines, as Natalie grieves her best friend Jules's death
by suicide, Jules's influencer mother plans to release a book about it, which causes
Natalie and Jules's boyfriend to band together and expose the truth behind Jules's tragic death.
Identifiers: LCCN 2022037479 (print) | LCCN 2022037480 (e-book)
ISBN 978-1-5476-0918-5 (hardcover) • ISBN 978-1-5476-1071-6 (e-book)
Subjects: CYAC: Grief—Fiction. | Social media—Fiction. | Suicide—Fiction. |
Friendship—Fiction. | LCGFT: Novels.
Classification: LCC PZ7.1.M37614 Re 2023 (print) |
LCC PZ7.1.M37614 (e-book) | DDC [Fic]—dc23
LC record available at https://lccn.loc.gov/2022037479

Book design by Jeanette Levy
Typeset by Westchester Publishing Services
Printed and bound in the U.S.A.
2  4  6  8  10  9  7  5  3  1

To find out more about our authors and books visit
www.bloomsbury.com and sign up for our newsletters.

*For Karl, my puppy.*
*We didn't get enough chapters,*
*but I will always love our story.*

Please note that this book contains depictions of depression, body shame, self-harm, suicide, grief, anxiety, cancer, death of a parent, and parental emotional abuse. If these topics will be particularly upsetting to you, please read with care.

REMIND ME TO HATE YOU LATER

# PART ONE

## JULES

# CHAPTER

## 1

There's no sound more recognizable than bacon sizzling in a pan. That staticky crackle. The pop and hiss. It's a delicious symphony.

There's a loud crack and I'm suddenly dodging flying molten droplets of oil.

"I don't think I've ever seen you move that fast, Jules," Natalie says, laughing.

I point my tongs at her while I creep closer to the stove to turn the heat down. "That sounds like someone who doesn't want her spaghetti carbonara," I say.

I glance over my shoulder at Carter. He's laughing too.

"You want pasta?" I ask him, wielding the tongs again. He nods. "Then stop laughing."

His smile slips for a second, but then he wraps his arms around my waist.

"I would," he says, pulling back to look at me, "but you love feeding us too much to follow through on that threat."

I refuse to back down, even if he's right. I twist in his grip, but he doesn't let go.

"Why are you so strong?" I say as I slap my free hand against his forearms. But my smile gives me away.

Carter blows a raspberry against my neck. "That's just one of the things you love about me," he says.

I freeze. We haven't said the L-word yet. But he's right. I do love him. I just don't want to say it for the first time with Nat here.

I glance up at her. She's looking at her phone, trying to ignore us. I don't want to make it awkward, so I kiss Carter quickly, and this time he loosens his grip so I can step away. Then I turn my back on them both and give the bacon a stir. The pasta water is boiling now, so I slowly lower in the spaghetti that Nat and I spent the afternoon making. There's still flour in her dark hair.

Nat's dad sticks his head through the kitchen door while I'm stirring. "You almost done? The smell of bacon is wafting down the hallway and I'm drooling so much, I almost shorted out my keyboard."

"Ten minutes," I say. "Have you met Carter?"

Carter puts his hand out for Nick to shake. "Nice to meet you, Mr. Nagler," he says.

Carter hasn't even met my parents yet, but it's way less intimidating to meet Nat's dad. Partly because unlike my mom, Nick doesn't write a monthly parenting column in one of the largest newspapers in the country detailing my biggest flaws and struggles. He doesn't have a blog that's essentially a diary of my entire childhood and that tells the world about how difficult I was to raise. And he doesn't have an Instagram account with half a million followers where he shares every intimate detail of his life with people who dissect and comment on every post.

At least my mom doesn't post pictures of me anymore, but it took a scandal to make that happen.

———————————

Once the pasta is ready, Nat's sister, Cordelia, and her dad join us at the kitchen table to eat. It is their house, after all—I just cook here. That's sort of our deal. We all get something out of it: the Nagler family gets a meal and I get to cook without my mom telling me how carbohydrates are like glue and that's why I haven't lost any weight. She doesn't seem to understand that I haven't actually tried to lose weight; I've only tried to eat more carbohydrates.

"Jules, this is incredible," Carter says after his first bite. The rest of the table agrees. And I can't argue. Spaghetti carbonara is hard to beat. But I just shrug and duck my head to stick another forkful in my mouth.

"Don't expect her to say 'thanks' to a compliment," Nat says. "But if you want to criticize her, she'll get out her phone and take notes."

I don't like the way Carter keeps laughing with Nat at my expense. I poke him in the ribs.

"Don't you dare," I say.

He squeezes my knee under the table. "What could I possibly criticize?" he says.

My cheeks get hot as I glance across the table at Nat. Her smile is forced. I know her well enough to recognize it.

"Wait until you try her chicken Provençal," Nick says, doing a chef's kiss.

"What's that?" Carter asks.

"It's this incredible dish with olives and tomatoes and white wine," Nick answers. "And Jules makes the best version I've ever tasted."

Nick and I share a love of olives, and really all things salty. He's my most appreciative audience. Which is good since I'm usually making a mess in his kitchen.

"I'm not a big fan of olives," Carter says.

There is a beat of uncomfortable silence as the Naglers exchange worried glances.

"Guys, it's okay if he doesn't like olives," I say. And I mean it. I think our relationship will survive.

Nick gives me a gentle smile and says, "Of course it is."

Carter looks more curious than nervous, but I pat his arm reassuringly. "I can forgive this one flaw."

He smiles and the dimple in his cheek makes me melt a little.

"So how did you guys meet?" Cordie asks me and Carter, changing the subject.

He and I look at each other, and I don't say anything. I want him to tell the story because I've never heard it from his point of view.

He clears his throat, then says, "We have Spanish together."

I raise my eyebrows when he doesn't elaborate. "That's it?"

Nat's smile is real this time, but she rolls her eyes in sympathy.

"What?" Carter says. He seems genuinely mystified.

The first time I saw Carter, I didn't notice his muscles or the soccer ball stuffed into his bag. I saw his hazel eyes behind his glasses, and the adorable curl to his dark blond hair, and the dimple in his cheek when he smiled at me. And then he stood and I saw that he was taller than me. I basically swooned.

But I can't tell him that.

"You're such a boy," I say with a sigh. Then I turn to Cordie. "Carter and his family moved here over the summer, so Spanish class was the first time we ever saw each other. He didn't talk to me for like a month, and then it was only because Señora paired us up to do a conversation exercise."

Carter gives me a smile that makes my stomach flip. "Yeah, but I'd been waiting for that opportunity to talk to you. And you didn't talk to me either."

That's because there are like five other girls in that class who are ten times prettier and skinnier than me who had no problem talking to him. I didn't think I could compete. I didn't think he'd be interested in me. But I don't say that either.

"Well, I won him over with my knowledge of Spanish curse words," I say, brushing imaginary dust off my shoulder.

Carter snorts. "You did not! You said you'd write out our conversation, and when I read my response, Señora almost had a heart attack."

Nat, Nick, and Cordie burst out laughing. I can't help joining in when Carter's cheeks flush and his ears turn red.

"Jules! What did you make him say?" Cordie asks.

"Well, I asked him, 'What do you like to eat for dinner?'" I pause for effect. "And he said, 'Shit sandwiches and penis salad.'"

Everyone starts laughing, including Carter. He wasn't even mad back then, even though he got detention for it. I waited for him in the hall until detention was over and, after he threatened to give me a shit sandwich, he asked if I'd ever seen *Office Space*. When I said I hadn't, he asked me to come over and watch it with him that weekend.

We've been together ever since.

---

After dinner, Cordie retreats to her room and Nick goes to watch TV in the living room, so Carter, Nat, and I take over the kitchen again. Carter volunteers to do the dishes. For some reason, the dishwasher is across the room instead of next to the sink, so he and Nat work together to pass the dishes across the kitchen. He rinses, she loads. Because I cooked, I get to just sit and watch.

"So how did you and Nat meet?" he asks me. His dark-framed glasses are sliding down his nose. He pushes them up with a muscular forearm.

Nat raises her eyebrows. "Have you really not heard this story yet?"

I shake my head. "Carter doesn't know about my past as a field hockey player."

The plate in Carter's hand slips into the sink with a crash that sets my teeth on edge. He checks to make sure nothing is broken before he turns to look at me.

"You played field hockey?" he says. His eyes are wide with surprise. "But you hate anything that even resembles a sport!"

I can't blame him for being shocked. It's even hard for me to believe.

So I nod. "It was a dark time."

"But it resulted in meeting me, so it had its benefits," Nat says.

I roll my eyes. She's actually good at field hockey. Good enough to make varsity as a sophomore last year.

Carter turns his gaze back to the water, but I can tell he's listening. He just knows that I'm better at talking when I don't have to look anyone in the eye.

"So when I was twelve, the summer before eighth grade, my mom decided I needed to take up a sport so that I might get good enough to play in high school," I explain.

I give Carter credit for keeping a straight face. Because the idea of me being even average at a sport is laughable.

"It was mostly an attempt to get me to exercise, but no matter how hard I pushed back, she wouldn't give it up." I sigh. The sting of her total inability to understand who I am still feels fresh. "I finally agreed to go to field hockey camp if she would also let me take some pastry-making classes."

Nat cackles. "That's still my favorite part of this story."

"Maybe she thought that once I fell in love with field hockey, I'd lose interest in cooking and baking?" I shrug. My mom is always wildly optimistic when it comes to her dream of turning me into a completely different person. It might be cute if it didn't make me question the necessity of my existence. "Either way, I learned how to make an incredible sfogliatella. And éclairs, and tarts, and so many other things."

That was a good summer. At first.

Nat clears her throat. "You're getting off track. You were telling Carter how we met."

Oh, right.

"I chose field hockey camp," I continue, "mostly because I felt better about my chances if I was hitting a ball with a stick rather than trying to throw it or kick it." I slump a little in my seat. "I should have realized that I would also be running and that's not really my strength."

"You also had no idea how to actually play field hockey though," Nat points out.

I grimace. "Yeah, that's true."

"Which is where I come in," Nat says.

"So I get to camp on the first day, and there are a few girls from my class there, but there are also a bunch of people I don't know. And I'm excited because I'm think-ing, 'Hey! Maybe not everyone here knows me and my whole life story!'"

I feel Carter's gaze on my face, but I don't look at him.

"And they didn't," Nat says. "At least not at first."

My jaw aches when I clench my teeth together. I wake up to that ache every morning.

"But as I was checking in, I said my name to the woman at the registration desk, and when she looked up at me, I knew instantly that she was a fan. Then she realized my mom was standing there with me and she literally screamed."

"Everyone turned to look," Nat says. "And then a whole line formed so that Britt could take selfies with all the other moms. Jules looked like she wanted to disappear. So I pulled her out a side door and down the stairs to the teachers' lounge where the snack machines were."

"She bought me Reese's Pieces, which instantly won my heart," I add. "And then she taught me the rules of field hockey so I wouldn't feel so lost. But she didn't ask about my mom once."

Nat just smiles as she dries her hands on a dish towel, then sits on the stool next to me at the counter.

"I didn't have to. I knew who Jules was," Nat says with a sympathetic glance in my direction. "And everyone else was going to learn soon anyway. She was one of the most well-known kids on Instagram."

I try to look smug instead of annoyed. "Not every kid gets the new American Girl doll the day it comes out."

Nat snorts. "At the cost of merely exploiting every moment of your life."

"A tiny price to pay for global fame, right?" I say. We've clearly had this conversation a few times.

Carter knows about the issues I have with my mom. He knows about my mom's Instagram notoriety, of course, and about the blog and the parenting column, both of which she still writes. But he doesn't know much of the background. When we first started dating, I asked him not to Google me, and so far, he says he's been true to his word that he wouldn't.

"Do you know why Britt doesn't post pictures of Jules anymore?" Nat says.

Carter shakes his head.

She glances at me to see if I want to tell this story, but we both know that I don't. I nod at her so she knows she can tell it.

"Well, it was that same summer, but it was after camp, and Britt was invited to a five-star resort outside of Austin," Nat begins. "She decided to make a family vacation out of it, but mostly spent the week posting photos and videos."

I haven't looked at the pictures in years, but I remember them. Among all the selfies Mom posted was a photo of me next to a campfire with a cotton candy sunset behind me. There was also one of her, me, and Dad riding horseback. The photo she took of me with my forehead pressed against a horse's nose ran alongside Mom's review of the resort in *Texan Traveler* magazine.

"And then she posted one of Jules in her bathing suit," Nat says ominously.

"You don't know this about me," I say, "but I used to love to swim."

"Used to?" Carter asks.

"Well, once your mom has shown the world a picture that outlines every single part of your body, it's hard to ever want to get into a bathing suit again."

Carter's eyes have widened. His eyebrows are raised above the frames of his glasses.

"She was jumping into the resort pool," Natalie explains. "You know the jackknife pose, where you have one leg tucked against your chest and the other pointed toward the water?"

Carter nods.

"I grew a couple inches that summer," I say, defending myself. "And I didn't know my bathing suit was that tight." It was a one-piece, but it lost a lot of modesty once I was in that pose.

I guess Mom didn't notice how much was actually visible in the photo. At least, I hope she hadn't noticed how much was visible.

But it took, like, ten seconds for someone else to point it out.

She removed the picture almost immediately, but the damage had already been done.

After we finish the dishes, Carter asks me to walk him to his car to say goodnight even though it's below freezing.

"So field hockey, eh?" he says. He brings our entwined fingers to his lips and kisses my hand. "I bet you looked cute in that little uniform skirt."

I laugh, but there's a sharp stab in my gut at the memory. "They didn't even have one in my size at the camp, so I just wore shorts. Everyone else looked cute though."

A crease appears between Carter's eyebrows. "I don't get it. How could they not have your size?"

And he means it. Because he's probably never had this happen in his life. He's probably never walked into a store and been afraid to even look at the clothes because of the fear of disappointment when nothing fit. He's probably never had to order something online instead of buying it in the store because he needed an "extended size." Carter isn't skinny, but no one would ever call him fat.

My own mother calls me fat.

"Let's not talk about it," I say.

"That's fine, because there was something else I wanted to tell you," he says.

I look up at him. I love that I can do that. "What?"

"I love you," he says. He twists our entwined hands behind his back, drawing me closer.

I think I might be floating as I say, "I love you too."

He kisses me, and I'm definitely hovering slightly in my sneakers.

When my teeth start to chatter, he kisses me one last

time and gives me a gentle push toward the front door. "Get inside before you freeze," he says.

I draw in close to him for another last kiss before hustling back into the warmth.

I could really get used to this feeling.

———————————➤

I close Nat's bedroom door behind me and lean against it with a smile. Nat rolls her eyes.

"I'm sorry," I say immediately. "I know we're gross."

She purses her lips. "Don't get me wrong, I love that you found Carter," she says. "But I think maybe you guys should hang out without me?"

Nat isn't making eye contact, so I know she's not joking. Natalie doesn't talk about feelings. The whole Nagler family avoids emotions, in fact. Maybe it has something to do with the fact that her mom died when she was five.

Although, terrible as this sounds, I can't help being a little jealous of her sometimes. The Naglers are such a tight family unit. They eat dinner together every night. They play board games on rainy days. They poke fun at each other, but they also hug regularly. They may not discuss their feelings, but there's no mistaking that they love each other.

But I have practice in hiding my feelings too. So I don't let on that it hurts that she doesn't want to hang out with me and Carter.

I sit at the foot of Nat's single bed while she unwinds her dark, wavy hair from its messy bun and starts brushing it. I motion for her to sit in front of me on the floor so I can braid it for her.

She tucks her legs under her and I have to stifle my jealousy that there's no cellulite on her thighs. No one would ever say anything mean about a picture of Natalie in a bathing suit.

I don't have any social media profiles, but Nat does and the only comments she gets on her photos and videos are full of praise about how pretty and athletic she looks. Must be nice.

"What if I give each of you one weekend night? Like, you get Fridays and he gets Saturdays?" I say. "Or we can alternate the nights."

I can't see her face, but I do see her shrug.

"Yeah, that's probably a good idea," she says. "And that'll give me a night to work on my podcast every weekend."

I have to stop myself from saying something I'll regret as I wrap a rubber band around the end of her braid.

Nat is super into true crime stories, and she has this dream of starting a podcast about cold cases and I just don't see the appeal. Who would want to listen to a depressing story that has no ending?

"Yeah," I say, trying to sound enthusiastic. Trying to sound like my feelings aren't hurt that she'd rather do research about unsolved murders than hang out with me. "That sounds like a good plan."

Apparently I fail in my attempt, because I can feel the tension in the air. But the tension isn't just about Carter.

"Do you want to hear about the episode I'm researching?" Nat asks as she sits on the bed next to me.

I feel her scrutiny even though I'm not looking at her. She knows how I feel about true crime, but she's watched hundreds of hours of food TV with me. And also listened to hours of me talking about food. The least I can do is listen to her talk about her passion. Even if it is super creepy.

"Yeah, sure," I say. "What's the case this time?"

She doesn't say anything for a few seconds. She just watches my face.

"Never mind," she says finally. "It won't interest you."

Nat and I don't fight often, despite how different we are. But this feels like it's been brewing for a while.

I try to hold in my sigh. "Look, I'm sorry that I don't want to hear about women being raped and murdered, or little kids being snatched out of their beds, or whatever. Especially when they haven't even found the person who did it. It's just going to give me nightmares."

She purses her lips, her eyes narrowed. "Better just to live in ignorance instead? You want to just pretend that bad things don't happen to innocent people?"

"Don't do that," I say. "You know that's not what I'm saying."

"True crime podcasts have helped solve cold cases," she says. "Did you know that?"

I did not. "But for the families in the cases that don't get solved, it's just salt in the wound," I say. "Their loved one's

17

murder becomes entertainment for bored hipsters on their commute to work."

Nat scoffs. "Your disdain for the human race is exhausting sometimes."

I don't know how to respond to that. I do hate people a lot of the time; she's not wrong. I have good reason to. People have been making judgments about me literally my whole life. And most of them aren't kind.

"Can you really blame me?" I say.

I watch Nat's expression soften and the boulder in my gut starts to dissolve.

"No," she says. "I just . . . I really wish your mom hadn't done such a thorough job at screwing you up." And then she looks at me with a hint of a smile on her lips.

I can't help smiling back. "You're telling me," I say.

I plug in the pump for the air mattress and start blowing up the bed that will soon take up the entirety of Nat's bedroom floor. The noise gives us a couple of minutes to let our anger dissipate, and by the time the mattress is blown up, the tension between us seems to have lifted.

We wash our faces and brush our teeth and climb into our respective beds. I put in my earbuds and open Netflix, picking a show to watch until I fall asleep. It usually takes about an hour. Nat is asleep before I've even pressed play.

I write a text message for Carter to read when he wakes up tomorrow morning.

*Did you know that in Switzerland, it's illegal to have fewer than two guinea pigs? Being social is so important to their happiness, there's actually a law about it.*

*I may not like most people, but I do like you. Kind of a lot. So thanks for coming to hang out tonight. Your presence was as welcome as a second guinea pig.*

I'm pretty sure he'll think that's cute and not creepy.

# CHAPTER

# 2

My mom loves to give me books that we can read together, as if we're in a mother-daughter book club. Unlike her followers, I don't think it's adorable. Because it's always a self-help book about how to make myself a better person through the use of crystals, or how to lose weight by being an active citizen in the community, or whatever her belief system is that month.

Like everything else Mom does, it's for show. It's so she can do a sponsored post, using me as her prop to show how involved she is as a mother. Her followers eat that stuff up with the yarn-wrapped spoons she claimed we made together the summer I was nine. She actually bought them at a flea market.

Her "New Year, New You" pick is *Living Vicariously: Why Online Culture Is Important for Healthy Self-Understanding.*

I don't need to read it to know it's complete crap.

So I'm hiding from Mom.

Problem is, everything in our house is white or beige—I saw it described as "dust bowl" colors in a *Vanity Fair* article about Mom once—and I am not. I mean, my skin is beige, but my clothes are almost always black, gray, or blue. Mom says I look like a bruise.

I feel like a bruise.

"Jules?" Mom calls up the stairs. I pause the episode of *Chopped* I have on.

When I don't respond, I hear her start climbing. I'm tempted to meet her halfway, not because it's the nice thing to do, but so she doesn't come into my room. I don't need her to tell me that "a messy room means a messy mind." Or "clutter makes the mind stutter." Or any of her other fake mantras.

I slide to the floor and roll under the bed just before she opens the door without knocking.

"Jules?" Mom says, sounding confused.

My car is in the driveway, the bathroom door is open, my phone is charging on the dresser. There's nowhere else I could be.

She sighs, but she doesn't bother searching for me. I watch her Tory Burch flats cross the room from under my dust ruffle. Her feet are tiny. If mine were as small as hers, I'd fall down all the time.

Mom sets the book on the floor and kicks it toward me with her heel.

"Please read this one?" she asks. "I think you'll actually like it. The publisher sent it with both of us in mind."

I close my eyes and plug my ears with my fingers and start humming random off-key notes.

After a minute, I unplug one ear to see if it's safe. Silence. And when I open my eyes, there are no tiny feet dangling over the edge.

I roll out from under the bed and find Mom sitting cross-legged, looking down at me. Her long, blond beachy waves are swept over one shoulder. A slim, tan shoulder. She's wearing a sleeveless jumpsuit that might fit one of my legs if I ripped out the seams and sewed them together.

"Are you ready to act your age?" she asks.

I roll back into the dark. "No."

Mom waits a minute before she stands and walks out of the room without another word.

---

Cordie drops Natalie off at eight-thirty on the dot that night. It's just enough time to say "hello" to Mom before she takes her nightly Ambien and drifts off in her California King. She's still frosty about the book thing, but she loves Nat. It doesn't matter that she's been ignoring me for most of the day, since I was avoiding her too, but I can't help the surge of jealousy when Mom embraces Nat. She always seems more excited to see her than she does me.

"I left a bunch of stuff downstairs for you, and for your dad and Cordie," Mom says. She looks at Nat, taking in her messy topknot of dark, wavy hair. "You should try out that conditioner on your hair. Your waves are so pretty, you just need a little more volume."

My jealousy fades, shifting to annoyance. "And good-night," I say.

I pull Nat out of the room and down the hall. We should have stayed at Nat's house tonight, but I slept there last night and Mom doesn't want me to "overstay my welcome" with the Naglers.

"Ignore her," I say. "Your hair is perfect."

Mom has given up on me at this point, letting my blond hair remain in the straight, boring ponytail it always is in. But she can't help trying to make everyone else "their better self."

She leaves us alone for the night, at least. And with the sleeping pill, she won't wake up unless an actual squad of firemen are carrying her out of the house while it burns down around them.

So with Dad away piloting a commercial flight from Dulles to Tel Aviv, the house is ours.

I take Nat's hand and lead her into the kitchen. "You are in for a treat tonight, my friend," I say.

Nat's blue eyes sparkle as I start pulling products out of the bags on the floor. Free things that companies have sent hoping Mom will post about them but that she has deemed unworthy. She uses them for giveaways on her Instagram or gives them to her friends, usually.

But she'd be thrilled to know that I'm even interested in looking at this stuff. Even though I pretend not to care, I actually love all the beauty products she gets. I just don't want her to get any satisfaction out of my enjoyment of the perks of her "job."

Nat sets aside a couple of sheet masks, some moisturizer, the conditioner Mom mentioned, and two sets of nail wraps. It barely makes a dent in the collection of products.

"There's also a bag in the hallway for you to take home. Mom mentioned you in a blog post last week, about how we met, and a few days later, a bunch of stuff showed up from a few different sports-type places."

She laughs. "Sports-type places, sure."

I laugh too. "You know what I mean. You're now the proud owner of several water bottles with logos of companies I've never heard of; some deodorant wipes made just for teens, whatever that means; a microfiber towel; and a whole assortment of energy bars in flavors that it's impossible they actually taste like."

Natalie's dark eyebrows tilt together. "Should we just put all of it in the giveaway pile?"

I nod. "I think you and your family have enough water bottles."

Mom posted a photo of me and Nat from field hockey camp once four years ago, and we were wading through boxes of sports gear and water bottles for months afterward.

We put the rest of the samples back in the bags, and I start pulling out the groceries I hid in the back of the fridge behind Mom's oat milk and a container of bell peppers. Tonight, we're having pasta Bolognese, garlic bread, and brownie sundaes for dessert. I originally wanted to make the noodles for the Bolognese by hand, but I realized we wouldn't be eating until midnight if I did that. But everything else, except the bread, I'm making from scratch.

While I cook, Nat actually does condition her hair and then comes back downstairs in her pajamas with her hair wrapped in a towel.

"So did you listen to my latest episode of the podcast?" she asks.

I wince. I haven't. And if I'm being honest, I'm not going to. Even though it's her podcast—a voice I love—I just can't make myself listen.

"Not yet," I tell her. "But I will, promise."

I can tell she doesn't believe me, but she lets it go. "What's Carter doing this weekend?" she asks instead.

My plan of splitting my weekend nights between them has been working, unless we go to the movies or a party or something all together, but this weekend, Nat has gotten me both nights.

"He's with Harry visiting one of the colleges that are interested in them," I say. "Apparently the coaches start recruiting pretty early and he lost some momentum when he moved here."

Nat looks annoyed. "No one's invited me to visit any schools for field hockey."

My stomach clenches. I don't like the idea of either of them going away for school. But I also can't help but wonder if Carter is enjoying this break from me. I wouldn't blame him.

My fingers itch to reach for my phone. To text Carter. It's times like these that I wish he actually used his social media accounts so I could see what he was doing. But he's never given me any reason to doubt him. In our relationship, the only person I lose faith in is me.

But before I can even start to panic, Carter sends a text.

*Hope you and Nat are having more fun than I am. Harry snores.* And then there's a picture of his friend Harry sprawled on his back on a twin bed, his mouth open.

I send him a picture of the Bolognese sauce simmering. He texts back the drooling emoji.

While Nat does her nails, I preheat the oven for the peanut butter and pretzel brownies and combine the ingredients, humming to myself.

When I look up, Nat is watching me.

"What?" I ask, wiping at my chin in case there's chocolate or flour or something there.

But she shakes her head. "Nothing. I just like to see you without RSF."

"RSF?" I have no idea what she's talking about.

"Resting Sad Face," she says, as though this should have been obvious. "You've had it as long as I've known you."

A laugh bursts out of me. "That might be the most accurate description of myself I've ever heard." But it doesn't take long for the laughter to fade. "I'm surprised no one's ever said it before. Or that Mom didn't use it as a hashtag."

I can feel Nat seething. She hates my mom's public persona almost as much as I do. And I love her for it.

"I'll never share it with her," she promises. "That one's just for us."

The timer buzzes. It's time for pasta and face masks.

That night, as Nat and I lie in my bed watching *Somebody Feed Phil*, I roll over on my side to face her.

"Does your face feel moisturized?" I ask her.

She shrugs. "I don't know. It didn't feel all that dry to begin with, so I don't know if there's much difference."

I touch my forehead. "The package said I'd feel restored. But I just feel kind of slimy."

Nat laughs. "I think restoration is gonna take more than just a sheet mask," she says.

"Yeah," I say with a sigh. "Do they make sheet masks for your soul?"

I feel her shaking her head. "I think that's called therapy."

My silence tells her how I feel about that. I've been in therapy for years, but I don't feel restored.

"But your nails look great," she adds.

I hold my hand up to admire it in the glow from the TV. Nat does the same. Then she wraps her fingers around mine and doesn't let go until she falls asleep.

## My Daughter Won't Talk to Me, and Other Complaints

Today, Jules hid under the bed so she wouldn't have to talk to me. My sixteen-year-old daughter hid.

Somehow, I thought we'd be past this kind of behavior by now.

When Jules was a toddler, if I left her alone for more than a few seconds, I'd come back into the room and find her gone. You can imagine my panic the first few times it happened. But it never took long to find her because she'd be humming, under a table or behind a chair, with her fingers stuffed into her ears and her eyes squeezed shut.

By the time she was ten, she had to sleep with the TV on. She walks around the house with earbuds in. She takes showers with music or a podcast blasting. There is always something streaming on the laptop in her bedroom.

Jules is incapable of being alone inside her mind. She has darker circles under her eyes than I had when she went through that sleep regression when she was two. (Link: "I Want to Throw My Two-Year-Old Off a Bridge")

And she refuses to tell me what's going on in her mind. Because I'm her mother, she acts as if I'm the problem.

It's hard not to take that personally.

Do your teenage children sleep all day and haunt the house all night? Do your adolescents ignore you, or even hide from you? Please tell me in the comments that I'm not alone.

—*Britt*

# CHAPTER
## 3

*Iron Chef* is on, but my eyes won't focus on the TV. I'm too busy seething with rage at my mom.

I pick up my phone and text Carter even though I know he's at the gym. *When will you be here?*

I could just leave. I could drive around the city aimlessly, or head for Nat's house, or go to the movies. But all I want is to be with Carter. He's the only distraction from my misery that actually works. And his love for me makes me hate myself just one fraction less. Sometimes that fraction is all it takes to keep me from breaking into pieces.

I see him writing back almost immediately. *Not for a while*, he says. *I'm just about to shower now. Why? You ok?*

The boulder in my gut is back. I hate that he has to ask that. That he knows I'm not okay without me saying anything.

I text him a pineapple emoji.

Pineapple is our code word. It means "I'm not okay, but

I will be." Carter picked it because he says I remind him of the spiky fruit. Prickly on the outside, sweet on the inside. It's pretty accurate.

*Be there as soon as I can*, he says.

—————————➤

Carter's car has barely stopped when I throw open the passenger door and climb in.

"Can we go to Olive Garden?" I say as I put my seatbelt on. "I need breadsticks and fettucine. Also, hi, and I love you."

Carter smiles, but it's a worried, placating smile. It's a my-girlfriend-is-scaring-me smile.

"I have to be home for dinner in an hour," he says. "But I can sit with you while you eat. Unless you want to come to the Graham house and dodge flying peas while trying to eat overcooked meatloaf. And hi, I love you too."

I try not to sigh, but Carter can sense it anyway.

"I can call my mom and tell her I'll be late," he amends as he pulls out of the driveway.

But I can't ask him to do that. He already spends too much time away from home, and from the twin toddlers who have taken over his parents' lives. Even if he'd rather be with me, he should be with them.

"No, don't," I say, placing my hand over his on the gearshift. "Just have a breadstick or two, or a dozen, before you go, and then I'll see if Nat can come get me. She might want a break from the sound of her dad's treadmill."

Carter laughs softly, his eyes catching mine for the briefest instant before turning back to the road. But with that one glance, I already feel a hundred times better. Somehow, he can fill one look with love and reassurance and then deliver it to my soul like a laser beam.

"You, Carter Graham, are the love of my life and the food of my soul," I tell him, hoping to make him laugh again. I love the way his eyes get all squinty and the dimple in his cheek gets extra deep.

"You, Jules Monaghan, are going to make me drive off the road if you don't stop making me laugh," he says.

I put my hand on his knee, moving it slowly up his leg. "What if I do this instead?"

He's not laughing anymore. His eyes are glued to the road in front of him, but I can feel his tense muscles through the denim of his jeans.

Carter and I had sex for the first time a few weeks ago and neither of us seems to know how to stop now that we've started. It's basically all I can think about, which has been super annoying to Mom because I'm even more distracted than usual. I worried at first that she might be able to tell I wasn't a virgin anymore, but she hasn't looked me in the eye for more than a few seconds in over a year. Her eyes immediately move to my uneven skin, or the wrinkles in my oversize sweatshirts, or the Eeyore slippers she can't stand. And then I disappear before she can ask me to try a new face mask or cleanse, or offer to take me shopping or to the dermatologist.

I know: *cry me a river, spoiled rich girl.*

But at least sex is a good distraction from the fact that my mom is the worst.

Carter pulls into the parking lot of Olive Garden. As soon as the car is in park, he turns toward me and cups my chin in his big hands. He brings his mouth to mine and I instantly forget my anger. But when his palm grazes my thigh, I can't help hissing through my teeth.

Carter immediately stills. As he pulls back, I can hear him drawing in a breath. He doesn't want to ask me why it hurts when he touches me. Because he knows.

My eyes flood with tears. One spills down my cheek as his gaze meets mine.

"When did you do it?" he asks.

I don't want to tell him. He'll only blame himself for not coming to get me sooner, even though it wouldn't have changed anything.

"Did you at least clean the cuts?"

I hate the disappointment he's trying to hide. But he sags a little with relief when I nod.

"I'm sorry," I whisper, falling against his shoulder. Guilt sits in my gut like a bad burrito.

He breathes in against my hair, his lips on my temple. "I know," he says simply.

There's nothing else to say.

Carter slumps back into the driver's seat. The sudden distance between us makes me shiver, like he turned on the air-conditioning.

He turns the car off. "Let's go get breadsticks," he says.

He doesn't wait for me to respond before he opens the door and gets out. I catch up to him at the entrance to the restaurant.

"Are we okay?" I whisper around the guilty, miserable lump in my throat.

He takes my hand and squeezes gently. "Pineapple," he answers.

———

Carter still feels distant as we follow the hostess to our table. But even though it makes me feel sick to my stomach, there's nothing I can do about it. I always feel this way after I've hurt myself. Like I'm a rich chili made of guilt, embarrassment, and relief. With an added dash of resentment for flavor.

"So do you want to talk about it?" Carter says over the top of his menu. I haven't even opened mine. There's no need. I know it by heart.

Nat and Carter don't really understand my love for Olive Garden. My mom definitely doesn't understand it. But there's just something I love about the consistency of it. There are no surprises at Olive Garden. There's just salad and breadsticks, and heaping bowls of pasta that are only mediocre at best, but they're the same every single time. You always know what to expect from Olive Garden, whether you're here in the suburbs of northern Virginia or in the middle of Times Square in New York City. Very few places in the world can say that.

"It's nothing new," I say with a soft sigh. "Just my mom,

writing about me again. This time, I tried to hide from her so she'd have nothing to write about, and guess what she did? She wrote about how I hid."

Carter doesn't answer. There's nothing to say, really. There's nothing to do.

Most of her blog posts these days are about her various projects like redecorating the house, or the beach house, or whatever clothes or makeup she's obsessed with, or the skin and hair products she uses (or says she does for the ad money). But she still catches me by surprise by writing about me from time to time. I check her blog once a week just to be sure.

There's no stopping her. Screaming hasn't worked. Crying hasn't worked. Going to Dad hasn't worked. Threatening to get emancipated hasn't worked. So I cut myself instead. And she doesn't know anything about it. I'm careful to keep my scars covered.

"The way she talks about me, it's pretty clear that all I've ever done is annoy her. Have you ever gone back to the toddler days of Minding Her Business?"

Carter shakes his head.

"She hated me, Carter. She really fucking hated me." And when I read the things she wrote about how I acted, I almost don't blame her. "She still hates me."

His hand covers mine. "She doesn't hate you."

He has to say that. But we both know the truth. She's hated me since the day I was born with a hole in my heart. I was imperfect from the very beginning.

Carter drops me off at home an hour later. He's going to be late for dinner at his own house and it's my fault.

"Will you be okay?" he asks as I lean in to kiss him goodbye.

I nod, but I don't actually know. I'm still angry. And I'm sure my mom and I will start fighting again as soon as I walk through the front door, but that's nothing new.

"Yeah, probably," I say.

He frowns. "Jules, that worries me."

I slump in my seat, trying to force back the tears that are threatening to spill over. "I'm sorry. I'll be fine."

"I don't want you to lie to me," he says, wiping away a tear that's escaped from my eye.

I shrug. "Well, I can't promise I'll be okay, so I don't know what else to tell you."

He sighs. "Will you tell your therapist about the cutting tomorrow?"

I'm silent for a few long seconds. I don't like talking about my cutting in therapy. It's partly why I do it on my thighs instead of my arms. My therapist can't see it there, and neither will anyone else. Except Carter.

But I nod. "I will, I promise."

He leans in to kiss me again. "Thank you," he says.

"Text me later," I say as I open the passenger door. "And tell your parents I say 'hi.'"

I leave my leftover fettucine Alfredo on the front seat.

"Don't you want that?" he asks, pointing at the container.

I shake my head. "If I bring that inside, I'll just have to listen to another lecture. Eat it as a snack later or something."

I close the door, but Carter rolls down the window. "I'll bring it to school for you for lunch tomorrow."

I almost start crying. I don't deserve him.

"I love you," I tell him instead.

# CHAPTER
## 4

On Friday, Carter is waiting for me at my locker. His face breaks into a smile as soon as he sees me and the weight on my chest lifts for a moment. It feels like floating. Sometimes I think he's the only good thing in my life. A lot of the time, really.

I kiss him three times, because once is never enough.

"Hey, baby," he says against my lips.

"Hi," I whisper back.

I let him take my backpack and hold it while I get my books out.

"You coming over tonight?" I ask him. It's his night. Nat's is tomorrow.

He grimaces. "I have to babysit the twins. Can you come to my house?"

I put my head into my locker, pretending to look for something. It's not that I don't like Carter's house, or the twins. I just always feel more comfortable in my own room. Where no one can see me. Where no one expects anything from me.

"Jules?" Carter says when I haven't responded for a minute.

I look up at him, working up to a smile. "Yeah," I say. "Of course I can come over."

His eyes crinkle adorably when he grins. I stand and lean into him, letting him wrap his arms around me. I love that he's tall enough that I can nuzzle against his neck without having to duck. I love that I don't feel like a giant monster around him. I love that he loves me.

"I'll bring the snacks," I say against his neck.

"Oooh, baby, you know just what to say," he says with a laugh.

"Cheese balls," I whisper. "Kit Kats. Salt and vinegar chips. And Tate's cookies."

He kisses my cheek, nudging me to tilt my face up until he can reach my lips. "Peanut butter and chocolate ice cream," he says against them. "And Funyuns."

I can't help laughing as he tries to kiss me. "You are so weird."

"That's why you love me," he tells me. And he presses his lips to mine before I can respond.

---

I nap while Carter's at the gym. He plays club soccer in addition to being on the school team, so he's expected to keep up with running and weightlifting, even in January when it's too cold to be outside playing soccer. Not that I can tell from inside my cocoon of blankets.

I know I should get up and get ready to go to Carter's.

I still need to stop at the store to get our snacks. I didn't want to bring them home because if Mom won't let me have pasta in the house, I can't even imagine the reaction she'd have to Funyuns. Probably something like seeing a black tarantula climbing her eggshell walls.

I can hear Mom and Dad talking downstairs. Dad must have just gotten home. He was gone most of the week. His time at home seems to decrease the older I get. I regularly wonder if he's planning to divorce Mom when I leave for college. I would if I were him.

My parents' marriage is depressing. For some reason, Dad puts up with all of Mom's crap and supports everything she wants to do. And she mostly ignores him, except to make him take pictures of her while we're on vacation. But if he left her, I'd have no one but Mom. And that would only end with one of us dead.

I hear Dad climbing the stairs, but Mom's still clacking around in the kitchen on her high heels, so I slip quietly down to the second level in my Eeyore slippers.

I knock softly on their bedroom door as I remove my earbuds. Mom's perfume hangs in the air, enveloping me in her familiar scent. It smells like judgment.

"Come in," Dad says. He's standing in front of the full-length mirror tying his tie.

When I was little, he'd tie his captain's uniform tie on me before putting it on his own neck. At some point, I talked myself into believing it was bad luck if he didn't. I'd have a meltdown if he left for a trip while I was at school and we couldn't perform our ritual. A few times, I even convinced him to stop by school on his way to the airport.

"Hey, kid," he says. He slips his tie off his neck and puts it over my head, his light blue eyes shining with amusement. "Looks better on you."

I slide the red silk through my fingers. "I don't think it matches my outfit," I say, gesturing to my pink, corgi-printed flannel pajama bottoms.

He takes the tie off me and pulls it over his own head again. "I guess you're not coming to this dinner with your aunt and uncle tonight?"

"That would mean going out in public," I say with a snort. I pick a piece of lint off his lapel. "I'm going over to Carter's. Where are you having dinner?"

His sigh sounds tired. "Some new place on H Street near the White House. We're going to sit in traffic for half an hour so we can eat tiny plates of food, and then your mom won't even let me get dessert."

"Shouldn't you get to decide if you eat dessert?" I say, knowing that I'm being naïve.

"That's not how marriage works," Dad says. He smiles, but it's a little strained. The wrinkles next to his eyes look deeper. "Will you bring me home a Snickers bar?"

I nod. "Sure."

I leave him to finish getting dressed and head back upstairs.

I don't really understand how Dad can spend time with Mom. I can't even be in the same room as her. It feels like a betrayal every time he leaves. Not just because he's not spending time with me, but because he's leaving me with her.

Once Mom and Dad are gone and I'm back in bed, I can't talk myself into getting dressed. I *could* go to Carter's in my pajamas; I have before, but I know his mom judges me for it. And I can't blame her. What does it say that I can't even get it together enough to put on pants? Who'd want that in a partner for their son?

But even though I may not even see his parents, I can't manage the twins. They're so loud. So sticky. So fragile and manic all at once.

I send him a text: *I can't tonight. I'm sorry. I love you.*

The dots showing he's replying stop and start a few times. Finally, he replies: *I'm sorry too. The twins were excited to see you. So was I.*

A tear slides down my cheek. I hate disappointing him. And using the twins to guilt me? That's a low blow. I hate myself just a little bit more now. But I can hate myself much better alone.

I don't want to subject him to me right now. *I* don't even want to be around me. But I don't get a choice.

My therapist says when I feel like this, like my depression has roots that wrap around my core, I should try to figure out the primary source. I should try to peel back layers.

But I don't have to peel back layers. I already know why I hate myself.

———————➤

I sleep until noon the next day and only get out of bed because I have to pee.

I'm disappointed with myself for not going to Carter's last night. I hate that I disappointed him. I hate that I get in my own way. I hate that I hate myself.

And with my pants off, I can see the healing cuts on my thighs and I hate those too. But I also don't want to stop hurting myself. When I push a blade into my skin, it's like opening a release valve, and a minuscule amount of pressure escapes.

It doesn't last. The pressure builds up again almost immediately. But in that brief moment, I feel better. Like there's finally physical proof of the scars that no one can see.

As I'm leaving the bathroom, there's a knock on my bedroom door, and then it opens before I can answer.

"Mom!" I yell. "Do you not understand how knocking works? You have to let the other person decide whether or not you can come in."

"It's my house, so I get to decide when I enter a room," she says defiantly. She even tosses her hair. Then she looks down at my trash can and sneers with disdain when she sees the candy bar wrappers and empty chip bags.

I just roll my eyes. This is not our first time having this argument.

"But I apologize," she adds. "I will try harder from now on to respect your privacy."

I'm speechless. My mouth is actually open, but no words are coming out. Finally, I manage to say "Thank you."

Mom pulls my duvet up over my wrinkled sheets and

sits on the bed. She pats the space next to her, inviting me to sit too. I sit at my desk instead.

"I wanted to talk to you about two things," she says. She crosses her legs even though her feet don't reach the floor. "The first is pretty exciting. I've been invited to be on *The Today Show* next Friday to make the sour citrus kale salad that we created!"

I can't help but be impressed. That's a really big deal for her.

"Congratulations, Mom," I say. "That's great."

I'm pretty sure I actually sound sincere. She posted that salad recipe on her blog about a year ago, and it has taken off. It was one of the few times she's asked me for help with a recipe and even though it's simple (and kale is gross), I am pretty proud of it.

"Well, I thought you might want to come to New York with me. We can make a whole weekend of it, maybe see a show, do some shopping."

I manage to keep the sneer off my face, but my response is immediate: "Thanks, but I'd rather not."

I was twelve the last time we went to New York for a weekend. Mom had been given tickets to see a new Broadway show in exchange for posting photos and a mention on the blog. By that time, I was tired of posing for photos and had been asking her to stop posting about me for over a year. She refused. She said this was her job and she was going to keep doing it.

We spent most of the weekend not talking to each other

and when we did, it always ended with me in tears. She'd take a dozen pictures of me doing something and then she wouldn't post them because I didn't look "slim" enough. She dragged me to Bloomingdale's and Saks, but nothing she picked out for me fit right, and she hated everything I picked out at Urban Outfitters and H&M. We ended up cutting the trip short and taking an earlier train home on Sunday morning.

This time, Mom looks disappointed, of course, but not surprised.

"Okay," she says.

"What was the second thing?" I ask. I just want to get this over with so she'll leave me alone.

"Well, a friend mentioned this nutritionist she's been seeing," Mom begins.

My stomach sinks.

"She says she's really helped her, and I thought maybe you'd want me to set up an appointment?"

What she's really asking is if I've seen the error of my carb-obsessed ways. She's never liked it when I bake pastries or cakes, or when I make pasta or rice-based dishes. She doesn't even let me keep the ingredients in the house. I had to hide the pasta attachment for the stand mixer in my closet so she wouldn't throw it away.

I close my eyes and take a deep breath, trying not to cry. "No," I say simply.

Mom lifts her perfectly shaped eyebrows, but only slightly because of the Botox.

"Why not?" she asks. As if we've never had this conversation before. As if I haven't asked her a hundred times to stop talking about my weight.

"Tell you what," I say. "Why don't *you* go see the nutritionist and then you can write a column about how awful it is to have a fat daughter. Because that's what you really want, right? Sympathy for having to look at my fat face all day."

I get up and walk into the bathroom, slamming the door behind me.

## Why Can't We Be Friends?

I know it's unreasonable to expect a sixteen-year-old girl to want to be friends with her mom, but can we talk for a minute about how Jules thinks I'm basically the worst person who ever lived? This is typical, I know. Classic teenage behavior. But somehow, knowing that doesn't make it hurt less.

It's almost phenomenal just how wrong it seems I always am when it comes to Jules. Everything I say is the wrong thing. Everything I do is embarrassing or weird. It's like having the Mean Girls clique around me all the time telling me how awful I am. I don't even want to be the cool mom; I just want her to not hate me.

She spent the entire weekend in her room because she's so angry at me. And all she did was eat. So yesterday, I brought up seeing a nutritionist. I know we've been down this road before and not all of you agree that I should be so worried about Jules's weight, but I just know how much happier she'd be if she lost a little of the weight she's put on since Thanksgiving. Or even a little bit more.

I didn't even ask her about doing yoga or going to spin class with me this time. But she still acted like I'd asked her to kick a bees' nest. Which I think she'd actually prefer to hanging out with me.

You guys would want to be friends with me, right? Can you tell Jules how great I am?

—Britt

# CHAPTER
# 5

Sad people are boring. That's what Mom says, anyway.

It's a shitty thing to say, but she's not wrong. I didn't leave my room all weekend. I spent Saturday and Sunday rewatching *Parts Unknown* with Anthony Bourdain. He was living the actual dream, traveling the world and experiencing—and eating—everything it has to offer, and it still wasn't enough to make him happy. He died by suicide.

What does that mean for me?

So, I'm sad and I'm boring. Even Nat was bored when she came over on Saturday.

She told me it was time to get out of my house. Out of my bed. Out of my head. She made it sound like it's easy.

"Just get up, take a shower, and then put on clothes," she said. "That's all I'm asking."

Sure, but once I'm clean and dressed, then I have to go out into the world and exist around other people. People who don't seem to struggle with the basics of hygiene.

People who can look at themselves in the mirror without wanting to break it. People who talk to each other and don't dissect every word, who don't think about their conversations for days afterward, making sure that they didn't say anything weird. People who can just exist, without wondering if it'd be better if they didn't.

So I ignored Nat's request and stayed in bed. She hung out with me for a couple of hours, but she didn't sleep over. I couldn't blame her.

And now it's Monday again.

Sometimes I'm almost relieved to have to go to school. I don't hate it. I'm an above-average student, so I don't have trouble with my teachers. And yes, people know who I am, but I don't give them any gossip to talk about, so they mostly ignore me. Which is how I like it. As long as I have Nat and Carter, I don't really need anyone else.

———

That afternoon, I drive myself to my therapist's office. I've been seeing Alice for a couple of years now. But I'm not sure we've made much progress. I mostly just complain about Mom, and she reassures me that I won't have to be around her for much longer.

"Two more years until you're eighteen and free," she likes to say. But we both know I won't ever really get away from Mom.

Today, I'm telling Alice about the invitation to New York, the nutritionist, and Mom's blog post.

"She thinks I spent the whole weekend in bed because

I'm angry at her," I say. "Can you believe how self-centered that is?"

But Alice just tilts her head and looks at me. "You spent the whole weekend in bed?"

*Fuck.* I didn't mean to say that.

"I mean, not just my bed, but in my room, yeah."

"You didn't have plans with Carter or Nat?" She doesn't sound judgmental, but I feel her judgment anyway.

"I did, but I didn't feel like doing them. I just wanted to be home. Alone."

Alice folds her hands across her lap. "I know we've discussed this before, but I have some concerns. Have you had any suicidal thoughts lately?"

I'm shaking my head before I've even considered the question. "No," I say.

It's a lie. I think about suicide all the time. But that doesn't mean I'm actually going to do it, so why worry her?

But I'm pretty sure Alice sees through me. "What about other types of self-harm?" she says. "I know you've struggled to control your impulse to cut yourself."

I consider lying again. But I can't do it.

"I'm still struggling," I admit.

"Have you hurt yourself recently?" She's so good at keeping her voice calm and regulated during these conversations. She could be asking if I've eaten breakfast today.

"Yes," I say. "Last week."

"Was there an incident that brought on that impulse?" she asks.

I give her a Look. "What do you think?"

Alice sighs. "A blog post?"

I nod. "She can't seem to stop herself. She just needs the constant validation from her fans."

"I'm sorry she does that," she says. "But I do honestly think that you're doing the best thing by not engaging with her as much as possible. Even though I know how hard it is for you."

I swallow painfully around the lump in my throat. I wonder what it's like to have a mom who doesn't hate you.

"When was the last time you did something fun?" Alice asks. "Like, something you actually wanted to do, not just something Nat or Carter wanted to do?"

I try to remember, but I honestly don't know. So I shrug. "It's been a while."

"Let's make that your homework this week. Your mom is going to be gone this weekend, so do something you'll enjoy. Something that has absolutely nothing to do with her."

I nod, but I'm picturing spending the weekend baking and then eating cookies in bed. Which is probably not what Alice has in mind.

It's like she can read my thoughts because she adds, "Make sure it involves leaving the house."

*Damn it.*

On Thursday, when I get home from school, my attention snags on the luggage next to the front door. Mom is leaving for New York tonight so that she can be at the studio first thing in the morning.

I try not to look too happy about her departure when I

walk into the kitchen. She's scrolling through her Instagram likes, as usual. I don't bother looking at what she posts anymore. As long as it's not about me, I don't care.

"What time is your train?" I ask.

"It leaves at four," she says. Then she looks at the time. "I should get going."

"Okay, good luck at the show," I say. I sound genuine because I actually want her to do well. I know it means a lot to her.

"Your dad is going to be home Saturday afternoon and I'll be home Sunday," Mom says. "I put money in your account so that you can order dinner for yourself tomorrow, but there's plenty of food in the fridge."

"If you can call that food," I grumble quietly. It's all quinoa and chia seeds and green juice. *Blech.*

"I know I don't have to tell you not to have any parties," Mom adds after a few beats. "Natalie can stay over. Carter cannot."

I think she enjoys the act of being a mom, saying the right parental things and judging others who don't. It's the unconditional love part that she has trouble with.

"Yes, mother darling," I say in my best Little Edie impression.

I've always felt like I understand Little Edie from *Grey Gardens.* The drive to get away from her mother while also feeling stuck inside her own house. But I'm not even allowed to have cats.

The next day at lunch, I tell Nat and Carter that they have to be at my house at nine on Saturday morning, and they look at me like I've grown antlers.

"What do you have planned?" Nat asks warily. Like I might drive them off a bridge or something.

"I was thinking we would drive up to Annapolis for homemade pop tarts at Iron Rooster."

Natalie's lips tilt into a small smile. "Ooh, can we also get milkshakes at Chick and Ruth's, and then drive to Pappas for Oprah's favorite crab cakes?"

"I feel like I'm only understanding half of the things you guys are saying," Carter says, "but those words are all about food, so I'm in."

I lean in for a quick kiss, then kiss him twice more before remembering that Nat is watching. She's looking away when I glance back at her.

I try not to feel annoyed that she hasn't gained any weight since Thanksgiving. She's been eating almost as much of the food I've made as I have, since I'm usually doing it at her house. I guess it helps that she's an athlete and her metabolism is a lot faster than mine, but it's always been a struggle not to be jealous of her narrow hips and flat stomach.

I've told her that I hang out with her and Carter on different nights so that they each get their own time with me and vice versa, but there's also a small part of me that wants to keep them apart in case they realize that they'd rather just cut out the middleman and hang out without me. They've actually got more in common with each other than either of them does with me. And they're both muscular and gorgeous in a way that I will never be. Never.

But that doesn't matter today. Or this weekend.

"It's a date," I say to the two of them with a grin.

I want nothing more than to eat my way through Maryland with my best friend and my boyfriend. But add in the fact that Mom will be out of town, and it's like Christmas all over again.

---

The drive to Annapolis takes about an hour. I let Nat drive my car and Carter sits shotgun so I can stretch out across the backseat.

"Is she asleep?" Nat asks.

I make an effort to look as though I am.

"I think so," Carter says. "It's pretty impressive how she can fall asleep in the car but not her own bed."

Nat sighs. "I wish there was something we could do to make things easier on her. I hate that she's so sad all the time."

Carter sighs too. "I know. I do my best, you know, to make her happy, to help. But I don't think it's anything we can help with. She needs to get out of her house. When we go to college, it'll be better."

Nat is quiet for a moment. "Will it, though? I worry about what will happen when we're not all together."

So do I. Sometimes the only thing keeping me alive is that I know how angry Nat and Carter would be if I killed myself. Most of the time, that works to pull me out of the depths of despair. But not all the time.

"I hope we all get into schools near each other," Carter says. "Do you know yet where you're applying?"

"State schools, mostly. UVA, JMU, Virginia Tech. And then I just have to hope I can get some scholarship money and financial aid. But you know Jules doesn't want to go to college. She wants to go to culinary school. Going to Le Cordon Bleu in Paris is, like, her ultimate goal in life."

I peek at Carter through my eyelashes when he doesn't respond. He looks like he just swallowed a lemon.

"I'm going to have to go to the best school that gives me a soccer scholarship," he says. "And that definitely won't be in Paris."

We haven't talked about this much, Carter and I. We mostly avoid the difficult subjects. There's enough difficulty in our relationship already, thanks to me. But the potential distance between us in the future is something that weighs on me all the time. Carter is such a huge part of my life right now—I can't imagine being without him.

But the reality is that I'm probably not going to Paris. If I'm lucky, Mom and Dad will agree to let me go to a school here in the States where I can get a hospitality degree. But more likely, they'll insist I study something like business or communications, something useful that they'll be proud to tell their friends about. My grades aren't good enough to get an academic scholarship like Nat, and since I don't play any sports, I'm not getting a sports scholarship like Carter.

I have to rely on my parents' goodwill to go to college, unless I want to be paying back loans for the rest of my life.

I close my eyes again and try to shut out the rest of their conversation. I don't want to think about what will happen when Nat and Carter go off to college to fulfill their dreams and I'm left behind.

Tears leak from the corners of my eyes until we pull into a parking space. Before Carter and Nat can see, I dry my eyes and sit up.

"Hey, baby," Carter says. "You ready for some breakfast?"

I nod. "Always," I say, even though I've lost my appetite.

I hope my puffy eyes look like just-woke-up face instead of crying face, but Carter squints at me. "You okay?" he asks.

I give him a tight smile. "Pineapple," I say.

He and Nat know enough to let it go. So I try to remember how lucky I am to have them, for as long as we get to be together.

Also, there are homemade pop tarts and crab cakes in my future, so it's hard to stay sad for too long. For today, at least, that's enough.

# CHAPTER
## 6

On the heels of our Annapolis trip, the next week is actually pretty great. The palpable awkwardness between Nat and Carter seems to have faded, and the three of us even start planning our next road trip.

Plus, Mom's segment went well on *The Today Show*, so she's in a good mood too, which always helps.

It feels like the universe finally realized I needed a break.

So I'm almost excited to go to this party tonight at Carter's friend's house. Almost.

Carter's picking me up in an hour, so I have to get out of bed. And shower. And get dressed.

I hate getting dressed.

People who aren't tall love to tell me how great it must be to be 5'9". But being tall is terrible. It means I stand out in a crowd when all I want is to be invisible. And being the tall, fat daughter of a tiny, perfect Instagram influencer is the actual worst. Take it from me.

I turn off *Chopped* and, after a moment of silence, drag myself out of bed and into the bathroom.

I'd feel proud of myself if it weren't the absolute bare minimum of what it takes to be a person in the world.

———————➤

Carter and I make terrible party guests. First, we arrive at Trey's house late, mostly because it took me thirty minutes of throwing clothes on the floor in frustration before I finally decided on something to wear. I still hate myself in it, but I'm dressed and I'm out of my house. That is serious progress.

But second, I have zero interest in talking to anyone at this party except Carter and Natalie, and she's already found her field hockey teammates.

So Carter and I each grab a drink and then head for the second floor to find a guest bedroom. I lock the door behind us.

Carter's hands are immediately on my waist, then sliding my shirt over my head. I shouldn't have even bothered to get dressed.

"Why do you think people even invite us to parties?" I ask when I'm curled up next to him with my head on his chest. "Actually, I take that back. No one invites me, they invite you. I'm just your arm candy."

Carter laughs, squeezing me against his side. "You're way better than candy. You're like chocolate soufflé. You're delicate and a little temperamental, and you need to be ordered in advance, but you're worth the wait."

I pull the pillow out from under his head to hit him with it. "I don't even know what you're talking about," I tell him. "But it sounds offensive."

He grabs the pillow from me and stuffs it back beneath his head. "It was the opposite, actually, but leave it to you to turn my positive into a negative."

There's a sour taste in my mouth. "And that's just one of the things my mom has written about me on her blog."

Carter's smile drops. "I didn't know that. I'm sorry."

I'm already shaking my head even before he apologizes. I know he didn't know that. And I know he was just trying to be nice and cute. And now I've ruined it. Just like I ruin everything.

"No, I'm sorry," I say, rolling onto my side so I can kiss him. So I can pretzel our legs and snuggle into the crook of his neck. He kisses the top of my head. "I know you didn't. I just can't get her voice out of my head sometimes, telling the world that I'm fragile and moody and hard to be around."

He nudges my cheek with his chin until I pull back to look at him. "I love you. You are perfectly flawed in all my favorite ways. And you are none of the things your mom has written about you."

Somehow, he always knows just what to say.

———————

Mom is waiting up when I get home. Her long blond hair is in a scrunchie on top of her head. She pats the couch next to her.

I hate being next to her. It just highlights how big I am in comparison. But I sit.

"I know you aren't going to want to have this conversation with me, but I'd like you to hear me out," she starts.

That's never a good sign. My muscles clench from my jaw to my toes. I'm poised to run away.

"I'm aware that you and Carter are having sex." She says it matter-of-factly, but not naturally. I'm pretty sure she's been practicing it aloud.

My first instinct is to deny it, but my cheeks are burning so hot, there's no point. I do wonder how she found out though.

She sets a box of condoms on the couch between us, and my mouth drops open. "I know I can't stop you, and I know that you love each other, so I won't try. But I really want you to be careful. You should use a condom every time, not just for pregnancy but for sexually transmitted infections too. And always pee afterward. It helps prevent urinary tract infections."

Before I can close my mouth, she adds, "No judgment, I promise. When you need more, ask. And I'll make you an appointment with my gynecologist on Monday to discuss getting on the pill."

And then she stands and heads upstairs. It is the least Britt-like conversation we've ever had, if you can even call it that. And if it hadn't been held over a box of condoms, I might have hugged her.

# PEAK MOM MOMENT

By Britt Monaghan

It took sixteen years, but I'm pretty sure I just peaked as a mom.

I had "The Talk" with Jules. Not the birds and bees—we covered that when she was eleven and got her period for the first time. This was a recap of the birth control talk, which means a lot more now than it did then.

Over dinner with a longtime friend on Friday, it came up that Jules was out with her boyfriend. And the friend asked how long they'd been dating. Four months is a long time in teen time, she pointed out. "Do you think they're having sex?" she asked.

Of course I'd considered it. It's impossible not to worry when your daughter has a boyfriend. But I guess I'd been in denial because the question hit me right in the solar plexus. "Am I bad mother if I don't know the answer to that question?" I wondered.

So I'm not proud to admit it, but I read her diary. And of course, this friend was right. She's having sex.

But instead of freaking out, I sent Chris out to get condoms.

When Jules got home, I sat her down and told her that I wasn't going to be mad or judge her, but I wanted her to be safe. I gave her the condoms and told her I'd make an appointment with my gynecologist for birth control.

And Jules didn't even get mad! It was such a civil conversation. There was no yelling or crying. She didn't hide from me or tell me to mind my own business. I almost didn't recognize her.

Chris struggled with it a little more, to be honest. He didn't like the idea of buying condoms for his sixteen-year-old daughter. But given the alternative—becoming grandparents in our forties—he came around pretty quickly.

I know this isn't going to be a popular column with some readers. I imagine there will be lots of opinions about how I handled this situation. But I'm proud of myself. And I'm proud of Jules.

# CHAPTER

# 7

This is a new all-time low. A deeper rock bottom than I knew existed. Of all the things my mom could tell her readers about, my sex life was never something I even considered being on the table.

I should have known. I should have expected it. Mom's never drawn a line before—why start now, when this is such rich material for the column?

She didn't tell me she was writing about it, of course. I found out the same way everyone else did: by reading her column.

I know they say not to read the comments. That's, like, the number one rule of the internet. And normally I don't. But the first comment catches my eye before I can stop myself.

*What kind of mother encourages her teenage daughter to have sex??? You should be ashamed of yourself. And discussing your daughter's personal business in public just makes you an even worse example for her. People like you are what's wrong with the world today.*

I feel vindicated. Supported. Embarrassed, sure, but at least people are on my side.

But then I keep reading.

*Sex before marriage is a sin! Your daughter is going to burn in H*LL and so will you for allowing it to happen!*

*You and your slut of a daughter are the reason abortion is still legal. Baby killers!*

*Jules Monaghan is fat and boring. Why would anyone want to have sex with her?*

*If Jules wants to experiment some more, feel free to send her my way!*

They only get worse from there. But the last comment is the one that makes me feel the sickest.

*For a good time with Jules Monaghan, call [my phone number].*

Almost immediately after I see the comment, my phone starts buzzing. And then it doesn't stop. Text messages are arriving at a rapid-fire pace, and calls from unknown numbers come in one after another. I scroll through the texts to see if any of them are from people I know, but none of them are. And half of them have photos that I don't have to open to know are not of people's faces.

I start forwarding them to Mom without reading them. Tears stream down my cheeks. I bet this is what she was hoping for: a viral moment at my expense. Mom of the Year.

Mom knocks on my door a few minutes after I finally turn off my phone. I ignore her.

"Jules? Honey?" she calls.

My door is locked, but she tries the knob anyway.

"Will you let me in, please?"

I slam the door to the bathroom behind me. I can still hear her knocking, but I don't care. I pull my shirt up to expose my stomach, then squeeze the rolls of fat between my fingers. And as Mom continues to knock and call my name, I push the sharp edge of a blade deep into my skin.

It doesn't make me feel better. Nothing can. But as I hold a wet washcloth to the cut, as it burns with pain, it feels like a punishment. And maybe that's what I deserve. For being fat and boring and sad and stupid. For believing, even for a brief moment, that Mom could actually care about me and not just herself.

The whole world has just learned one of my biggest secrets, that Carter and I are having sex, and while I'm not ashamed of it, I wanted it to *stay* a secret. I wanted this one thing for myself. And Mom couldn't even let me have that.

Like it's not bad enough that she violated my privacy by reading my diary (which I've now shredded every page of), it feels like the whole world is watching and judging every move I've ever made. And inviting them into my sex life is a whole other kind of violation.

A little while later, I hear a different knock on my bedroom door, louder, more insistent. A little bit panicked.

"Jules?" Carter calls. "Baby, will you let me in?"

I don't answer.

He knocks and calls to me for another few minutes, but I cover my ears with my hands. When he finally stops, I wipe tears from my face with the back of one hand. And then I hear the door open.

The bathroom door is locked too, but like the bedroom door, it's not difficult to unlock. And within a few seconds, I hear the click before the door slowly swings inward.

Carter and Nat stand in the doorway, looking down at me.

"Thank God," Carter breathes as he pushes through the door. He drops down next to me on the tile and pulls me into his arms, ignoring the blood that's soaked my shirt and smears on his.

I look up at Nat through the blur of tears in my eyes.

"I really fucking hate your mom," she says. She sinks to her knees on the floor in front of me.

"Me too," I say.

There's nothing either of them can do to make this better. And I hate that they're seeing me like this. I hate being like this.

"Are you okay?" Nat asks. Then she sees the blood. Her face pales. "Oh God, Jules. What did you do?"

Carter has seen my cuts, new and old, because it's unavoidable, but I've always been careful to not let Nat see anything I'm able to hide. So when she reaches for the hem of my T-shirt, I push her hand away.

"Don't," I say. "Just leave me alone."

She frowns. "You need to clean that," she says. "You may even need stitches. That's a lot of blood."

"Yeah, I know," I snap.

She rocks back on her heels, putting some space between us. Carter holds out a hand and motions for Nat to give us a little privacy, so she stands, stepping out of the bathroom.

It annoys me that she listens to Carter and not me. Can't anyone just do what I've asked? Is that just another one of my defects?

"Just go home, Nat," I say, without looking at her. "You don't need to babysit me."

She doesn't respond, but I hear her close the bedroom door behind her when she goes. I immediately feel worse. And I can see on Carter's face that he wants to admonish me for being mean to my best friend. It's almost worse when he doesn't. I'm too fragile, apparently.

"You can go too," I say, pushing him away and standing. "I can take care of myself."

When I pull my shirt up to inspect my stomach, Carter sucks air through his teeth.

"Oh, baby," he says sadly. "That looks painful."

He opens the medicine cabinet, removing the alcohol and gauze pads he bought for this purpose, then goes to work cleaning me up. The cut isn't deep enough for stitches, but I wouldn't go to a doctor even if it was. I've been seeing a therapist for long enough to know that this would be reported and I could be deemed enough of a threat to myself that I'd be put in the hospital for days, maybe even weeks.

I've never been a very good liar, and right now, if some-one asked if I was thinking of harming myself and if I was having suicidal thoughts, I'd have to say "yes."

"I'm sorry this happened," Carter says as he finishes tap-ing gauze to my stomach.

I look up at him. "You mean my mom reading my diary and finding out that we're having sex? Or telling the world about it? Or someone publishing my phone number so every creep and nutjob in the world can tell me what a horrible person I am for sleeping with my boyfriend?"

He closes his eyes and takes a breath. "For all of it, Jules. You don't deserve any of this."

But I'm not sure he's right. My mom's been writing about me for years, which means she has plenty of material. If you believe the things she writes, I'm a terrible daughter. And now I'm a slut too.

"I just can't believe she would write about this," I say. "I didn't think she had anything left that could surprise me, but she just keeps finding new ways."

"None of this is a surprise to me," he says, shaking his head. "Your mom is who she is and she's not going to change."

"You say that like you're just going to accept whatever she does," I say. I cross my arms over my chest. "Like noth-ing she does will change anything for you."

He's quiet for a moment. "I don't care who knows that we're having sex," he says finally. "I care that you care, but no, it doesn't change anything for me."

And yet for me, it feels like the entire internet has been

invited into our relationship. To comment on. To dissect. To judge.

"Well, it changes everything for me," I say around the hard lump in my throat.

Carter's face hardens. "So, what? You don't want to have sex with me anymore because people know about it?"

I want to say "no." I want to say "I don't care what people think." But I do care.

"That's right," I say quietly. "I won't. Not for now."

"That's ridiculous," he says.

I shake my head. "It's not," I say. "Don't you understand what this feels like? My mom has been sharing things about me without my permission for my entire life. How am I ever going to go to college, or get a job, or make new friends without everyone knowing my entire life history?"

I'm shouting now. "Every person who Googles me will know how old I was when I lost my virginity, or when I got my period, or when I started gaining weight! I will never be able to remove the things she's said about me from the internet, but even if I could, I'll never be able to scrub them from my own mind."

I double over, sobbing into my hands. "Don't you see, Carter? You get to tell people your secrets when you choose to, and even this one will just be a funny way to show off to your friends in college. But this will stay with me for the rest of my life."

I feel Carter's hands on my shoulders, but I can't look at him. I can't even breathe, I'm crying so hard. I just want to curl up and sleep for a year. I wish I could just sleep and never wake up. I'd rather be dead than deal with this anymore.

Carter pulls me against his chest, shushing me and telling me it'll be okay. But I know it's only because he doesn't know what else to say. There isn't anything else he can say.

But there's one thing I can do.

"I don't want to do this anymore," I say, pushing him away. I've left dark, wet spots on his shirt.

"What do you mean?" he says. He's frustrated with me. Tired of dealing with my mood swings and tears. Tired of patching me up and putting me back together when I fall to pieces.

I'm doing him a favor.

"This. Us. I don't want to do it anymore." My voice is flat and unfamiliar. I know this will hurt tomorrow, just like the wounds on my stomach, but I don't care. This is for his own good.

Carter looks stricken. He opens his mouth, but nothing comes out. And then his forehead creases and I see the tears in his eyes.

"You don't mean that," he says.

I nod. "I do. I can't do this. I'm too broken."

He reaches for me, but I slap his hands away. "Just go, Carter," I say.

I can't look at him. I don't want to see the pain on his face. Or worse, the relief.

His resigned sigh echoes off the tile. "I'll call you in the morning," he says.

I won't answer. But I don't say so. I just let him walk out. I don't even watch to see if he looks back. I don't want to see that either.

# CHAPTER
# 8

I didn't sleep last night. Instead, I watched Anthony Bourdain travel the world, fighting his own misery and self-doubt. I watched episode after episode of *No Reservations* and *Parts Unknown*, looking for a reason that he would want to die. Looking for something in his eyes that showed how miserable he was. And finding nothing.

I've turned off my phone, but I can't seem to stop reading the comments on Mom's column. There were some people demanding that the comments section be closed, but the newspaper didn't listen. The column has gone viral now and they're probably loving the free publicity. I'm sure their advertisers are loving the click-throughs. Or maybe not. Maybe they'd rather not be tied to the story of a teenage girl losing her virginity.

Yeah, well, neither would I.

Because I'm a glutton for punishment, I pull up Mom's Instagram too. Her post promoting the column has more than ten thousand comments. People are arguing about whether I should be having sex, whether Mom should have written about it, and whether the newspaper should have published it. People love to argue, especially when they're feeling morally superior.

Dozens of people from school have also posted their take on the situation. They wonder why Carter is even dating me, much less sleeping with me. They wonder whether I was actually adopted since I don't look anything like my beautiful mother. They wonder why my mom writes about me when clearly I haven't done anything worth writing about until now. They wonder why I haven't killed myself because I'm fat and stupid and boring. They wonder whether this will be the thing that sends me over the edge.

I don't have to wonder.

———————

Dad arrives home a few hours later. He's been on a flight for the last twelve hours, but the slam of the garage door tells me he's seen the column. I can hear him and Mom arguing downstairs, but I don't bother to listen. I don't want to hear her excuses. And I don't want to hear it when he forgives her. Because he always does.

But not long after he gets home, I hear his heavy footsteps climbing the stairs to my room. I unlock the door and leave it open a crack.

He knocks softly, and I tell him to come in.

"Hey, kid," he says. "How are you holding up?"

I just shrug miserably.

I'm sitting on the edge of the bed, so when he stops in front of me, I can lean my forehead against his belly. He kisses the crown of my head.

"She's gone too far this time," he says. "Your private business should be just that: private."

I tilt my head back so I can look up at him. "And what did she say when you told her that?" I ask.

He sighs as he sits down next to me. "She's defensive and still trying to justify it, but she admits that it was a violation of your privacy."

I gesture toward my silent phone. "And what does she think about all the things people are saying about me? What does she think about the fact that someone posted my phone number so I'm getting harassed and called names and sent dick pics?"

Dad's eyes widen. "Give me your phone," he says. "I'm going to alert the police. Sending a nude photo to a minor can be considered a crime. And they should be aware of the harassment too."

He wraps an arm around my waist and pulls me against his side. "I'm sorry," he says.

But I can't answer. My throat is too tight. And there are no words for the sorrow and anger and embarrassment I feel.

"Do you want to go get something to eat? Or do you want me to bring you something? I can go to the Portuguese bakery and get pastéis de nata."

My favorite custard tarts. He's really trying. But there

aren't enough pastries in the world to bury my feelings in. So I shake my head.

"I'll set up a new phone number for you with the cell phone company in the morning," he says as he picks up my phone. "You don't have to go to school if you don't want to."

For some reason, this is what makes the tears start again. Because there was no way I was going to school anyway, but to be given permission just shows how bad this situation really is. It's not just in my head. Not this time.

This time, the whole world is watching. And their eyes are on me.

As he promised, the next morning, Dad came home with a new phone for me, and a new phone number. Then he promptly left the house again.

I'm not sure where he went, but at least it means there's no one to force me to do anything. Mom has no power over me anymore. But she doesn't even knock on my door, so I figure she doesn't really care if I leave my room or not.

I didn't sleep the night before, but even if I had, I'd still be lying in bed all day while *The Great British Bake Off* (my number one comfort show) played in the background. Occasionally, I check Mom's column to look for fresh comments and then I torture myself by searching the Minding Her Business hashtag on Twitter and Instagram. Ten minutes is about all it takes for me to hate myself even more. But I can't seem to stop. The comments validate all the things I've thought about myself throughout my life. And as much as it hurts, I do like being right.

For some reason, the supportive comments just annoy me more. No one should have to be standing up for me. This never should have happened.

I don't regret sleeping with Carter, but it doesn't feel the same anymore. I hate that people know about it. It makes me feel dirty. It makes me feel judged. And I've had enough of that throughout my life.

But I guess it doesn't matter anymore anyway.

I bet he called this morning, just like he said he would. So reliable. So dedicated. So wrong for me. I ignored it.

We only dated for five months. He barely even knows me. And we never would have lasted. He's going to go to college and be a jock. A smart jock, but still a jock. And I want to go to Paris, to Le Cordon Bleu, where hopefully no one has ever read my mom's blog. But even if I don't move to Paris, Carter is going to realize pretty soon what a miserable piece of garbage I am.

I just helped him get there a little early, that's all.

⟶

Around four, there's a knock on the door. A quick double tap. Nat's knock.

I drag myself out from under the covers and open the door, but I turn around and immediately climb back into bed without looking at her.

I'm out of tears. I'm out of rage. I'm out of fucks to give.

I'm like an ugly, threadbare bathing suit; I have no elasticity left to accommodate what other people want from me.

The mattress dips as Nat slides in next to me. She even gets under the covers, pulling the duvet up over our heads like we're in a blanket fort. Then she curls against my side, resting her chin on my upper arm. She knows I like this position because she can't see my face. I don't have to look at her when I'm spilling my secrets. Or tears.

"I missed you today," Nat says. Her voice is a little muffled.

I sigh through my nose. "How bad was it?"

I don't have to elaborate. She knows what I'm asking.

"It was bad. People have capital-O-pinions. But they're mostly on your side," she adds quickly.

"Did you see Carter?" I ask. My stomach takes a sharp left when I say his name.

"Yeah," she says slowly. "But he didn't say much. Is everything okay?"

I don't lie to Nat. Not usually. But I don't want to explain why I broke up with Carter. She wouldn't understand. She's always acted like he was infallible. She was always taking his side when I told her about our arguments, then claiming she was playing devil's advocate.

Well, he can date her instead. They've always had more in common than he and I did anyway.

"It's fine," I say. "We're fine."

Nat is quiet for a few minutes. We lie there, breathing next to each other in silence.

"You're not really fine, are you?" she asks.

I shake my head. "No," I whisper around the tightness in my throat.

Her arm snakes around my middle and she wraps her legs around mine. I feel like I'm being squeezed by a very loving boa constrictor.

"I hate this," I say.

"What?" she asks into my armpit.

"Everything. The world, my mom, her followers, the people at school." I bring my free hand up to cover my eyes. "I hate myself more than anything else."

Nat squeezes me harder. "You shouldn't," she says. "You're so damn lovable."

I laugh mirthlessly. "Yeah, so lovable that the entire internet hates me."

But they loved me once, when I was a kid. I just had no idea. I thought I was just posing for pictures and enjoying being the center of Mom's attention for a while. But when I look back now, it's hard not to be at least a little impressed with what Mom was able to build. I looked adorable in the outfits she put me in. Before puberty, I was only a little chubby and most of her followers found it endearing. They liked that I wasn't perfect. For a little while, anyway.

But the internet always turns on you.

I squeeze my eyes shut to stop the tears from leaking out, but it doesn't work. My heart is pounding, my breathing is shallow and quick. I can't seem to take a deep breath.

Nat squeezes me harder. "Oh, Jules," she whispers. "What can I do?"

I hate that question. There's nothing anyone can do.

"You can let me go," I sob.

She releases me, retracting her limbs, and sits up cross-legged, looking down at me. But that's not what I meant.

"I don't want to do this anymore," I say. I roll onto my side so she can't see my face.

"What don't you want to do?" she asks gently.

I press my fists against my eyes until I see stars. "Anything. I don't want to do anything anymore. I just want to be dead."

I've said it before, but Nat's sharp intake of breath means she can tell I'm serious this time.

"Don't say that," she says. She climbs off the bed and kneels on the floor next to me, even though I won't open my eyes.

"Why not?" I say. "What difference would it make?"

"A huge one," she says. Her voice is trembling. I want to feel guilty about making her sad, but I just can't. "It would make a difference to a lot of people."

I snort callously. "I have a really hard time believing that. If I died, nothing would change."

Nat grabs my hands and pulls them away from my face. Her eyes are streaming tears and her pale skin is red and blotchy.

"Listen to me: you can't kill yourself," she sobs. "I need you. Carter needs you. You have so many things left to do! You have too many things to cook! And bake! You have a whole life ahead of you that has nothing to do with your mom."

But all I can do is shake my head. She doesn't understand. No one does. None of that matters. It's not enough to cancel out how much I don't want to deal with any of this anymore.

I don't care how much she thinks she needs me. She doesn't. Carter definitely doesn't.

I'm a weight that keeps them from flying. How can I possibly live with myself? I might as well be deadweight.

Nat won't see it that way. At least not at first. But maybe eventually she will.

I pull my hands from hers. "You don't need me," I say. "You just don't have any other friends."

It's cold and cruel, but it's enough to make her stop plying me with lies.

"You don't mean that," she says quietly, almost to herself. Her mouth is slightly open, her brows knitted in confusion. Her long eyelashes are clumped together by tears. I've always been jealous of those lashes.

"You're right," I lie. But I can't seem to make my voice sound normal. It's flat, monotone. Just like my heart. "Fine. I won't kill myself."

Nat stares at me, her expression skeptical. "You promise?" she says finally.

"I promise," I say. I can't even feel guilty for lying to her. It's better this way.

"I love you." Nat wraps her arms around my body, squeezing me so tight it hurts.

"I love you too," I say. This, at least, isn't a lie.

"I can stay for a while," she says. "It's Cordie's night to cook dinner, so I'd be happy for an excuse to not go home."

But I shake my head. "Thanks, but I just want to be alone."

I can see the conflicting thoughts running through her mind. She doesn't trust me, but she's also too kind and too good a friend to not do as I've asked. It's one of her greatest strengths. And one of her biggest flaws.

She slowly stands and backs toward the door as if she's afraid to take her eyes off me.

"Remember your promise," she says. "I will hate you forever if you kill yourself."

I just nod. Because it won't matter anyway.

# CHAPTER
# 9

I didn't sleep again last night. That's not unusual for me, but it always makes things worse. Because I love nothing more than sleep. Not even pastries. Or olives. Or Nat.

Even at my worst moments, when I'm out of breath from crying and my hands are shaking, if I can tuck myself under the covers and force my eyes closed, I will usually fall asleep. It's like my brain needs a reboot. And when I wake up, I feel better. Not hugely better, but any incremental amount is an improvement.

But when I can't sleep, worst piles on top of worse, and the more exhausted I get, the more I hate myself. Which is really saying something because I hate myself a lot already every second of the day.

Finally, around 7 AM, I give up and decide to make myself breakfast and take my antidepressants. It's early enough that Mom should still be in her room, even if she's not asleep. She has a coffee maker in there, so she usually doesn't come downstairs before nine.

I pad quietly down the stairs in my Eeyore slippers. But when I reach the landing outside the double doors to her bedroom, I freeze. I can hear Mom talking on the phone.

I'm hungry enough that I'm willing to risk it, but I hope she'll be on long enough that she won't see me. I'm still not ready to talk to her. I'd prefer never to even have to look at her again.

"She's angry at me," I hear Mom say. "But she hasn't left her room in two days. I don't think she's eating." There's silence. And then, "Yes, she's self-harmed. Her best friend told me last night that she's been cutting herself and she's having suicidal thoughts."

I gasp as I sink to the floor. I feel like I've been punched in the gut. When I press my hands to my stomach, I hiss through my teeth. The cuts there are still tender.

I can't believe Nat told Mom about my cutting. I can't believe she told her I was talking about suicide. The betrayal stings like a slap to the face.

"This isn't the first time," Mom continues. "Jules's best friend says she's attempted suicide once before. I didn't know about that. And she's been self-harming for years."

My cheeks burn. No one but Nat knew about my previous suicide attempt, not even Carter.

I wonder who Mom is talking to. Am I going to be carted off to a psychiatric hospital? Will I be locked up because my mom is an asshole who can't keep my private life private? Because my best friend tattled on me?

But then she says, "I'll send you an email with some notes and we can figure out how to proceed from here."

And I realize with a sinking feeling: She's talking to her editor. She wants to write about my depression. She wants to exploit my suicidal ideations for her column.

I shouldn't be surprised. This is completely in character for Mom.

What really gets me, though, is that this is happening because Nat told her about all of it. The person I trusted most in the world told my secrets to the person I trust the least with them.

I wish I weren't surprised. I wish I'd come to expect the worst of people. But I only expected the worst of Mom. I never expected this from Nat.

I'm such an idiot.

———————————>

I turn and walk back up the stairs in a daze.

My hands are shaking so much that it takes a few tries to actually call Nat. But as soon as she answers, I start yelling.

"You told my mom?" I shout.

"What?" her sleepy voice responds.

I'm almost hyperventilating. "You. Told. My. Mom," I wheeze.

"Jules, what are you talking about?"

"I just heard her on the phone, Nat. She said you told her that I was threatening suicide. That I've been cutting myself."

There's silence on the other end for a few long moments.

"Yes," Nat says finally. "I did."

I squeeze the phone so hard, I'm surprised it doesn't shatter in my hand. "How could you do that?" I ask. My voice is shaking. "*Why* would you do that?"

"I was worried!" Nat says. "I didn't want to leave you there without someone who knew the kind of thoughts you were having."

I snort. "Can you really blame me?"

"Yes!" she shouts. It's so unexpected that I nearly drop my phone. "Are you kidding me? I know that your life is hard, Jules, believe me. Your mom has done some serious psychological damage to you. I'd never tell you that you didn't come by these feelings honestly. But it isn't a reason to kill yourself!"

Nat has never yelled at me before. But it seems like she has years' worth of pent-up frustration to get off her chest.

"You're being immature and melodramatic, Jules." She's practically panting, like she just ran laps. "You have so many things that most people would kill for. You have two parents, a massive house, an amazing boyfriend, ridiculous skills in the kitchen. What more do you want?"

I don't even know what to say. But Nat isn't finished.

"You can do anything you want to do," she says. "And your mom, no matter how misguided, loves you. And she even has a platform to support you if you wanted to do something someday, like my podcast."

That snaps me out of my silence. I'm so tired of hearing about her damn podcast.

"Oh my God!" I shout. "Were you trying to get into her good graces so she can promote your stupid podcast? Is that what this is about?" I'm not even making sense, I know that. But it doesn't matter.

Nat is silent for a few seconds. "If you think that, then you don't know me at all. And you definitely aren't my friend."

"You know what, Nat?" I snap, knowing I'll regret it later. "Maybe not. And maybe I don't care."

I hang up before she can say anything else. I didn't think it was possible to feel any lower, but it turns out I was wrong.

The worst part is that nothing she said is untrue. Maybe I am so focused on my own pain that I don't see what I really do have. Maybe I don't see the pain I cause other people. Maybe I really don't care. And what kind of a monster does that make me?

All I want is to close my eyes and forget. I need a reset. I need relief.

I climb back into bed and pull the covers over my head.

Maybe I'll sleep this time. Maybe I'll feel better when I wake up.

## PART TWO

# NATALIE

# CHAPTER
## *10*

It takes a few moments before it registers, through the haze of sleep, that the incessant, shrill ringing noise is my phone. It's not the gentle *ding* of a text message. It's an actual phone call.

It's past midnight. No one should be calling.

When I pick up the phone, I see Chris Monaghan's name on the screen and my hands start shaking so much that it takes me a few tries to stab the right button. Chris has never called me. I only have his number saved in case of an emergency with Jules.

*Oh God. Jules.*

"Chris?" I say. "What's going on?"

He's silent for an excruciating moment, then I hear his sharp intake of breath.

"It's Jules," he finally manages. Another sharp breath.

"What happened?" I whisper.

"She's gone," he says.

Maybe she's run away from home. Maybe she's on her way to my house. I check for a text from her. But there's nothing new.

"We think that it was suicide," Chris says. His voice is so quiet I can barely hear him. Or maybe it's the blood rushing in my ears. "She's dead, Nat. She's gone."

I barely register the *thunk* as my phone hits the carpet.

This can't be happening.

My cry is a scream of disbelief, unrecognizable to my ears. I yell for as long as I can before I have to take a deep, shuddering breath. And then I do it again. And again. And again.

Dad throws open my bedroom door. His hair is wild, his eyes squinting in the dark, glasses askew.

"What is it? What's wrong?" he asks as he rushes to me. "Are you okay?"

"Daddy," I sob, "Jules is dead."

I can barely see his face, but I recognize the disbelief in his shocked gasp.

Slowly I realize that Chris is saying my name. I can hear his tiny voice coming from the phone on the floor.

I feel boneless as I slide off the bed, then rest my face next to the phone. The coarse fibers of the carpet scratch against my cheek when I say, "Chris, I'm so sorry." I say it again and again. I sob it. "I'm so sorry."

"I know," he says. His voice catches. "I am too. I'm really sorry." I hear him crying softly on the other end of the line.

Dad sits down next to me on the floor and pulls my head into his lap. He gently strokes my hair while I cry too.

"What should I do?" I say.

I think what I'm really asking is "What do I do now that my favorite person in the world is gone? How do I keep going?" But he can't answer that.

Then Chris asks, "Can you call Carter? I haven't told him yet."

I almost say "no." But how can I? His daughter is dead. This is the least I can do. And I think I'd rather Carter heard it from me.

"Of course," I say. Tears are streaming down my cheeks.

"Thank you," he says. He takes a shaky breath. "And thank you for being such a wonderful friend to my girl. You were the best thing that ever happened to her."

He doesn't know how untrue that is.

I will never forgive myself for yelling at her. I will never forget that our last words to each other were angry ones.

I will never stop wondering if I'm the reason she's dead.

I know Dad is talking to Cordie, but I can't hear him over the ringing in my ears. I'm out of tears for the moment. I can't seem to move. I can only stare at the wall in disbelief. In confusion. In rage.

And then Dad is pulling me into a sitting position. He's kneeling in front of me. His mouth is moving. The ringing fades as I focus on his lips.

"What do you need?" Dad is asking.

I blink a few times. And suddenly there's a cold glass of water in my hand. I look up at Cordie in silent thanks.

The water helps me focus a little more. It washes the salty tears from my lips.

"What do you need, Bug?" Dad asks again.

I search for my phone and find it on the floor next to me.

"I have to call Carter," I say. "He needs to know."

Cordie's brow wrinkles. "Are you sure? Maybe Dad or I should call him."

But I shake my head. "No, it needs to be me. He needs to hear it from me."

Dad and Cordie exchange a look, but I stand and hug them both to me for a few seconds.

"We'll be in the kitchen when you're done," Cordie says when I release her. She leads Dad out of the room, closing the door behind her. Then she pokes her head back in and tosses me a box of tissues.

I hold my phone in one hand and a tissue in the other. My thumb hovers over Carter's name. It's nearly one now. He's going to know this isn't a friendly call.

"Nat?" his sleepy voice says when he answers. "What's going on?"

My throat closes as I start crying, and I can't talk for a few seconds. "I'm sorry, Carter," I finally sob, not sure if I'm apologizing for crying or because I'm about to ruin his life. I guess it doesn't matter. "I have to tell you some awful news. Jules is dead. Her dad says it was suicide."

The sob that follows will echo in my mind for the rest of my life. It's like listening to his heart shatter.

He just keeps saying "no" over and over again.

I cry silent tears for several long moments as the truth sinks in. Carter has moved the phone away from his mouth, so his voice is far away, but the anguish in his cry is clear even at a distance.

"How did this happen?" he says finally.

I press my lips together, steeling myself for the lie. "I don't know," I say. "I really don't."

I hear his parents in the background now; he's telling them what happened. He starts crying again while his parents say soothing, undistinguishable things.

"I have to call you back," I say. And I hang up. His pain on top of my own is too much for me right now.

I stare down at the soggy tissue in my hand.

This moment is now a bookmark in my life. There is a before and an after. I'll never get to go back to the before. But I don't want to live in the after. Not without Jules.

I don't want to do this.

I can't.

# CHAPTER
# *11*

The steady hum of the treadmill on the other side of my bedroom wall has been the soundtrack of my afternoon.

Dad works from home as an IT help desk manager. A couple years ago, he decided he was going to get back in shape and bought himself a treadmill desk. Now, if he's not on the treadmill or playing basketball with his friends, he's shooting hoops with Cordie in the driveway. I get tired just thinking about it.

At six, I knock on his door.

"Dad?" I call.

"Come on in, Bug," he calls back, sounding winded.

I push the door open. Dad is moving at a steady pace, just slow enough that he doesn't have to move his arms to stay balanced and can type while he walks.

"Hey," I say. I lean against the treadmill desk's corner. "Are you almost done? It's Cordie's night to make dinner so you should probably come up with an excuse now to get out of it."

Dad grimaces as he checks the time on his phone. "Oh, man. Can I say that I have a doctor's appointment?"

I shake my head. "You need to come up with something better than that. I already told her that I'm going to visit Jules tonight with Carter. It's been three months."

Dad presses a button on the treadmill and glides to a stop. "I know, Bug. How you doing?"

I shrug, but I'm not even convincing myself. The truth is that there's a persistent tightness in my chest, like a piece of dental floss tied around my lungs. Every time I think of Jules, the floss gets wrapped around some cosmic dental hygienist's finger and half of my air supply gets cut off.

"I think Carter needs this more than I do," I lie. "He hasn't been to her grave since the burial."

Dad nods, pretending to agree with me. We're pretty good at this dance.

"And can I take your car?" I ask. I know he can't really say no, given the reason.

"Sure," he says. "Tell your sister it's just the two of us for dinner, and take a twenty from my wallet to get yourself something edible, okay?" And then he turns the treadmill back on.

———————

Carter's waiting for me outside Olive Garden at seven. Jules loved Olive Garden. It didn't seem to matter that she could make pasta dishes that were ten times better than anything she could get there.

I think it was partly because a carbohydrate hadn't been

allowed in her house since the year we went trick-or-treating when we were thirteen. That year, when we got home, we sat in the living room still in our costumes while Britt picked through Jules's bag, pulled out five pieces of candy that Jules was allowed to eat (including a bag of Raisinets), and threw the rest in the trash.

Britt Monaghan is a boil on the ass of the world.

Carter waves at me as I pull into a spot near the entrance. I notice his hazel eyes are a little puffy behind his dark-framed glasses. He's got the hood up on his sweatshirt.

"So how many people have asked how you're sleeping today?" I ask him as I get out of the car.

There has to be a list somewhere that people keep referring to called "How to handle someone who's grieving." And that question must be first on the list because at least six people have asked me that just this week.

Carter winces. "I hate that question. It makes me feel guilty that I sleep fine. I'm so exhausted from being sad all day that by the end of the night, I just put on an episode of *Parks and Rec* and I'm asleep before it's over."

I envy him. I haven't gotten a full night of sleep since before Jules died.

Maybe Carter can sleep because he and Jules weren't fighting when she died. He'd probably said "I love you" only a few hours before her body was found.

"People have stopped bringing me food though," he says as he holds the door open to the restaurant. "Which is a bummer."

I roll my eyes, but I can't help smiling a little too. "You would focus on the food," I say.

Carter just shrugs. "Still. No one cooks like Jules did."

It's true. No one cooks like Jules did. And no one has brought the Nagler family food in a while either. I wonder if anyone is still sending food to the Monaghans. Not that Britt would eat it.

Which reminds me: "Did you see Britt's post today?" I blurt out once we're seated at the table.

Carter keeps his gaze on his water glass, but I hear his heavy sigh.

"You know I didn't," he says. "What did she do now?"

Carter deleted all his social media accounts after Jules died, but he was never all that active on them to begin with. It was one of the things Jules loved about him. And one of the only things she and I fought about. Jules didn't care what other people were doing with their lives. Because she knew how easy it was for them to only share the good parts. She knew how often the good parts are a lie. I know that too, but I still like to follow my favorite podcasts and bands, and even Britt.

Britt had also taken a "hiatus" from social media after Jules died. She lasted almost a month.

"She's writing a fucking book," I say.

Carter's eyes snap to mine. "About Jules?"

I nod. "About Jules, and also about the 'metamorphosis' she's undertaken since her death. Her post said it was going to be 'part memoir, part self-help, and part how-to.'"

He scoffs. "How to what? Drive your daughter to suicide?"

I wince at the word but shake off the memory of calling him to tell him about Jules. It was one of the worst moments of my life.

"No, how to be *her*. How to turn yourself into a commercial for a life no one can actually achieve."

Carter's fingers curl into fists on the table. I'm tempted to reach over and wrap my hands around them, but despite how much time we've spent together, we're not that close. Carter and I are only friends because of Jules.

But that was how she was: magnetic. Once she had a grip on you, once she pulled you into her orbit, it felt secure. Unmovable. It didn't matter how different we were, or how different she and Carter were, we were together in her pull. I'd just hoped she'd never get bored enough to let go.

But she didn't get bored. She got angry. And that was even worse.

---

The cemetery closes at nine, but we make it with about thirty minutes left. The parking lot is empty, and the slam of my door echoes off the gravestones that stretch before us. The chill that makes goose bumps perk up along my arms is only partly from the early spring air.

Carter places a container of fettucine Alfredo at the base of the gravestone that reads:

*Julianne Bethany Monaghan*
*Beloved daughter*

When Carter texted me to ask if I'd come with him tonight, I knew why he wanted to come so late: Jules was happiest at night. Well, maybe not happy, but it was when she was most comfortable. It was the only time she felt like she could be herself in her house. While Britt was asleep.

So it seems right to come to the cemetery in the dark, bearing her favorite pasta. I feel bad that I never thought of it. But that's probably because I don't have the money to waste on an entrée. Dad's twenty didn't even cover *my* meal.

"Do you want to go first?" Carter asks, gesturing toward the headstone.

I clear my throat. "Uh, hey, Jules," I start awkwardly. I've never been good at this. "I miss you. But you haven't missed too much lately. Dad is still using the treadmill desk, if you can believe it."

We both thought that would last a month, two tops, but it's been over a year.

"Cordie is using every annoying thing Dad and I do to tell us how much she can't wait to move out of the house in the fall, but I can tell she's getting nervous." I pause for a second, trying to think of something else to say. "That's kind of it. I don't leave the house much, but I've been watching a lot of your favorite TV shows."

My throat burns as my eyes water. "Netflix is so confused," I say, laughing and crying at the same time. "Anyway. I love you."

I turn to go. "I'll give you some time with her," I say to Carter.

But before I take a step, Carter puts a hand on my arm.

"Stay?" he says. His voice catches.

I've seen Carter cry before. I've heard his sobs on the other end of the phone and echoing through a church. But with his grief so close, it doesn't take long before I'm choked up too. I try to smile, try to pretend, but my lips aren't cooperating. I miss Jules so much, and being around Carter makes me miss her even more.

The thought I can't seem to shake, from the moment she died, is that I want to talk to her about it. She was the person I'd go to when I needed comfort, or humor, or sarcasm, or whatever healing balm. We talked about everything. And now all I want to do is curl up in bed next to her and whisper across the inches separating us. I want to cry into her long, dark blond hair. I want to hear her tell me that I'm not the reason she's dead.

I want that more than anything.

Carter takes a deep breath. "Hey, Jules," he says. He glances at me just as a tear catches on the frame of his glasses. "I miss you so much."

He covers his mouth with his hand to stifle a sob. I rub his back until he takes a long, shuddering breath.

"I can't believe you've been gone three months already," he starts. "Every day I wake up thinking that you will have texted me overnight, telling me that you love me. I miss those morning texts."

Jules didn't sleep much, so I woke up to those texts too. She could be so bitingly sarcastic, so withering and bitter, but she was also hilarious and clever. And when Jules took the same way with words to express her love, it felt like she'd composed you a sonnet.

And now tears are streaming down both of our faces.

"I just wanted you to know that I love you enough to buy you fettucine Alfredo, even though you can't eat it."

And that has us crying even harder. Which makes me start laughing, because of all the things that are awful about this situation, the fact that she'll never eat Olive Garden again definitely isn't the saddest. And then Carter is laughing with me, but we're both also crying, and it suddenly feels right to pull him to me. He stiffens for just a moment before relaxing against me, pressing his face into my shoulder. He tightens his grip around my middle. And I notice that he smells like clean laundry and citrus, like he ate orange slices after a game and then wrapped me in a fluffy towel.

We may be a mess, but at least we have each other. He's the closest thing to Jules I have left. I think he probably feels the same way about me. I hope he does.

When we separate, Carter looks a little embarrassed, but I feel comforted. Jules would have really enjoyed this moment.

"Should we go?" I ask after we've collected ourselves.

Carter nods. He kisses his fingers and touches them to the top of Jules's gravestone.

"'Bye, Jules," I say.

"'Bye, baby," Carter whispers. And for some reason, it makes my chest ache.

We're quiet as we reach the parking lot. Carter walks me to Dad's car.

"Thanks for coming tonight," he says.

I give him the tight-lipped smile I've used a thousand times in the last three months.

"You're not alone," I remind him. "You can always text me or even call me. Or just come by. I'm literally always home."

He nods. And then we just kind of stand there awkwardly. We did so much hugging tonight, but that doesn't make it less weird. We didn't hug when Jules was alive.

But Jules isn't alive.

"I miss her every day," I say. "But I feel like she's still here when I'm with you. Like she just went to the bathroom or something. So maybe we could hang out a little more?"

Carter's smile isn't tight at all. "Yeah, that'd be good."

I nod and get into the car. Carter waits until I'm buckled in and driving away before he heads for his own car.

What I couldn't say to him—won't say—is that I'm still mad at Jules. I'm pissed as hell. Because she didn't only take her own life. She took the life we had together. She took my best friend, Carter's girlfriend, her parents' daughter. And she left us to deal with what was left behind.

And I don't want to deal with any of it.

## Influencer Monaghan sells memoir

In a world rights acquisition, Ampersand Books has bought lifestyle influencer and parenting columnist **Britt Monaghan**'s memoir *Minding Her Business: A Mother's Tale of Love, Overexposure, and Grief.* The memoir, says editor **Susan Loh**, "reveals the unseen side of social media fame and the heartbreaking consequence for Monaghan: the suicide of her daughter." **Spencer Hill** at The Hill Agency represented the author in the deal.

**BrittMHB** I have some big news! I am so honored to announce that I've sold my book! As you all know, this has been a difficult time for me. Jules's death still hurts Every. Single. Day. But I've learned SO much in the last three months, about myself, about what I wish I could have done differently, and what I still have to learn. I've undergone a metamorphosis since losing my sweet baby, but there will always be more to learn about myself. And I hope you'll join me on that journey next year when this book comes out. It's part memoir, part self-help, and part how-to, but it has all of my heart.

# CHAPTER
## 12

"The most annoying part is that Britt can actually write," I say to Cordie as I help her load the dishwasher.

Our kitchen was apparently designed by someone who'd never cooked or cleaned before, so the dishwasher is next to the washing machine along the back wall. You either have to walk a few feet to put each dish in, leaving a trail of water each time, or you put dish towels on the floor and hand your sister the dishes over them. We've lived here ten years, so it's a finely honed system, which Cordie is rudely disrupting by going to North Carolina for college on a basketball scholarship in the fall.

She hums her half-hearted agreement. She's heard me say this before.

"She's a decent photographer, but she can write too. Which means she'll do a pretty amazing job of dissecting her daughter's life and death for strangers. And it already has buzz because of who she is and because of the case. You know how much people love a good gossipy death story."

"You certainly do," Cordie says with a pointed look. I used to have a podcast about cold murder cases called *Dead Unburied*, but no one listened. Not even Jules.

The reminder makes my stomach sink.

"Do you think someone's going to make a podcast about Jules's death?" I ask. "Or wait—do you think someone already has?"

Cordie raises one dark eyebrow. I hate that she can do that and I can't. It's just so efficient.

"Why would you care more about a podcast than the *Dateline* episode?" she asks. "You never even watched it anyway."

The idea of some random stranger just saying anything they want about Jules, with no recourse if they're wrong and no network fact-checkers, makes me want to throw things. Heavy things.

But I ignore the question and return to my favorite topic: hating on Britt Monaghan.

"Why would she want to write a book about this anyway?" I'm shouting at the running water now. "Her whole persona has been about showing what an amazing mom she is, and now she's basically outing herself as a failure. I mean, she's not even a mom anymore."

This, for some reason, makes my eyes fill with tears. I don't want to feel sorry for Britt, but that's just so damn sad. And I'm pretty much always on the verge of crying these days anyway, so it doesn't take much to send me over the edge.

Cordie dries her hands on her shirt before wrapping her arms around my shoulders.

"I know," she says soothingly. "I think you have to stop following Britt, or reading her blog. This obsession isn't healthy."

I blow out a shuddery breath. "Yeah," I say noncommittally.

My therapist says the same thing, but every week, I go in and admit that I haven't taken her advice. I don't know how Carter has been able to cut himself off so completely.

I suddenly feel the need to read through the archives of Minding Her Business, looking for hints into when things started to go wrong in the Monaghan family. Looking for proof that Jules's suicide was Britt's fault.

Because if it was, that means maybe it wasn't mine.

---

Later that night, I finally do what I haven't had the nerve to do since Jules died. I Google her.

Most of the articles are from the day after. News stations worldwide ran the story. Then there's the article from *People*, which went into more detail and included interviews with people "close to the Monaghans." (I'm sure.) The *Washington Herald* ran several follow-up articles, but because they were the publisher of Britt's column, I have a hard time believing that they could be impartial.

The most startling thing is the number of photos that come up when I click to the Images tab. Jules hated having her picture taken. I only have a handful of pictures of the two of us together and even fewer of her alone. But the internet seems to have hundreds.

Most are taken from Britt's Instagram feed and are of Jules as a kid. She once told me she didn't really know what her mom did for a living until she was seven or eight. She just thought all kids got to take the train to New York City for movie or theater premieres, or were sent random gifts from strangers or companies hoping for promotion.

There are a handful of photos of Jules more recently, from school picture day last year and from Britt's fiftieth birthday celebration. Those weren't on her Instagram because Britt would never publicly admit to being fifty, but Jules allowed Britt to post them on her private Facebook profile.

But there's a photo that I know better than any of the others, because I've stared at it on my own camera roll at least once a day. It's a photo of Jules that I took, on a rare occasion where I got her to play basketball with me. Because of her height and hand–eye coordination, she was pretty good; she just hated to run. So in this picture, she's lying on the asphalt, having just attempted and missed a shot from the ground. The sun is bright on her face, her hair is splayed behind her like a golden crown. Her mouth is open in a laugh and her eyes are squinted against the light. She's happy.

And it was posted on my Instagram feed. My *private* feed. I only have twenty-five followers. And one of them is a traitor.

My blood boils as I check my followers and see Britt's username, @BrittMHB. I block her immediately, but it doesn't quench the lava in my veins. I want to expose her as a terrible mother, as a liar and a fraud. I want to poke holes in all the stories about Jules she told on her blog, or on Instagram, or in her column.

But as I move deeper into the search results, my gaze snags on a Reddit thread. "Did Britt Monaghan stage Jules's suicide?"

The stutter in my chest tells me I believe the answer is "yes."

I did not see that coming.

I call the only person I can: Carter. And he picks up immediately.

"Hey, Nat," he says. His tone is guarded. We haven't talked on the phone since the week after Jules died, and that was only because there were logistics that were easier to plan over the phone. Or, more accurately, there were logistics to thwart. Because Britt had tried to stage a vigil at the school, which her fans would have flocked to, which Jules would have hated. So we got the students to sign a letter stating that we wished to grieve "as Jules would have: privately."

"Do you think Britt killed Jules?" I spit out.

His silence makes me realize how paranoid and ridiculous I sound. But I still need to know his answer.

I manage a short breath and start again. "Sorry, I mean, I just ran across a theory in a Reddit thread about Jules and . . . well, do you?"

I hear muffled voices, and then Carter says, "Hang on."

Sweat prickles at my hairline as the silence stretches.

I jump when Carter asks, "Where are you?"

I want to object; I want to say I don't need him, but since I've carved half-moons into my palms with my fingernails, I tell him I'm at home. My fingers unclench as I hang up.

———————→

Carter knocks on my bedroom door twenty minutes later, interrupting my descent into Britt's blog posts.

"Hey," he says, drawing out the word warily. "Your dad let me in. He told me to keep the bedroom door open a foot."

Blood rushes to my cheeks. "Sorry," I say. "He was probably trying to be funny. He knows you and I aren't . . ." My voice trails off. Because I don't even know what we *are*.

But Carter just shrugs. "Don't worry about it. My mom was the same way about Jules being in my room."

The weight of her name hangs heavy between us.

Carter sits. It's weird to see him on my twin bed, sitting on the teal bedspread next to the stuffed dog that I still sleep with every night. There's never been a boy in my bedroom before. It's a pretty small space already, but it feels smaller with him in here with me. And not just because he's so tall and broad-shouldered.

I do a quick glance around the room, searching for anything embarrassing, but it's just a desk, a dresser with a framed photo of me and Jules on it, and my bed. Everything else is tucked away. I'm too organized to leave something like a bra or underwear lying out. Jules used to make fun of me for being so uptight, but who's laughing now?

Oh, right: no one.

"So . . . ," Carter begins. "What were you talking about before?"

I bite my lip. It's somehow harder to say to his face.

"Do you think Britt had anything to do with Jules's death?" I say after a pause. The lack of surprise in his expression tells me that he heard what I said on the phone earlier. "Do you think she could have killed her?"

He sighs, scrubbing his hands over his face. "No, I don't. Why would you think that?"

And this is the part I've been most nervous to bring up. Because Carter doesn't know about Jules's previous suicide attempt. And I don't want to put that in his mind if he doesn't have to know. But he does.

I take a deep breath. "Jules had attempted suicide before," I say. I pause to let that sink in.

Carter's mouth opens, but he doesn't say anything. His eyebrows lean toward each other. "When?" he finally whispers.

"Before she met you," I say. "Freshman year."

"How?"

I don't want to get into the specifics. I've tried for two years to block that memory from my mind. So I just shake my head.

He nods once, silent. His fists clutch my bedspread on either side of him.

"Britt didn't know until I told her," I say. "Two days before Jules . . ."

Carter looks up at me, his eyes shining with tears. "Why didn't she know?"

I swallow loudly. "Jules begged me not to tell," I say.

I know I made the wrong decision. I know I should have told Britt right away. But Jules made me swear not to. She promised me she'd tell her therapist and her parents. I should have known she wouldn't.

I'll never forget the way she looked at me that night. Her eyes bloodshot and her cheeks streaked with tears.

But she knew I was coming over that night. She knew I would walk in. She must have known I'd stay up all night if she needed me. And that I would watch her when she finally slept. Which is exactly what I did.

I didn't think she actually wanted to die. I thought it was like the cutting—a cry for help. A way to hurt herself. A way to show people she was hurting without having to say the words.

I was wrong.

"But that's my point: it's not unreasonable for me to think that Britt could have done this, right?"

Carter just stares at me.

"Okay, maybe it's a little unreasonable. But it's not completely out of left field."

He still says nothing.

"Britt knew Jules had tried to kill herself before, and she knew that she was having suicidal thoughts again. And she either didn't do anything to help her or she took the opportunity to get her inconveniently depressed daughter out of the way. And to gain a whole new level of fame while she was at it. She has over a million followers now."

He exhales loudly, then seems to shake his feelings off, sitting up straighter. "You can't actually believe any of that," he says.

My shoulders slump. I don't. I just really need this to not be my fault.

"Maybe not."

Carter stands and walks toward me. He squats down in front of me, putting a hand on each knee. He angles his head so he can look me in the eye.

"I was hanging out with some people when you called," he says. "Want to come back with me?"

I don't say anything.

"I think you could use the distraction."

He's not wrong. I look down at the plaid flannel pajama pants and T-shirt I'm wearing. At eight-thirty on a Saturday night.

"Can you give me twenty minutes?" I say.

"No problem," he says.

While I head to the bathroom, he sits at my desk and closes my laptop, shutting out Minding Her Business and Britt Monaghan.

⌒

Carter slowly pulls his mom's Subaru out of the driveway. He's always been a careful driver, but he got even slower after Jules died. Like he had to try extra hard to stay alive.

In the soft glow of the dashboard, I study his profile. I wonder if he ever wishes he could be with Jules.

In the first few weeks, I thought about death constantly. I just wanted Jules back, but if I couldn't have that, then I wanted to be where she was. Wherever that is. If there is a wherever.

My eye catches on the crucifix hanging from the rearview mirror.

Dad's never been particularly religious, not even after my mom died when I was five. We seem to follow the religion of capitalism, in that we celebrate Christmas and Easter, but we don't go to church or even say grace before dinner.

So the afterlife is kind of blurry in my mind. Are we just gone? Or does the consciousness hang on somehow? Or is it like *The Good Place*, with neighborhoods and pets? I don't believe in God, I don't think, but I wish I had some sort of faith to hold onto, some belief about where Jules is. I think it would be comforting. Instead, I fall asleep imagining Jules floating around in space, alone, frozen in time.

"So where are we going?" I ask to distract myself.

"You know Harry Chu?" Carter says. He glances at me as we pull up to a red light.

I nod. "By reputation," I say. "I doubt he knows who I am."

Our school isn't that big, but I've never really made myself a part of it. I never had to. I had Jules. We were enough.

Carter scoffs. "I'm pretty sure everyone knows who you are now."

But not because of anything I've done.

It's almost a cliché how everyone stops to look at us when we walk into Harry's house. The music doesn't screech to a halt, at least, but it takes a good ten seconds for people to return to their conversations.

Right. This is why I haven't been going out. Carter and I are a walking sideshow.

*Step right up! Gaze upon the Puddles of Grief, the best friend and boyfriend of the deceased! Watch as they pretend like they aren't made of tears!*

I look up at Carter. "You thought this would help me how?"

He reaches for my hand. "Ignore the stares. They'll get used to having you around."

I slide my fingers into his and he squeezes them. "We'll see."

Carter leads me into the kitchen. I'm relieved that this isn't a big party. There are maybe a dozen people here, including two girls from the field hockey team who come over as soon as they see us.

Adriana and Louise, I remind myself as they each give me a quick hug. I shouldn't have to remind myself; we've been teammates for three seasons now. But grief does weird things to the brain.

"I'm so happy to see you out!" Louise says. There are bright pink spots on her cheeks, meaning she's been drinking.

"Me too," Adriana says, but quieter. She gives me a small smile. "I know it's the wrong question to ask, but how are you?"

It is the wrong question to ask, but it's almost more awkward not to ask it. Because that's how conversations work. You ask how people are. They ask you back. It's a thing.

I manage a shrug. "I'm hanging in."

My standard response.

Adriana nods, but her dark brown eyes are slightly narrowed. "If you ever want to go for a run or something, let me know. After my grandma died last year, I would run for miles." She leans in and adds quietly, "Tears are less noticeable when you're sweating."

I can't help smiling, even though I hate it when people compare losing a grandparent, or worse, a pet, to losing my best friend. "I haven't run since the season ended. I'm a little out of shape. But that does sound kind of appealing. Thanks."

Louise has gotten distracted by Harry, who's trying to set up a Jenga set for some reason. He keeps knocking it over halfway through, so Carter walks over to help.

Adriana leans in again. "You don't have to reach out, but is it okay if I maybe text you sometimes to see how you're doing?"

I'm not sure what to say. Obviously the polite thing is to just agree and give her my phone number. But it feels like charity.

I nod anyway and type my number into her phone.

She sends a text to me that says *Hi, it's Adriana*, so I have her number too.

"Thanks," I say. Though I don't really expect to hear from her. And then I wave awkwardly and escape to Carter's side.

I had worried it'd be weird if I didn't drink, but as I look around, I realize that only about half of the people are drinking. I don't really have a problem with alcohol; I'm just always nervous I'll make an ass out of myself at parties. If Jules had been here, she could have kept an eye on me. Or we would have skipped the party entirely and just snuck a bottle of Britt's wine up to Jules's room and gotten drunk and giggly on the floor while we wore sheet masks and watched *The Great British Bake Off* for the fifteenth time.

Carter and I team up against Harry and Louise for Jenga. It's really not a fair match given their inebriation, but Harry and Louise don't seem to notice that Carter and I have soda in our cups.

"So, Nat," Harry says. His black hair has fallen over one eye and the other is squinted as he tries to push the first block through.

I can't believe he even managed to get the tower built.

"So, Harry," I say when he doesn't finish his thought.

He laughs, and his finger pokes the block clean through to the other side without knocking the tower over. *How?*

Then he picks up the block and squints at it. "Your question is: if you had to eat only one thing in this room for the rest of your life, what would it be?"

I stare at him. Then I look at the rest of the blocks and realize there's writing on all of them.

"What is this, Truth or Jenga?" I ask Carter.

He laughs. "Basically. But eventually, Harry will try to make up a question on the fly that makes no sense or he'll knock over the whole thing, so it never lasts that long."

Harry points a long finger at Carter. "You shut your mouth," he says. Slurs, really. "I always don't make sense."

Carter catches my eye and laughs.

"Okay," I say with a shrug, looking around the kitchen. I guess I could go open cabinets or something, but I see gummy worms, the sour neon kind, in a bag on the counter. And I point to them. "Gummy worms. That's my choice."

Carter motions for me to pull our first block. "You get to decide who you want to ask the question to, Louise or Harry," he says.

"What color is your underwear?" I read to Harry.

He opens his mouth and closes it again. "I—" He pauses, putting a hand in his waistband. His eyebrows knit together in confusion. "I'm not wearing any!"

We all groan.

"No!" Louise scoots her chair farther from his. "You're telling me that there's only a thin layer of denim between me and your junk?"

Harry nods proudly. "Laundry day," he says, looking at me. "What are you gonna do?"

I can't help laughing. "What *are* you gonna do?" I agree.

It's Louise's turn and she's less wobbly than Harry, so she only struggles a little to get a piece out.

"Okay, Carter," she says. "If you had to kiss one person in this room right now, who would it be?"

Carter's cheeks redden, and so do the tips of his ears. It's kind of adorable. He stubbornly refuses to look around the room. "Harry," he says after a short pause. "It's gotta be Harry."

I see him glance at me out of the corner of my eye. And I feel a dropkick of disappointment that he didn't say my name.

Harry, of course, is delighted by this news. "Bro, you already know I'm going commando, so I can't blame you for wanting to test the merchandise."

As he leans over the table to try to kiss Carter, he knocks over the Jenga tower. The calamitous crash is followed by a chorus of groans from around the room. The loudest are from the three of us who were still playing.

"That's my cue, folks!" Harry says, putting both hands in the air. "You don't have to go home, but you can't say here!"

———

After a quick stop for a drive-through cheeseburger, Carter takes me home. As he pulls into the driveway, he turns to me. "Are you going to be okay tonight?"

I'm honestly not sure what he's even asking.

"Yes . . . ?" I say unconvincingly.

The corners of his lips tilt. "If you can't sleep, text me. I'll be up for a while. But don't go down any more conspiracy theory holes, okay? No Reddit."

I nod. "I promise. No Reddit."

And I mean it. Because I see how ridiculous jumping on the murder theory was. I guess maybe that was the denial part of the grief process. I just don't want my best friend to have killed herself. I don't want her to be dead at all.

As I open the door and step out of the car, Carter ducks his head so he can see me. "I'm serious. I'm here."

I nod again. "I know. Thanks."

The warmth in my chest as I walk up the front path is unexpected. Jules was so lucky to have him.

And just like that, I'm back to anger.

———————➤

Monday afternoon at four-thirty, I'm sitting in my usual chair across from Lisa, my therapist of three months. Dad booked the first appointment pretty much as soon as his tears dried after hearing about Jules.

"So you can see why I'd be angry about this, right?" I say. I've just told her about Britt's memoir.

"I do see," Lisa says. "I know you think a lot of Jules's depression stemmed from the way her mom treated her."

I don't like the way she phrased that. "You don't?"

She doesn't take the bait. "Jules isn't my patient. You are. But I understand why you don't want your best friend's life exploited any more than it already has been."

"Yes!" I say, relief flooding through me. "No one else seems to have as big a problem with this as I do."

Lisa waits for me to continue.

"I mean, Carter didn't like the idea of it, but he doesn't seem nearly as angry as I am. Cordie basically brushed it off. I didn't even bother to tell Dad."

"Do any of your other friends have opinions about it?"

I sigh. I know what she's trying to say. Maybe if I had other friends, Jules's death wouldn't continue to hurt quite so much.

But I can't think about that right now. I don't want new friends. I want Jules. And maybe, if I'm being honest, I want Carter too.

"Would it be weird if I had a crush on Carter?" I ask without looking at Lisa.

I see her head snap up in my peripheral vision. "Jules's boyfriend?"

I nod.

"No. I'd say that's fairly natural. Do you think it's weird?" She loves to turn my questions back on me.

"A little, yeah."

She tilts her head. "Why do you think you have a crush on him?"

I shrug. But I've been giving this a lot of thought. "I think it's maybe because he's the closest thing I have to Jules. And I want to, like, claim him as mine. So he can't leave me too."

Lisa raises her eyebrows.

"You're impressed with my self-awareness, right?" I say proudly. "I've been practicing that."

She chuckles. I know Lisa likes it when I joke with her. The first few sessions all I did was cry.

"How was it being at a party without Jules?" she asks.

Pain stabs me in the gut. I hadn't been practicing for that one.

"Not as hard as I expected it would be," I say, trying not to sound winded, "but we didn't really go to that many parties, you know? So it's not like I was upsetting some big tradition."

Lisa doesn't say anything.

"Now, if I were watching *Top Chef* and eating tiramisu on the floor of Jules's bedroom without her, that might bring up some hard memories."

She doesn't laugh. "How was it, really?" she asks.

My throat squeezes shut. "Hard," I manage.

Lisa nods. "Were you able to enjoy yourself at all?"

As I dab at my eyes with a tissue, I say, "Well, yeah. How else do you think I got a crush on my dead best friend's boyfriend?"

I get a smile this time. And Lisa takes the cue to move on to a different subject.

# CHAPTER
## 13

I didn't see Carter at school Monday, but I can't miss him on Tuesday morning when he's waiting for me at my locker before first period. His glasses reflect the fluorescent overhead lights so I can't see his eyes very well, but his smile makes my stomach do a dumb little dance.

"Morning," I say, trying not to sound too happy to see him.

"Hey," he says.

As I open my locker, he gestures for me to hand him my backpack. He used to do this for Jules: hold her bag while she loaded up the books she'd need for the morning. I try not to feel weird about it as I slip the straps into his hands and squat down to pick out my books.

"So listen, I'm glad you came to Harry's on Saturday. It was fun, right?"

I glance up at him. "Yeah, it was. Thanks again for bringing me."

He waves me off. "Oh, no, you don't have to thank me.

I just wanted to see if you'd be interested in going camping with a few of us this weekend. Adriana and Louise are coming and they said you can share their tent."

I don't know how to respond. I've never really been camping before, except for that one year when I decided to try being a Girl Scout. It didn't last. And I'm not sure how Dad will feel about letting me go out into the wilderness with a bunch of underage kids he doesn't know. But when I stand and look into Carter's hopeful eyes, I can't say no. I don't want to say no.

"I'll ask my dad," I say instead. And my stomach dances again when Carter grins.

"Great." He holds out the straps of my backpack so I can turn around and put it on. I feel every millisecond that his fingers are touching my shoulders.

"See you later," he says.

But before he can turn, I grab his sleeve. "Are you busy this afternoon?" I ask.

He shakes his head.

"Do you want to maybe go for a run?"

Adriana's suggestion to run off my grief wasn't a bad one. I do need something to occupy my time. Something to take me away from Minding Her Business and Britt's Instagram, at least for an hour or so.

Carter smiles. "Yeah, definitely."

"I might slow you down," I warn him, already regretting this decision. He's going to hate this. "I haven't run in months."

He looks down at my fingers where they grip his sleeve. I let go, but he grabs my hand.

"We don't have to go fast," he says. I wonder if he can feel my rapid pulse in my fingers. "I'll meet you at your house after school?"

I swallow loudly. "Yeah, see you then."

When his fingers release mine, I can feel how clammy my palms are. Gross.

But maybe this is a good way to get over Carter. Let him see me sweaty and red-faced, out of breath and out of shape. I'll be too embarrassed to ever want to see him again.

***

At lunchtime, I head to the library. I spent most of Sunday combing through Minding Her Business, bookmarking the posts where Britt talked about Jules. There aren't that many of them from the last five years, but the ones that she did post walk a fine line between complaining and cruel. I mean, Britt might not have known that Jules still read her blog, but there was always the chance that she could. That alone should have been enough to keep her from sharing so much. But Britt didn't care about Jules's privacy or her feelings.

Today, though, I'm looking at her early columns from the *Washington Herald*, since the school has a subscription. It's not like I was going to subscribe myself just so I could comb the archives.

The most recent byline from Britt is the column that served as Jules's obituary. It's glaringly obvious how little

Britt actually knew about her daughter. She describes Jules as "kind to everyone she met," saying "her classmates seemed in awe of her." Our classmates ignored her, for the most part. Until Britt's second-to-last column. Her "Peak Mom Moment."

Britt spent five hundred words talking about her daughter's sex life and how cool Britt was when she found out about it. She got eviscerated in the comments section, which was satisfying, but so did Jules. Which destroyed her.

She didn't go to school the next day, but I did. I heard the things people said. They wondered how they were still single when a fat loser was getting laid by a hot jock. They wondered why Jules kept a diary because who even writes on paper anymore?

Some of them were on Jules's side and thought Britt had crossed a line, but even those people also wondered why Jules didn't ask Britt to stop writing about her a long time ago. Like Jules hadn't thought of that.

I email myself the remaining columns from the last ten years while I eat my lunch, but my appetite wanes with each one. It's Britt's tone that I hate most. It's so clear how much she despised her daughter. I have to wonder why she ever had Jules in the first place.

---

That afternoon, I change into leggings and a T-shirt, lace up my sneakers, and head to the kitchen to fill a water bottle. But I pause at Dad's room. The silence is alarming.

I knock on the door.

"Hang on," he calls out. I hear him moving around for a minute before the door opens. His hair is a little mussed.

"Hey, Dad," I say warily. I kind of don't want to know what he was doing that's left him breathing a little too hard.

"What's up, Bug?" he says, acting casual.

"I just wanted to let you know I'm going for a run with Carter. I'll be back in about an hour."

He nods, then glances at his watch. "I'm going out to play basketball and then have dinner with some of the guys tonight, so I might be home kind of late. You and Cordie will be okay on your own, right?"

I nod slowly. "Yeah, sure. We'll order pizza or something."

"Use my account and order two so I can have some for lunch tomorrow," he says. "Have fun with Carter."

And then he closes the door, leaving me to puzzle through what just happened. In seventeen years, I've never seen Dad flustered.

But then Carter texts to say he's outside, so I grab my water, phone, and earbuds and send Cordie a text telling her to order dinner when she gets home. My heart is already racing as I open the front door and see Carter. He's looking at his phone, but when he hears me close the door, he looks up and smiles, tucking it into his pocket along with his glasses.

"Hi," he says. "You ready?"

I shake my head. "Probably not. Take it easy on me, okay?"

Field hockey season ended in November, so I haven't run in almost five months. But I also haven't had much of an appetite since Jules died, so I've lost a little weight. Probably all muscle. Sometimes I feel like I'm liquid inside and the only thing holding me together is a plastic Natalie shell.

Carter and I stretch for a minute, and then he opens his running tracker app and shows me the route he planned for us.

"It's only three miles," he says, like that's nothing. To him, it probably is. Because while I spend the off season in front of the TV, he still lifts and runs almost every day.

I snort. "Right. 'Only.'"

"It gets easier after the first two." His grin tells me he knows that I want to hit him.

"Not if I throw up first."

He takes a step back. "Does that actually happen?"

I shrug, trying not to laugh at his expression. "I guess we'll find out."

And then I start jogging out of the driveway, leaving Carter to follow behind. For a few steps at least.

---

I manage the three miles, but by the time we're back at the end of the driveway, I really do think I might vomit. I'm drenched with sweat and I'm sure that my face is bright red. It takes me a good three minutes to catch my breath enough that I can talk without gasping.

Another good thing about running: no one expects you

to hold a conversation. After the first few minutes, Carter and I just put our earbuds in and kept pace alongside each other. He was wrong: it didn't get easier after the first two miles. By the end of it, I was almost crying from exhaustion.

"Thanks for not leaving me in the dust," I say when I can talk again.

He nods, removing his glasses from his pocket and sliding them on. "Anytime," he says. "Maybe tomorrow?"

I can't stop my lips from turning up at the corners. "Yeah, sounds good."

Carter waves as he heads for his car. "I'll text you tonight to make sure you're not too sore," he says.

And my stomach does its jig again.

---

Even after a hot shower, my muscles are angry and protesting. But when I get in bed, I'm too tired to read Britt's blog or even scroll through social media. I don't have the energy to do anything more than watch TV. So I curl up with my laptop and put on GBBO.

I'm not too tired to miss Jules though. *The Great British Bake Off* was her favorite comfort show. And it had the added bonus of being inspiration. We'd watch an episode and suddenly she'd be on Instacart ordering the ingredients for Mary Berry's princess cake or Paul Hollywood's iced buns, and then we'd spend the rest of the night in the kitchen. I mostly contributed by doing dishes and making comments about how delicious everything tasted, but Jules had a gift. Most people are either bakers or cooks, but Jules was amazing at both.

She could have had an incredible future ahead of her. But she knew Britt never would have approved of her working in the culinary industry. Britt didn't even let her cook in their house. Not when she was awake, anyway.

When Jules was little, Britt posted lots of pictures of Jules cooking and baking. She seemed proud of Jules, even writing a column about how she won their neighborhood July Fourth pie baking contest when she was eight. But when Jules started growing, and gaining weight, Britt took her to a nutritionist who told them Jules had to learn to cook healthier meals and stop eating sugar entirely. Britt wrote a column about that too.

Jules was ten.

So unless it was the middle of the night and we were doing it in secret while Britt slept, Jules did most of her baking at my house. Much to my dad's and Cordie's delight.

My phone dings with a text from Carter. *How are you feeling?* he asks.

I hesitate, wondering if I should mention Jules. But it's not like avoiding the subject keeps either of us from thinking of her.

I send a picture of my laptop screen. *I'm sad*, I tell him. *And I can't move my legs.*

He sends a picture back of his own laptop, the screen filled with Paul Hollywood's face. *I miss her too*, he says. *Think it will ever get easier?*

I simultaneously hope that it does and that it doesn't. I don't want to stop missing Jules, or remembering her. I don't want to forget the way her laugh echoed through the house, or the way her long fingers crimped pastry, or how she'd sing off-key, loudly and with no embarrassment, as she drove me home from school in the afternoon. But I also can't imagine living the rest of my life with her loss sitting so heavily on my chest that it hurts to breathe. I can't handle falling asleep with my pillow wet with tears and then waking up every few hours hopeful that it was just a nightmare, only to remember that it wasn't. That my best friend is dead.

*I hope so*, I write back. And then, *But I also don't want it to.*

Carter doesn't respond.

# IN LOVING MEMORY
Julianne Bethany Monaghan

I've been writing about my daughter, Jules, since before she was born. But I never anticipated talking about her in the past tense.

Since she was conceived, Jules has been difficult to describe. She defied expectations at every turn. Her father, Chris, and I weren't sure we'd be able to get pregnant after multiple miscarriages and two failed rounds of IVF. But Jules was so strong.

She was a night owl even in the womb. Just as I'd climb into bed, she'd start rolling around, pressing her little head against my bladder. She kept me up all night.

Then she was born with a small hole in her heart. The doctors said it would close up on its own with time, but I couldn't sleep for months. I would just watch her all night, breathing in and out. After a while, she stayed up with me. We'd end up falling asleep as the sun rose.

She never got over that habit of staying up all night.

Once when Jules was eight, I came downstairs at three in the morning and found her sitting in front of the TV, a bowl of cereal in her lap. She smiled up at me when she saw me.

"Look, Mommy," she said, pointing at the late-night infomercial. "Can I learn how to make pasta?"

She loved to cook. I don't know where that inclination

came from, as neither Chris nor I is the domestic type, but Jules seemed to enjoy both the process of creating something out of nothing and the creativity of changing what the recipe called for to make something new. She was inspired, and so were her creations.

Jules had a spirit that could light up a room, even if she was standing in the corner. She was always shy, so her dad and I worried about her social life, but she was kind to everyone she met and no one ever had a mean word to say about her. Her teachers loved her, her classmates seemed in awe of her, and her friends and boyfriend couldn't seem to get enough of her.

I wish I'd understood the depths of her depression. I wish she had shared with me just how hard things had been for her lately. I wish she had talked to me, or her therapist, or someone else. I wish for a hundred things that could have changed the outcome of the night that Jules took her own life.

She will never come back. That fact will never change. But she will live on in the hearts of those who loved her. And for that I will always be grateful.

# CHAPTER
## 14

The next morning, Carter's waiting for me at my locker again.

I hate myself for being so excited to see him. I hate that I put concealer under my eyes to cover up the dark circles so I'd look better for him. I hate that I wore my hair down instead of in a ponytail. I hate that I have on my favorite pair of jeans with Jules's favorite sweater.

Everything I do feels like a betrayal. But nothing feels worse than the fact that I know that and am doing it all anyway.

"How are you?" Carter asks. He puts out his hands to take my bag and I let him.

"I've been worse," I say, groaning as I squat down to gather my books. "But maybe not much."

He offers a hand to pull me back up to standing. I try not to read too much into it when he squeezes my fingers before letting go.

"Do you want a day off?" he asks.

I shake my head. "No. Last night was the first time I've fallen asleep before midnight since . . ." I let my voice trail off.

"Yeah," he says. "Okay, I'll see you around four, then."

Carter hands me my bag and slips into the parade of people walking past. They're all careful not to look at me.

I'm sure they think they're doing me a favor by not acknowledging my pain. Or they're doing themselves a favor by ignoring their own uncomfortable feelings about death. I get it. I never thought about it either before Jules.

I've never said anything to my dad about how hard it must have been to raise two daughters alone after losing my mom. I was too young to notice when he packed up her clothes for donation, or when he put away the family photos. I didn't really miss having Mom at my school plays or take me trick-or-treating on Halloween.

Cordie and I don't talk about her either, even though I know she remembers Mom better than I do. She has some of those memories that I'm missing, but she doesn't offer to share them.

In the Nagler house, we just tuck those feelings away in a drawer. Or sweat them out.

---

Carter and I are panting in the driveway that afternoon after our run when Cordie pulls up with her friend Kayla in the passenger seat. As she gets out, Cordie holds up a bag from my favorite Tex-Mex restaurant.

"I brought dinner," she says triumphantly. "Carter, you want to stay? I got enough to feed an army of taco lovers."

His eyes are round behind his dark frames. "Hell yes," he answers, practically bounding up the front steps. He holds the storm door open for Kayla and Cordie, and I can't help the hot streak of jealousy that runs through me as he watches Cordie's long legs. She doesn't even notice.

"Should I get Dad?" I ask as she sets the bag on the table.

Cordie glances at her phone. "No, he's gone already. He said he had a meeting or something."

I look up at her. Two nights out in a row? That is not the Nick Nagler I know. But Cordie just shrugs.

"Let's eat in front of the TV," she says, filling her plate with four tacos and grabbing the bag of tortilla chips before heading for Dad's recliner. Kayla does the same and then sits on the arm of the recliner, leaning against Cordie.

Carter and I follow, our plates piled high with tacos too. I grab the container of guacamole. I would eat it with a spoon if Cordie would let me.

We crunch loudly while Cordie browses through Netflix. None of us mention that Jules would have hated this meal. She felt like the flavors and ingredients were too similar in tacos and burritos and fajitas. She liked to get creative instead with a kimchi-brisket taco or a Frito pie burrito. They were delicious, but sometimes I just really craved a classic taco.

I didn't usually argue with her though. I just ate tacos without her.

Carter's phone dings as he finishes his last bite.

"Do you have to go?" I ask as he glances at it.

But he shakes his head. "No, my mom's just reminding me to pick up milk on the way home."

"Okay, good," I say without thinking. My cheeks heat with embarrassment, but Carter doesn't seem to notice. He just pulls my feet into his lap and goes back to watching TV like we've been doing this for years.

———

On Thursday, I run the whole first mile without feeling like I want to throw up. Through the second mile, I basically just follow Carter, whimpering a little while trying not to keel over. But halfway through the third, the familiar first notes of a song make me stumble. Jules's favorite: "The Bed Song" by Amanda Palmer.

Carter glances back at me, removing an earbud. "You okay?" he asks.

I take out one of my own. "Yeah," I gasp.

I pretend to stretch for a few seconds and then jog up to meet him. But the song is still playing in one ear. And tears are building in my eyes.

I start running again so he doesn't see. I don't want to talk about it. I'm tired of talking. I'm tired of crying. I just want to run.

Tears drip down my cheeks, but I don't bother wiping them away. And by the time the song is over, we're almost home.

When we get to the bottom of the driveway, we both lean over and put our hands on our knees, breathing heavily. The tears have dried on my cheeks and my face feels stiff and tight. I rub my hands across my eyes.

When I remove them, Carter is standing in front of me. He's sweaty and red-faced too, and, with his glasses on, he can probably see how bloodshot my eyes are. But he doesn't say anything about it. He just opens his arms and wraps them around me.

"Ugh, gross!" I complain. "You're all sweaty!"

He lifts me and spins me around a couple of times before setting me back on my feet. "You are too," he says. "So just accept my hug."

Before he can let go, I wrap my arms around his neck. He somehow still smells like clean laundry, but also sweat.

"You sure you're okay?" he says against my ear.

I nod into his shoulder. "Yeah," I whisper, breathing away the tightness in my chest. "Thanks."

Carter stays for dinner again. He showers and gets dressed in my room after our run, and it is really hard not to think about him being naked so close to my bed. Or to feel awkward about being naked while he's in the house when it's my turn to shower.

It helps that Dad is in the kitchen making meatloaf.

Since he didn't get home until I was in bed the night before, I corner Dad while he's making the boxed mashed potatoes and heating the canned string beans.

"So, Dad," I say, aiming for nonchalant. It doesn't quite work.

"So, Bug," he answers with a raised eyebrow.

I clear my throat, which makes me seem even more nervous and weird. Definitely not a good way to reassure him that nothing is going to happen if he lets me go into the woods with a bunch of kids he doesn't know.

I take a breath and try again. "Some friends are going camping on Saturday night, out at Shenandoah National Park, and they asked me to go."

Dad's other eyebrow meets the raised one. "You? Camping?"

I shrug. "It wasn't my idea, but Carter invited me. And I figure maybe it'd be good to get out of the house."

His face relaxes. "Yeah, Bug, it probably would. And Carter will be there?"

I'm not sure why he's asking, but I nod.

"I feel better knowing that, but you're not sleeping in the same tent, right?"

"No!" I say, trying to keep the disappointment out of my voice. "I'm sharing a tent with two girls from the hockey team. And Carter says someone can loan me a sleeping bag."

Dad looks like he's warring with himself internally. I can't tell which side is winning.

"Will there by cell phone reception?" he asks.

I shout the question to Carter, who's sprawled across the couch in the living room. He calls back, "Yep!"

Dad still looks skeptical. "And who's going to be driving?"

I call out that question too and hear the squeak of the couch springs as Carter hauls himself up. He leans against the doorframe, his curly, damp blond hair sticking up a little in the back from being matted against the couch cushions.

"I'm driving a few of us, including Nat, and my buddy Harry is driving a couple others. There are six of us who are going, so it's not a huge group."

Dad's raised eyebrow makes a repeat performance. "That's not a *small* group either though."

I roll my eyes.

"Are you planning to drink out in the woods?" he asks. "Or smoke some weed, maybe?"

Carter's mouth opens but I jump in. "Dad, no. That's not what this is about."

He looks between us. "What is this about, then, if not to go out into the woods to get drunk and high? I thought that was what camping was for."

Carter snorts a laugh before my glare shuts him up.

"Maybe it was for you, Dazed and Confused. But for us . . . Well, I'm not sure how I got invited, actually. But for Carter, this is supposed to be a distraction from, you know, Jules."

I don't know that for sure, but when in doubt, play the dead best friend card. Works every time.

When I look at Carter, I can see that he hadn't thought

of it that way—that his friends were just trying to distract him from his sadness—and my stomach plummets.

But Dad distracts us both when he says, "Okay, you can go. But you're going to call me when you get to the campsite, before you go to bed, and when you wake up. Call. Not text."

The apprehension I feel about camping momentarily fades as I smile. Dad's face lightens when he sees it.

"It's a deal," I say.

Carter and I retreat to the couch before Dad can change his mind. We exchange conspiratorial grins, like we just pulled off a heist.

It's only been a few months since Jules died, but she wasn't really her old self for months before that. I'd almost forgotten what it was like to have someone to do things with, things out in the world that involved making plans or even other people.

And each night this week since Carter and I started running, I've crawled into bed before midnight and fallen asleep before my pillow was soaked with tears.

I haven't had the chance to read through the archives of Minding Her Business once.

---

Saturday morning, Dad knocks on my bedroom door.

"Come in!" I call.

"I can't, my hands are full," he says.

That doesn't bode well.

I open the door slowly, peeking around it. Dad is

standing in the hallway holding bug spray, a flashlight, an electric lantern, a travel pillow, a yoga mat, a first aid kit, and two MREs.

"Dad. Really?" I say as he walks past me and dumps his bounty on my bedspread.

He starts packing things into my backpack. "Bring a few extra pairs of socks. You can wear them like mittens if your hands get cold while you sleep. And it's just always good to have a clean pair of socks. You should also bring a hat and some long underwear. It'll get pretty cold up there at night."

I squint at him. "Where did this stuff come from?"

Dad is no more a camper than I am, and the yoga mat is purple. Dad has never done yoga or owned anything purple for as long as I've known him.

"A friend loaned it to me. So be gentle with it." He doesn't meet my eyes. "Are you excited?"

I shrug. "I think Carter only invited me out of pity," I say as I sit down on the bed. Dad sits next to me. "He knows I don't have a life without Jules."

Dad pats my knee. "I doubt that. He wouldn't hang out with you this much if he didn't actually want to be around you."

I swallow the lump in my throat. "I think he just misses Jules too. I'm the closest thing he has left. A poor facsimile."

He shakes his head. "You're not a copy of Jules. You never were. You just have to let the shock of losing your best friend fade. When it does, you'll see you're more than just one half of a pair."

I look up at him, trying to read his expression. "How long does that take?"

His sigh isn't encouraging. "I don't think there's a set amount of time. It doesn't happen all at once. But one day, you'll start to notice that you don't think of yourself as a 'we' anymore. You're just 'you.'"

"And then what?"

"And then you figure out what comes next," he says with a casual shrug. Like it's that easy. "But you're allowed to find some happiness in the meantime. Just because Jules is gone, that doesn't mean you have to be sad all the time."

Tears burn at the back of my throat. "What if I don't know how to stop being sad?"

Dad reaches out and pulls me against his chest. "You don't have to know how. It'll happen naturally. Just don't lock yourself inside. Keep going out, keep seeing your friends, seeing the world. Talk to your old dad from time to time, maybe."

I lean back so I can roll my eyes at him. But when I see that his eyes are moist, I hug him again.

"Do you still miss Mom?" I ask into his shirt.

I feel him nod against the top of my head. When he releases me, he wipes his eyes with the back of one hand.

"I still think about her every day," he says. "Your mom was my favorite person in the whole world. She had the most incredible sense of humor, and she was always laughing. Even at the end." His voice catches. "And she wanted to be a mom so badly. She said having you and Cordie was the best thing she ever did."

I manage a small smile, but my chest feels full of rocks. I don't understand how she could think that, and yet I don't know even the smallest things about her. I don't know what her favorite song was, or what she looked like when she danced, or how she smelled, or whether she was a night owl like me or an early bird like Cordie.

Until Jules died, I didn't think about those things very often. I didn't like thinking about what a massive hole there was in my life or how there was nothing I could do about it. I just wanted to pretend like everything was okay.

And it was, for the most part. If I ignored the way Dad sometimes stared at nothing for a few minutes before snapping out of it. Or if I pretended like I didn't want to go to school dances so I wouldn't miss out on having a mom to help me get ready. Or if I focused on the negative parts of having a mom, which was easier to do when Jules complained about Britt.

But eventually, reality catches up.

"People say there's no right or wrong way to grieve, but I think I did it wrong," Dad says. His voice is a little wobbly. "Not talking about her, not sharing her with you and Cordie, was the wrong way. I just . . . I couldn't even think about her without feeling like I was going to lose it, and you girls needed me to keep it together." He sighs. "I needed you to keep *me* together."

I squeeze him around the middle again, and I can't help noticing that he's firmer and a little thinner than he used to be.

"You did a great job, Dad," I tell him.

He kisses the top of my head. "Thanks, Bug."

And then he stands and goes back to packing my bag full of things I probably won't even remove. But if it'll make him feel better to know I've got a burn kit and a hand crank radio, I'll bring it all along.

# CHAPTER
## 15

Carter picks me up an hour later; his friend Trey is already occupying the front seat. I climb in the back of the Subaru while Dad stores my bag, pillow, yoga mat, and a collapsible chair in the hatchback with a gallon of water ("Just in case"). Then he taps on the window. I roll it down.

"Remember: Call me when you get there. No drinking. No drugs. No sleeping in the same tent as the boys."

"So no fun," Trey grumbles, but quietly enough that Dad can't hear. I don't know him very well, but I have the sudden urge to kick the back of his seat.

"I promise," I say. "I'll call you soon."

I try to ignore the lead ball sitting in my gut as Carter pulls away from the curb. I wish Jules were here sitting next to me. And since she's not, I wish I were sitting in the front seat next to Carter. But at least from the backseat, I can gaze at his profile without being super obvious about it. And I can berate myself silently for even thinking about him that way.

It takes an hour to get to the campsite, and Carter lets Trey be the DJ, so we listen to his terrible EDM playlist the whole time. I'm ready to throw myself from the car by the time Carter pulls up to our assigned campsite.

Harry, Louise, and Adriana are already in the process of setting up the second of two huge tents. Louise squeals when she sees me get out of the car. She drops the pole she's holding and races toward me. I wonder for a second if she's already been drinking, but it's only noon, so that seems unlikely.

"I'm so glad you came!" she says as she throws her arms around my neck. "Adriana and I set up a sleeping bag for you between us. I'm not gonna lie, I kick in my sleep and Adriana snores, but no one sleeps well on the ground anyway, right?"

I grit my teeth and smile. "I guess not?"

Adriana walks up behind Louise and rolls her eyes. "I do not snore," she insists. "Louise does. She wakes herself up snoring sometimes and convinces herself it's me."

My smile is genuine this time. I grab my stuff from the back of the car and follow Adriana to our tent while Carter and Trey take over helping Harry with the second one.

Harry waves at me around an armload of weatherproof fabric. "Hey, Nat!" he calls. He's even better looking when his eyes aren't glassy and his face isn't red from drinking.

"Hey, Harry," I call back. "Thanks for the tent setup!"

He grimaces. "I only take responsibility for one side. If half of it collapses when a leaf falls on it, that's Louise's side."

Louise gives him the finger as she ducks into the tent.

My stomach feels a little lighter now that I'm here. The anxiety of doing something new is hard enough without Jules. She was always my buffer in these situations. Not that she was ever any less anxious than I was, but at least we had each other to talk to.

After I call Dad and assure him that I'm alive and well, I step into the tent and set my things down on the sleeping bag in the middle. Louise is already stretched out on hers. Adriana's sleeping bag has a little pile of multicolored rocks sitting in the middle of it.

"What are these?" I ask as I reach for one. Then I pull my hand back. It's probably not polite to just start touching her things.

But Adriana sits down and scoops up a few, handing me a flat purple rock that fits perfectly in my palm.

"These are my crystals," she says. "That one is purple lepidolite. It helps with anxiety. And it can help with sleep, which is why I brought it."

I don't really understand how a rock can help with anxiety, but I like the way it feels in my hand. It's cold and heavy, and the perfect shape to squeeze in my palm.

Louise rolls her eyes. "You don't have to pretend to believe in Adriana's weird crystal energy. I just smile and nod, and occasionally I wake up with a crystal under my pillow."

"I brought this one for you, actually," Adriana says, ignoring Louise. She hands me a small, rough black stone.

"It's black obsidian, a volcanic rock that's supposed to absorb grief."

I look up at her with surprise. "I can keep this?"

She nods, looking a little relieved that I didn't laugh.

"Thank you," I say. I hand the purple stone back to her as I rub the black one between two fingers.

"I keep one in my pocket pretty much all the time," she says quietly. "Most of these were my grandma's. No one else in the family believes in crystals, but she did. She did yoga every day and meditated and read tarot. She loved to tell me what each crystal does, and she'd buy me one every year for my birthday. So I figure even if they don't actually do anything, what harm can it do to have them around?"

A sudden slap on the outside of the tent makes us all jump.

"Come on, ladies!" Harry calls. "We're going for a hike!"

Louise jumps up and dashes out, already pointing a finger. "See? The tent is still standing!"

"For now!" Harry says with a laugh.

Adriana shakes her head. "Don't be scared. The tent is fine. Louise may not know what she's doing, but I do."

I want to hug her for so many reasons, but instead I just tuck the obsidian in my pocket and stand up, then follow her out of the tent.

———————

Hiking with five other athletes makes me glad to have had a few days of training with Carter this week. We're only climbing small inclines, but the group is moving faster than me. And they're all wearing backpacks. I'm just carrying a water bottle.

I pick up the pace to catch the rest of the group just as we reach the crest of the hill. Harry climbs to the top of a boulder and poses for a selfie. Trey immediately tries to push him off. The rest of us gaze out at the view below.

Spring is still new, so the leaves are the yellow-green of new growth. A lake sparkles under the early afternoon sun at the base of two mountains. It feels like a Bob Ross painting.

"Anyone hungry?" Harry asks as he jumps down from the boulder. "We came prepared."

Adriana removes her backpack and pulls out a small cooler. Inside are cold cuts, cheese, packets of mayo and mustard, and apple slices. Harry opens his backpack and reveals a bag of sandwich rolls. Louise is packing paper plates, napkins, and cutlery. Even Trey came prepared with a backpack full of bags of chips.

Carter and I look at each other guiltily. I'd blame him for not telling me about this, but it's clear he didn't know we were supposed to be bringing lunch either.

"Does anyone want a sip of my water?" I offer with a grimace.

They all hold up their own bottles.

"Don't worry," Adriana says as she lays out the food on a blanket. "This was a surprise for you guys. We've been feeling kind of guilty."

I glance back at Carter, but he looks as baffled as I am.

"Why would you feel guilty?" he asks.

Adriana pats the blanket next to her. I sit, and everyone else follows until we're in a circle, passing plates and sandwich rolls.

"We didn't know you very well when Jules passed," Adriana says to me. "But none of us reached out, not even after the funeral. And Carter, I know you've hung out with Harry and Trey a little since January, but not enough. If there's anything I learned from my grandma's passing, it's that distraction is the only comfort. So we're here to distract you. Currently, we're doing that with food."

Harry holds up his sandwich. "To Jules," he says.

The rest of us lift our sandwiches in the air too. "To Jules," we echo. Or at least, the four of them do. Carter and I are both a little too choked up to do more than mouth the words.

———

The walk back to camp is both easier and harder than the climb up was. Climbing downhill is hard on the knees but takes a lot less energy. Even so, we're all pretty quiet on the walk back.

After Harry's toast, we didn't talk about Jules. True to their word, the group did their best to distract me and Carter from our grief. But as we reach the flat trail to our campsite, Carter hangs back to walk next to me.

"Jules would have hated this," he says.

I laugh. "Jules never would have come on this trip at all."

We're quiet for a few moments. It's strange to be with Carter and his friends instead of in Jules's bedroom or my kitchen. My world was so small with her. It was cozy and comforting but also sometimes a little stifling. The newness of this experience, of being with new people, makes my chest feel fizzy with both anxiety and excitement.

"Do you ever feel guilty when you realize you haven't thought about her for a few hours?" Carter asks.

I nod. "At first, I couldn't go more than a few minutes without thinking about her and crying. I spent a lot of time on the floor. It was like my body needed to find the lowest point possible to reflect where my mind was at."

Carter smiles a little. "Same. And then eventually I'd realize that I had cat fur stuck to my cheek or I'd find a Cheerio in my hair, and it would distract me long enough to get me off the floor. Maybe even into the shower if the Cheerio was old enough."

I laugh, and Carter does too. And for a minute, I don't even feel guilty. But like a heavy blanket, the guilt settles back over my shoulders and wraps around my middle. I'm breathless for a few seconds. When I look back at Carter, his smile is gone too.

I instinctively reach for his hand, intertwining our fingers. We walk silently side by side until we're back at the campsite. But he drops my hand before anyone sees us.

As I duck into my tent, my palm feels cold and empty. A little bit like my heart.

It turns out Carter and I lied to Dad. The main point of the camping trip is, in fact, to drink in the woods. Because that's what camping is all about. Or at least that's what Harry claims when he pulls the bottle of Goldschläger out of his backpack after we finish our dinner of hot dogs and baked beans. There are actual gold flakes swirling around in the bottle. I can't help but wonder where the hell Harry gets the money to buy things like this. But I'm a scholarship student among rich kids. I may never understand.

He brought paper Dixie cups to use as shot glasses and he pours six, but Adriana declines hers.

"Someone should be sober in case anyone cuts off a finger or something and we have to drive to the hospital," she deadpans.

Harry doesn't give her grief; he just pours her shot into his and lifts the tiny cup with Donald Duck on the side. Mine has Minnie Mouse I notice as I hold it up next to Harry's. Carter's has Chip from Beauty and the Beast.

"Cheers," Harry says as Louise and Trey join us.

I've never tried Goldschläger before, but I try not to overthink it as I toss it into my mouth. The burning sensation is almost as bad as the cinnamon taste. My chest and throat are on fire. My stomach revolts at the idea of containing the shot, but I breathe in through my nose and manage not to vomit.

Harry puts his arm around my shoulders. "You okay there?"

I nod, but I don't trust myself to talk.

"Here!" Louise says, frantically shoving a marshmallow at my face. "Eat this, it'll help."

I want the marshmallow to absorb some of the liquor still in my mouth and get rid of the burning sensation, but my stomach churns at the thought of swallowing it. I nibble an edge to see how it goes, and when I don't throw up, I take a bigger bite. I catch Adriana's eye across the campfire. She's shaking her head.

"You're all ridiculous," she says.

Harry, Carter, and Trey go back for seconds, but Louise and I sit next to Adriana. We each skewer a marshmallow on a stick and hold it over the flames. Louise's immediately catches fire. Adriana holds hers at a distance so that it gets perfectly browned. I go halfway, trying to brown mine before getting impatient and letting it catch fire for a few seconds; then I blow it out and shove it in my mouth. It's hot enough to almost burn my tongue, but the sickly sweet sugar finally gets rid of the liquor taste in my mouth.

"I brought chocolate and graham crackers for s'mores," Adriana says after she swallows her perfectly toasted marshmallow. "You want one?"

"I think you meant to say 'You want s'more?'" Harry calls across the fire.

"No, I did not!" Adriana shouts back with more patience than I think he deserves.

He and Trey laugh as they do another shot. Carter sits this one out, opting to join us for dessert instead.

After a s'more, my throat doesn't burn anymore and my

stomach isn't churning, but my chest is warm and my head feels slightly cloudy, and it's a pleasant, happy feeling. I sidle up next to Harry and hold out my tiny paper cup.

He raises his eyebrows, or tries, but his head tips backward instead. I take the bottle and pour myself another shot.

"Carter!" I call out to him.

He hands his stick and marshmallow to Trey and joins me on the other side of the fire. I pour a shot into his Chip cup.

"We're supposed to be getting distracted," I tell him.

He holds his cup up, his eyes locked on mine. "To distraction," he says. And we down our shots.

It doesn't burn any less the second time around. But when I don't vomit (again—yay, me!), I pour us another.

As I move to pour yet another, Carter lowers his cup. "I'm pretty sure this cup will disintegrate if it has to hold another shot of this. Let's have some water."

Wise words. But it's too late. I'm drunk.

———

The fire swims in front of my eyes when I stand an hour later. And I sway a little, until I feel a hand on the small of my back and turn to see Carter behind me, keeping me steady. The way he has for the last few months.

"Where you going?" he asks. He sounds a little more sober than I am, but there's still a slur to his words.

"I have to pee," I say. My cheeks heat with embarrassment, but luckily he can't see in the darkness.

I bend over to grab the lantern Dad gave me, but I have

trouble making it back up. My head is foggy and my vision dims as I flail my arms. But Carter grabs me around the middle and pulls me to standing until my back is flush with his chest, his arms wrapped around my stomach like we're posing for a prom picture.

"You okay there?" he asks in a low voice. His lips are so close to my ear, his breath sends goose bumps down my neck.

I nod, but I don't move out of his embrace. I don't even care how it looks.

Carter runs one hand down my arm until he reaches the lantern, which he takes. When he steps away, the cold air hits my back like ice water. I feel a little more sober as I turn to look at him.

"I'll come with you so you don't get lost in the woods or trip over a tree root. I promised your dad I'd bring you back with no broken bones." He holds the lantern up and leads the way toward the tree line.

I don't love the idea of Carter listening to me pee in the woods, but I also don't want to go alone in the dark while I'm drunk, so I follow behind him, sticking close to the small circle of light the lantern gives off.

Carter stops at the entrance to the woods and hands me the lantern. I make him turn around before I walk the remaining twenty feet to the designated tree. Harry bungeed a roll of biodegradable toilet paper to the trunk and stuck a shovel in the dirt next to the hole he dug, so it's clear that I'm in the right place. But it's also really quiet. Way too quiet. I can hear Carter shuffling his feet while he waits.

"Could you, like, sing a song or something?" I call to him. "I don't think I can do this with you listening."

He laughs. "Any requests?"

"Something loud," I say as I set the lantern a few feet away and pull down my jeans, focused on balancing.

Carter starts singing "Brown Eyed Girl" by Van Morrison. He's slightly off-key, but it helps take some of the pressure off.

Jules had blue eyes, but mine are brown. I wonder if he knows that.

When I'm done, I use the hand sanitizer I slipped into my pocket. And by the time I reach Carter, he's started really getting into the song, singing at the top of his lungs. Back at the campsite, I can hear Adriana, Louise, Harry, and Trey singing along with him.

Carter takes my hand, and instead of walking, he spins me out and back while he sings "Sha la la la la la la la la la ti da." I'm laughing as he dances his way back to the campfire, still holding my hand. But before we reach the clearing of our campsite, while we're still in the dark outside the circle of firelight, I pull him to a stop. He quirks an eyebrow in a question.

But I don't respond. Instead, I take a step closer. And as I look up at him, placing one hand on his chest, he breathes shakily, unevenly, and closes the distance.

His lips are warm and soft against mine and when he opens his mouth, he tastes like cinnamon and chocolate. His fingers slide up my neck to cup the back of my head, and

I'm pressing my mouth against his hungrily when he suddenly breaks free, stepping backward to put space between us. He puts one hand to his mouth, holding the other up as if to ward me off. The evil temptress.

"I'm sorry," he says. His words are muffled by his hand. "I shouldn't have done that."

My head is spinning, from the kiss, from the alcohol, from the song. "Why?" I say. My throat is tight, and it comes out a whisper.

But he doesn't answer. He walks away, leaving me standing alone in the halo of light from the lantern.

---

When I stumble back into the campsite, I keep my head down and walk straight to the tent. Harry and Trey are still taking shots, but Carter isn't with them. Louise is passed out in her chair, her sleeping bag draped over her. So only Adriana sees my tear-streaked face.

She gives me a minute to get myself together before following me.

I sit cross-legged on my sleeping bag and hug my arms around me, trying to stop shivering. It's cold away from the campfire, and I can feel every rock and stick beneath me. Sleeping tonight is going to be impossible for so many reasons.

"Are you okay?" Adriana asks as she sits next to me.

She hands me the purple lepidolite. I squeeze it in my palm until my fingers hurt.

"Not really," I say.

"Did something happen?" she asks gently. "Or is this about Jules?"

My throat is too clogged with tears to answer. I drop my head into my hands, holding back tears until I can take a deep-enough breath to talk.

"It's Carter," I say finally. "I thought we were . . ." I feel so stupid saying it out loud. And callous and deceitful and wrong. So fucking wrong. "I thought he liked me, but after he kissed me, he looked like he realized he'd just made the biggest mistake of his life."

Adriana's silence doesn't help. I can feel her judgment without looking at her.

"I know. I'm a horrible person. You can say it."

But she doesn't. She just reaches out and puts her hand on my knee. "Grief causes some strange responses," she says. "And you've both been drinking. I don't think you should assume anything just based on this one . . . interaction."

I scoff, but I can't help looking at her thoughtful expression without a little bit of hope.

"I don't know how it happened," I tell her. "He's always been Jules's boyfriend, and I tried really hard not to think about him in any other way. But now I don't know how to stop."

"I don't think you're doing anything wrong," Adriana clarifies. "And I know I didn't know her, but I don't think Jules would think so either."

I look up at her with watery eyes. "Really?"

She tucks her thick, dark brown hair behind her ears. "People have to move on. It's the only thing you can do. And if you find comfort in each other, if you really like being with him, I don't think there's anything wrong with that. Jules loved you both for a reason."

The dental floss around my lungs releases just a fraction. "That's true," I concede. "She always said he and I were more alike than they were."

But Carter pulled away from me. He didn't mean to kiss me. It was just a moment of drunken sadness. He was probably just missing Jules.

"I have to call my dad," I say. It's true, but I also just want a little time to myself. To cry into my pillow.

Adriana stands. "Yeah, I should probably try to get Louise to bed too. Maybe Harry can carry her in here." She pauses at the door. "You're okay?"

I nod. Put on my brave Nagler face. "Yeah, I'm okay. Thanks."

When she's gone, I zip up the tent and call Dad. But he doesn't answer.

That's not like him. He would definitely want to be sure that I wasn't drunk or high or eaten by bears. But I didn't really know how I was going to talk to him without slurring my words, so I'm mostly relieved. I text him instead and let him know I'll call him in the morning.

It's gotten pretty chilly, cold enough that I can see my breath, so I change into my long underwear. Then I pull on sweatpants and a sweatshirt, two pairs of socks, and my hat.

I stow a pair of socks under my pillow in case I need them as mittens in the night. And then I curl up on my side and zip my sleeping bag up to my neck, ignoring the rock that's jabbing my hip.

When I close my eyes, I see Carter's face as he leaned in to kiss me. And the horror in his eyes when he realized what he'd done. I pull the socks over my hands and use them to dry the tears that leak from my eyes.

I guess Dad was right: it's always good to have a clean pair of socks.

# CHAPTER
## 16

Carter drops me off at home on Sunday before noon. Trey rode shotgun again, but I didn't mind this time. I put in my earbuds and stared out the window the whole trip.

Carter tried to act normal over breakfast. Everyone was hungover and quiet as we ate cold Pop-Tarts around the firepit that was now just ashes, so it didn't seem so unusual that we weren't talking. But I saw Adriana's eyes flick between us, back and forth like she was waiting for one of us to apologize or crack a joke.

Aside from asking if I wanted to stop for coffee on the way, though, we barely spoke.

And now that I'm home, and Dad and Cordie are both out, a whole silent day stretches ahead of me. A day to think about how I screwed everything up between me and Carter. A day to think about what a terrible friend I am, to him and to Jules. A day to think about all the ways I could have tried to help Jules. To save her.

But instead of wallowing, I know what I'm going to do to fill it: revenge.

I pull my laptop onto my bed and open a Word document; then I open Britt's most recent column from the *Washington Herald*. Jules's obituary. And I catalog every lie in it.

Like how Jules had a "spirit that could light up a room, even if she was standing in the corner." Jules was usually in a corner, sure. But she didn't light up a room. She darkened those corners with smirks and snark. And she wasn't "kind to everyone she met." She hated being around people and avoided conversation at all costs. But she hated no one more than she hated herself.

I move onto the next column, and the next, and the next. I get so caught up in the lies that I forget to eat lunch, so by five, my stomach is growling an angry protest.

I put a sweatshirt over my tank top and pad out into the hallway. I haven't heard Dad or Cordie come home, but they must be around somewhere. But Dad's room is quiet and there's no sound from the living room. The kitchen is empty as I pour myself a bowl of Frosted Flakes and sit at the table to scroll through Instagram.

An hour later, the front door finally opens. I know from the heavy footsteps that it's Dad. When I talked to him that morning before we drove home, he apologized for missing my call, but he didn't say where he was.

When he steps through the door to the kitchen, he seems surprised to see me.

"Hey, Bug!" He sounds almost guilty, like I caught him at something.

"Hey. Where have you been?" I say, with a hint of suspicion.

Just as he says, "How was camping?"

We both wait for the other to answer, but he holds out longer. He's had more practice.

"It was fine," I say finally. "A little cold last night. Thanks for the sock tip."

He nods. "Always glad to share the wisdom of the elders," he says with a smile.

"So where were you today?" I ask again. He was vague on the phone that morning when he told me he wouldn't be home when I got there.

Dad exhales loudly, not quite a sigh, and pulls out the chair next to me, then drops into it. I notice for the first time that he's a little dressed up. Collared oxford shirt, dark jeans, new sneakers. And he got a haircut. Was he asking for a loan or something?

"I was on a date," he says.

I stop breathing for a second. My first thought is *How?* But I manage not to say that. Instead I say, "With who?"

Dad's cheeks flush. I don't think I've ever seen him blush before. "Her name is Hannah," he says. "We've been dating for a few weeks."

It shouldn't be so shocking that Dad wants to date again. It's been over a decade since Mom died. But it feels wrong somehow. Not a betrayal of Mom as much as a betrayal of our family. It hurts that he would think about bringing someone new into our dynamic without asking how I felt about it.

But I don't want to discourage him, so I manage a smile. "That's great, Dad. I'm glad you're happy."

The words aren't a lie, but the bitter aftertaste in my mouth tells me they're not completely truthful either. I know this feeling. It's jealousy.

"Thanks, Bug," he says. He breathes a heavy sigh of relief, and I can see how much telling me has been weighing on him. "You can meet her whenever you're ready, but there's no pressure, okay?"

I nod, swallowing the bitterness in my throat. "We'll see," I say. "I left the yoga mat and stuff by the door—oh. Those are hers."

I feel like an idiot. How did I not see this was happening?

Dad clears his throat. "Yeah, Hannah's pretty into camping. I had to talk her out of loaning me her solar shower and camping stove and a dozen other things."

It's impossible to miss the smile he's trying to hide.

I don't really understand my reaction. It's not that I don't want Dad to be happy. But maybe I don't want him to be *this* happy when I'm so miserable. And yet I don't want him to feel like he has to hide it either.

So I force a smile. "I'm really happy you've found someone," I say. It even sounds like I mean it.

———————

Dad orders Chinese for dinner, but to avoid having to talk again, we eat in our rooms. I can hear a basketball game on the TV behind his door when I walk by to put my plate in the kitchen sink. I shake my head. It's not even basketball season, but he still finds a game to watch.

I sit at my desk with my laptop and go back to reading "Minding Her Business." The succulent Jules bought me for my birthday sits on the shelf in front of me at eye level. I almost killed it right after she died. I kept trying to nurture it, but I was just overwatering it.

A couple hours later, I've made my way through most of the newspaper columns, but there's still plenty of lies about Jules to go through on Britt's blog and Instagram. I don't know what I'm going to do with this information when I'm done. Maybe I'll send it to Britt's publisher, or write an anonymous letter to the *Washington Herald*, or just post it all online somewhere. But I know one thing: Britt doesn't deserve to tell her side of the story without putting Jules's out there too.

And since Jules can't stick up for herself, I will. I'm the only one who can. I owe her at least that.

---

When I wake up Monday morning, I want nothing more than to burrow back under the covers and sleep through the day. I contemplate telling Dad that I'm sick and need to stay home from school, but he'd be suspicious after the camping trip.

The thought of seeing Carter makes my chest burn like

I've eaten a ghost pepper. But I drag myself out of bed and into the shower. I get my morning cry out of the way under the stream of hot water, only wrapping it up when Cordie bangs on the door and yells that it's her turn.

I haven't had the chance to talk to her yet about Dad's new girlfriend. She got home late last night, when I was already too deep in my pile of blankets to pull myself out.

But on the way to school, I casually broach the subject in case he hasn't told her yet.

"So do you know where Dad was this weekend?" I ask her.

She glances at me out of the corner of her eye. "Yeah. Do you?"

I nod. And then we're both silent for a minute, each waiting for the other to talk.

"So what do you think?" I say finally.

She shrugs. "I think it's about time. He's been single too long and I'm super tired of my friends telling me they think he's hot."

"Ew, no!" I yell, putting my hands over my ears. "No, no, no!"

Cordie cackles. "I think that's why he let you go camping," she says. "Because he knew I'd be gone Saturday night and he could sleep over at her house."

"No!" I yell again. "Why do you say things like that to me? My poor ears!"

Now we're both laughing, our hands clutching the other's across the armrest as she stops at a red light. Cordie squeezes mine three times, then checks her makeup in the visor mirror, swiping a fingertip under her eyes.

It suddenly hits me how few of these mornings together we have left. Cordie's graduation is less than two months away.

I look out the window so she doesn't see the tears pooling in my eyes. But she's not fooled.

She squeezes my hand again. "You okay, Bug?"

I squeeze hers back. "Not really," I answer honestly. But mercifully, she turns into the school parking lot then so I don't have to go into why.

Before I open the door, Cordie says, "Hey."

I turn back to her.

"You don't have to be okay," she says. "But you'd tell me if you were, like, really *not* okay?"

She means if I were suicidal, like Jules. She doesn't have to say it.

I nod, swallowing around the lump in my throat. "Yeah."

"Promise?"

"I promise," I tell her.

I'm pretty sure I mean it, but as I walk into school and lock eyes with Carter before he turns a corner, I can't help thinking for just a moment that maybe I'd rather be dead than deal with what's coming.

———

Mercifully, I don't see Carter for the rest of the day. And when I see Adriana in English, she doesn't mention him, or anything else about the camping trip. I notice, however, that she occasionally wraps her fingers around the amethyst that hangs on a delicate silver chain at her collarbone.

I left the black crystal she gave me in my backpack, so I fish it out and put it in my pocket. For some reason, it makes me feel a little better. A little less alone.

But I don't mention it to Lisa that afternoon when I get to her office. She wouldn't make fun of me, but I think she'd be skeptical about using crystals as a coping mechanism.

"So, how have you been?" she asks. Normally I have almost nothing new to report, but this time I'm not sure where to begin.

I start crying instead.

Lisa holds out the box of tissues that's always next to her armchair. "Hard day?" she guesses.

I nod. And then I tell her about camping, and Carter.

"We had just gotten to a place where we were friends, sort of," I say. "It was so nice to not be alone all the time, and having him around was a little like having Jules around. And now it's all ruined."

She tilts her head. "I don't know that it's ruined," she says. "Carter may just need more time before he can contemplate what his feelings for you might mean. Jules hasn't been gone that long."

If my chest cracked open right now, a swarm of angry bees would burst out.

"I know," I wail. "What's wrong with me? Why couldn't I just leave him alone?"

Lisa narrows her eyes. "There's nothing wrong with you. You're grieving."

"How long do I get to use that excuse for being a shitty friend? I wasn't grieving when I told Britt about Jules's depression. I wasn't grieving when I betrayed the trust of the person I loved most in the world."

"Are you sure?" she asks. "Because I think if my best friend were threatening suicide, I'd be pretty grief-stricken. I'd be hurt and angry and sad and worried, and I would have done the exact same thing that you did."

I can't talk because I'm crying too hard. So I just nod. I was all of those things.

"I know you feel guilty," she continues, "but you didn't do anything wrong. Telling Britt was the only thing you could do. And you knew Jules would be mad about it, but you did it anyway because you knew she needed help more than you cared about keeping her secrets. That makes you an amazing friend."

I sob into my soggy handful of tissues.

Since Jules died, I've been sort of paranoid that everyone else in my life is hiding something from me too. Her suicide showed me that no matter how well I thought I knew her, I never really knew everything. She hid how miserable she was from me most of the time. And then she took away the most important thing in my life: hers.

All I want now is to expose the truth, for my sake and for Jules's.

"I've been working on something," I say when I've caught my breath and can talk again.

Lisa raises her eyebrows.

"I know you told me to stop following Britt on social

media, but since she announced the memoir, I just can't shake the feeling that she's just going to publish a bunch of lies about Jules. And I can't let that happen."

She still doesn't say anything, so I continue.

"I'm working on a counternarrative that exposes the lies in the stories that Britt's been telling for years. I want the truth about Jules out there before Britt can publish her memoir."

"Do you think Jules would want the truth out there?" Lisa asks. "Would she want those stories rehashed and reexamined?"

I suck in a breath. I hadn't actually thought about what Jules would want.

"I . . ." I pause. "I don't know."

"I want you to just try something," she says. "Next time you want to stalk Britt's social media or read the archives of her blog, or anything else like that, look at pictures of Jules instead and think about a good memory you have of her. Do something positive instead of focusing on the negative."

I can't keep the skepticism from my face.

"It feels easier to be angry and sad than it is to heal and forgive because it takes less work," Lisa says. "But I don't think it's healthy. And I don't think it's what Jules would want."

Anger boils up inside me. "You know what?" I yell. "Maybe I don't care what Jules would want! She didn't seem to care what I wanted when she killed herself, so why should I?"

Lisa's eyes are wide. I've never yelled at her before. But I don't care.

I stand. "And I don't care what you think either," I say. And then I walk out of the office, slamming her door behind me.

———————

Lying in bed that night, I stare at the ceiling while tears leak from my eyes and roll into my ears until I can't see or hear, and it's exactly what I want. If I could turn off my feelings, my guilt and anger, I'd do that too.

I suddenly understand Jules in a way I never did before. I understand why she felt suicide was her best option. I've never felt suicidal before, but now, all I want is to not be part of this world. I want to close my eyes and drift away.

But I don't want to miss Cordie's graduation, or her first season of playing basketball at UNC. I don't want Dad to be alone next year after she's gone. Even if he has a girl-friend, it's not the same.

And if I'm being honest, I still have hope that things will get better. I don't know why—I have no proof of it—but I can't seem to squash it. Even when I imagine what the world would look like without me, I can't help wanting to be a part of it.

I just don't want to do it alone.

# CHAPTER
## 17

I wake up the next morning feeling like I didn't sleep at all. I'm achy all over, my head feels like an overinflated balloon, and my eyes are swollen and dry. Again, I'm tempted to try to take a sick day, but staying home alone all day isn't much more appealing than going to school. At least school is a distraction from my misery.

Once there, though, I realize just how alone I really am. All around me, people are talking and laughing, making plans and living their lives. I'm just trying to get through each minute.

My swollen eyes fill with tears. I turn my face into my locker and use the small magnetic mirror to see how pathetic I look. It's worse than I thought. My hair is limp and messy. The dark circles under my eyes make me look like I was in a fight and lost, badly.

When I close my locker, I see Adriana at hers just down the hall. She gives me a small wave.

I take a deep breath and walk over to her.

"Hey," she says. "Did you read the first two acts of *Hamlet?*"

I nod. I may be miserable, but I'm still too responsible to let my homework go undone.

"Louise told me that Mrs. Barrett always assigns a group project when she teaches *Hamlet*," she says with a frown. "And I'm afraid Trey will ask me to be his partner. He never does any work; he just draws skateboards and boobs in his notebook."

I make a disgusted face.

"Would you want to be my partner, maybe?" she asks.

I look up at her, surprised. Jules was always my de facto partner on school projects when we had classes together. No group projects have been assigned since she died, so I haven't had to confront this until right now.

My stomach feels like it's full of worms.

I think Adriana might be covering, trying to help by not making me confront this situation in front of our whole class. I think she's trying to be my friend, which is what I need right now. More than anything.

"Yeah," I say. "Sure."

Her smile widens. "Great! Thank you. I really appreciate it."

"Don't worry about it," I say. "I, um, I'm glad you asked."

She shrugs, but there's a slightly pink tinge to her cheeks. "Do you want to come over this afternoon?" she asks. Her voice is quiet, shy. "We can plan our project, but also, I could show you my recording studio." Then she ducks her head. "I mean, it's not really a studio—it's a walk-in closet with foam on the walls. But it's kind of cool."

I tilt my head quizzically. "Studio? For what?"

Her cheeks flush brighter. "My podcast?"

I rack my brain, replaying our recent conversations. I don't remember her mentioning anything about a podcast. "Your . . . podcast?"

"Yeah, um, I told you about it last fall on the bus back from our game against Holy Cross." She tucks her glossy, dark hair behind one ear. "But it's not like anyone listens to it. So I wouldn't expect you to."

I'm a terrible person. Clearly it meant a lot to her to tell me about her podcast, and I must not have even been listening.

"I'm so sorry. My brain has been a little foggy since Jules . . ." And now I feel even worse for using Jules as an excuse. But it feels kinder than telling Adriana that I wasn't listening. "What's it about?"

The bell rings then, so we start walking toward class.

"Oh. Well." She pauses. "I always feel kind of silly talking about it."

I do my best to smile. "I know that feeling. I kind of miss my podcast, but whenever I'd tell people about it, I could tell they thought there was something wrong with me for being so obsessed with murder."

Adriana offers a smile in return. "But if they'd actually listened to it, they'd have seen that it was about so much more than that. The unsolved cases you chose were so

176

important. And the way you told the stories of the girls who were murdered was so personal. It seemed like you really got to know who they were. I think that's amazing."

I don't know what to say. I had no idea she'd even listened to my podcast. Almost no one else did. Not even Jules.

"Wow, thank you," I manage to say after a few stunned seconds.

"I just think sometimes people get so caught up in someone's death that they forget to remember their life," Adriana says. "It's important to remember the person. It always means so much to me when people tell me stories about my grandma that I didn't know. It's like she's still telling me about her life, even though she's gone."

I suddenly feel like the wind has been knocked out of me. I want Jules back so badly, but I want people to stop focusing on her death almost as much. She was so much more than just the depressed daughter of Britt Monaghan. So much more than her suicide.

But I also realize that maybe I'm just as bad. And maybe I should stop looking at Minding Her Business as proof of why Jules is dead and instead embrace it as a chance to learn things about her that I didn't know. In a way, it is sort of nice to have this archive of stories about Jules. And maybe that's why I've been so obsessed with reading them. I get to keep learning things about her, even though she's gone.

Adriana doubles back when she realizes I've stopped walking and am leaning against the nearest row of lockers. I just need a minute to let all of this sink in.

The second bell rings then, though, so we hustle to the

door and slide into our seats silently as Mrs. Barrett starts teaching.

But when she assigns our group project, I turn to Adriana with a relieved smile and mouth, "Thank you."

---

That afternoon, I'm glad to have the trip to Adriana's to distract me from the fact that I'm not going for a run with Carter. We'd only been running together for a week, but I had already gotten attached to the routine. To him.

Adriana's house isn't too far from mine, it turns out. Only about a half a mile. Like mine, her house is a small one-story, but hers has a broad front porch with a swing in one corner that I immediately want to sit on. There's a breeze that lifts the loose strands of hair off my neck like fingers, curling in an invitation to bask in the warm spring afternoon.

But I know Adriana wants to show me her studio, so I follow her inside.

Her house smells like home-cooked meals and unfamiliar spices. I'm not sure what our house smells like, but it's not food, unless we've just brought home takeout. A few years ago, Cordie and I agreed to each cook once a week to take some of the burden off Dad, but I usually just had Jules over to cook on my nights. Sometimes on Cordie's too. Ever since she died, we've been eating hot dogs, or sandwiches, or pancakes and bacon for dinner most of the time. Dad usually doesn't complain as long as he doesn't have to cook.

A woman who looks like an older version of Adriana walks out of the kitchen. Her hair is the same deep brown, thick and wavy, and cut bluntly across at the center of her back like Adriana's, but hers is streaked with silver. She has the same warm brown eyes that crinkle when she smiles. And she immediately wraps her arms around Adriana, speaking Spanish rapidly enough that my three years of classes are useless.

Adriana kisses the woman's cheek and turns to introduce us.

"Mami, this is Natalie," she says.

I assume Adriana must have told her mom I was coming because she doesn't seem surprised to see me. She takes the hand I offer, but wraps both of hers around it and pulls me in so she can kiss me on both cheeks.

"Welcome to our home," she says. "Make yourself comfortable. I'll bring you girls some food."

I open my mouth to say that she doesn't have to trouble herself—I can tell she's already in the middle of making dinner—but Adriana shakes her head.

"It's not worth fighting it. She'll make it whether we want it or not," she says.

I wonder what it's like to have someone waiting with a hug and a snack when you get home from school. I don't usually see Dad until he finishes with work and emerges from his bedroom around six, but sometimes it's much later. And there's never a snack waiting for me. He just gives Cordie free rein to buy whatever granola bars or chips or yogurt she wants at the grocery store as long as he doesn't have to do the shopping. I guess next year, I'll be in charge of the groceries.

We wind our way through the living room toward the hallway. The Rodriguez house looks a lot like ours on the inside, with slightly worn furniture and carpets, but it's clearly a place where people are loved. The couches all have throw blankets draped over the backs and piles of pillows that are misshapen from use. I imagine the Rodriguezes all snuggled up together watching movies. And there are framed family photos on the side tables and on top of the piano. Adriana's an only child, and there are photos of her at every age lining the hallway walls.

When Adriana opens the door to her bedroom, though, it's like stepping into another world. The walls are painted a deep pink ("I was nine when I chose the color," she explains), and the single bed in the corner is covered in a vibrant multicolored blanket with embroidered flowers all over it that match the walls. But there's so much stuff covering every available surface, it's hard to even take it all in.

Along one wall she has a row of bookshelves loaded with books and things I hardly know how to describe. There are little statues of deities from every religion I know, and even more that I don't. There's a shelf that holds a voodoo doll with pins in uncomfortable locations in front of books about voodoo, hoodoo, Santeria, and candomblé; a shelf with guides to tarot cards, crystals, and spells; a shelf that holds yoga gear;

and another one for board games. There are shelves full of books on meditation, UFOs, paranormal encounters, cults, ghosts, reincarnation, and so much more. And there are candles everywhere, on every surface, as well as fragrant, half-burned sticks of wood and sage bundles.

On top of her dresser is where Adriana keeps most of her crystals, including a tall rose quartz pillar and several dishes full of smaller stones. Next to her bed is an amethyst pillar and a dish with a few more stones.

Adriana's been watching me take all of this in while chewing on her bottom lip.

"Have you read all of these?" I ask, moving toward the shelves.

She nods. "Yeah, most of it's research." And then she opens the closet door.

The closet is small, but it fits a chair and a desk that holds a microphone equipped with a pop stopper in front of it and a headset that hangs from a hook. The walls and ceiling are covered in yellow egg crate foam, and the shelf that runs along the top is full of even more books. The hanging rods are empty, though, so I can't help but wonder where she keeps her clothes.

"Wow," I say. "This is awesome! You have so many books!"

Adriana stands outside the door while I run my gaze along the spines.

"What are you researching, exactly?" I ask.

"All the things I do my podcast on," she says. "It's called

*Unexplainable* and it's about unexplained phenomena. But I also get into different spiritual practices and beliefs. For me, it's not about the subject so much as it is the stories. Like, I don't need proof that aliens exist; I just want to talk to people who say they've experienced an abduction."

I try to keep my expression neutral. "That's fascinating," I say.

Adriana laughs. "It's okay. I know it sounds weird."

I don't laugh though. I can see how much this means to her, and it really *is* fascinating. I don't know if I believe in alien abduction, but it seems pretty egotistical to think that we're alone in the universe. So why not talk to people who claim to have experienced it?

"I mean, yeah, it sounds weird," I say, "but weird is my favorite. Normal is boring. What other things have you done episodes about?"

Her eyes shine. "Some of the weirder ones have been about people who hunt for Bigfoot or the Chupacabra. I did one recently about the phenomenon of karaoke rage. But one of my favorite episodes has been about past lives and reincarnation. Did you know there are kids as young as two who remember exact details about lives they claim to have lived that there's absolutely no way they could know about?"

I know why that was her favorite. I like to think about Jules being reincarnated too. But not before I get to wherever she is and can squeeze her tight for about a century.

I swallow around the lump in my throat and blink away the tears. Adriana seems to be doing the same.

"I didn't. I'll make sure I listen to that one," I say.

She beams. "Actually, sort of in the same vein, I'm doing an interview with a medium this weekend," she says. "If you want to, you can come over and listen?"

I glance around the tiny closet space. "Won't that be a little crowded?"

Adriana laughs. "No, it'll be virtual. She's based in Salem, Massachusetts."

"Oh!" I laugh too. "Okay, then yeah, I'll definitely be here."

Adriana's mom calls down the hall that she has our snack ready for us, so we head for the kitchen.

"Why don't you girls sit outside?" Mrs. Rodriguez says, shooing us toward the front door. "At least until the sun starts to set. I'll bring the food out to you."

I get the feeling she just didn't want us eating in Adriana's room, or hanging out in the kitchen. It's not a large space. But I don't care what the reason is. I sit with a contented sigh on the swing while Adriana sits on the porch and leans back against the railing.

Mrs. Rodriguez brings us a bean and cheese dip with tortilla and plantain chips and then leaves us to finish making dinner. We open our laptops and put our copies of *Hamlet* in front of us so that it looks like we're working, but we mostly just chew quietly.

"Jules would have loved it here," I say, without thinking.

Adriana tilts her head. "Why?"

I gesture around at the fresh herbs in the pots next to me, the snack lovingly prepared, and the beautiful sunny afternoon. "It's so normal," I say, hoping that doesn't sound insulting. "And lovely," I add just in case. "Jules's life was kind of . . ."

"Anything but normal?" Adriana provides.

I nod, caught between laughing and crying. "Exactly."

"I love it too," she says. "My abuela and I spent a lot of time out here. I haven't actually been out here much since she passed. It's hard."

I jolt, nearly toppling my laptop. "Why didn't you say something? We don't have to be out here!"

But Adriana is shaking her head. "No, it's good for me. I can't keep avoiding the things that hurt. I think my mom knew I wouldn't say no if you were here. She's been sort of worried about me."

I picture Dad's face as he told me about Hannah. "Yeah, my dad is too."

We're quiet for a few minutes. I don't know what else to say, so I start reading through a scene in *Hamlet*. It's early in the play, but I know what's coming. Ophelia will die, and it will be because she's spent her life being manipulated by the people around her. She won't have the will to save herself from drowning.

I close the book, blinking back the tears that burn in my eyes.

"Do you want to go for a run with me tomorrow afternoon?" I say.

Adriana blinks, snapping out of her own thoughts. "Yeah," she says. "That sounds like a good plan."

It is a good plan. We can cry side by side and no one will ever know.

———————➤

That night, as I lie in bed scrolling through Britt's Instagram feed, I pause at a photo of Jules from when she was ten. She's dressed as a fortune teller for Halloween with her head wrapped in a scarf, her hands poised over her crystal ball (actually a glass bowl). She even used a cardboard box to make it look like she was inside an old-school coin-operated machine.

She's trying not to smile in the picture, but you can see how delighted she is with her work.

The comments on the picture were not kind, for the most part. People said that Jules was being insensitive and called it cultural appropriation.

I don't disagree with the comments, but Jules was a kid. She had just seen the movie *Big* and she wanted to be Zoltar. Her motive wasn't to offend anyone, but scrutiny is part of being a public figure. And you don't get to decide who you offend.

The photo makes me think about Adriana's interview with the medium on Saturday.

Like my feelings about aliens, I don't necessarily believe that mediums are able to connect to the spirits of dead people, but there's a fluttery feeling in my chest that tells me I hope it is possible. And maybe I'll see some proof of that when Adriana does her interview.

Or maybe I'll just be disappointed. At least that's not an unfamiliar feeling.

———————➤

The next day after school, I meet Adriana halfway between her house and mine.

"I'm pretty out of shape," I warn her, as I did for Carter. "So if you want to run ahead of me, I'll understand."

But Adriana is already shaking her head. "I've been running a few miles a couple times a week since my abuela died, but I'm not in anything close to the shape I was this fall during the season."

I'm relieved. "Okay, good. Running with Carter felt a little like being an old dog on a leash. He was always looking back to make sure I wasn't stopping to sniff a fire hydrant or something."

Adriana laughs, but I can see her watching my face.

"How are things between you guys?" she asks as she leans over to stretch the back of one leg.

I do the same. "Things are awkward," I say honestly. "We haven't talked since he dropped me off on Sunday morning. And it's not like we were best friends or anything, but we texted almost every day since Jules died. And for the last couple of weeks, we were starting to hang out more and it was just . . ." I don't know how to finish the sentence.

"Comforting?" Adriana supplies.

I nod. "Yeah. Comforting, and familiar. And, if I'm being honest, a good distraction."

"Distractions are key," she says, stretching her other leg. "There's no way to forget your grief permanently, but if you can find a way to stop thinking about it for even a few minutes, it helps."

I wonder if throwing herself into her podcast is Adriana's way of being distracted. But kissing Carter seems like it'd be a lot more fun. If he wanted to kiss me.

"Ugh, let's stop talking about him. Carter isn't interested in me. Period."

Adriana shrugs. "Okay. You ready to get going?"

I nod. "Let's do this."

We jog down the block and make a right, heading toward the running trail. It's not like it was with Carter. We keep the same pace, but Adriana and I are silent and awkward as we breathe heavily next to each other. I'm not sure if it'd be rude to put in my earbuds, so I don't, but I can't just spend the next three miles in silence.

"What are some of the weirdest things you've learned in your research for the podcast?" I ask her finally.

Adriana smiles, and I can tell that I hit on the right topic. "Well, did you know that in southwestern Virginia, they call Bigfoot a Woodbooger?"

I turn my head to look at her. "I'm gonna need you to repeat that."

"It's true!" she says. "There's even a Woodbooger festival every fall in a place called Norton."

"We should go!" I say. "Maybe you can do an on-location episode!"

Adriana grins, even though she's breathing as heavily as I am. "I would love that so much," she says. "Louise wouldn't go with me last year."

"I can't imagine why," I say. "There are so many questions that need to be answered. Why is it called a Woodbooger? How is it different from Sasquatch? What kind of food will there be?"

Jules would have loved to go to this festival. One of her favorite activities was going on road trips to eat local cuisine, but it was even better if there was a festival and she could try all kinds of different foods. We went to the oyster trail in the northern neck and up to the eastern shore of Maryland for crabs. We went to Smithfield to see the world's oldest edible ham and the world's oldest peanut. We visited seven of the top ten diners in Virginia. We even drove to Philadelphia for cheesesteaks once, but I made her take a tour of the Eastern State Penitentiary while we were there. Meat and murder: a perfect Jules and Nat road trip.

Adriana looks like she wants to hug me. "All great, perfectly valid questions," she says. "We will find out!"

I glance down at my phone and notice we've already run a mile and I don't feel like puking yet. Distraction is clearly a winner.

# CHAPTER
# 18

Carter and I avoid each other the rest of the week—or at least, I avoid him, and because I don't see him, I assume he's avoiding me. So I lean into the concept of distraction as a coping mechanism.

To start with, rather than eat in the library alone, I sit with Adriana and Louise and a few other girls from the field hockey team at lunch. I feel a little out of place—they've all been hanging out together since freshman year, while I was off hanging out with Jules—but they don't seem to hold that against me.

Adriana and I go running again on Thursday and Friday afternoon. It's less awkward now that we've gotten into a bit of a rhythm. We talk until we can't manage it anymore, usually after about a mile, and then we put in our earbuds and listen to the same podcast for the rest of the time. Afterward, we talk about what we heard and what we liked and didn't, what we'd do differently or adopt for our own podcasts. She's been encouraging me to restart mine, but I don't know if I have the energy anymore.

I invite her to come over Friday night to talk about it, but she has to prep for her interview, so instead, I knock on Cordie's door when I get home.

"Come in!" she calls out.

I open the door and find her curling her hair in front of the mirror.

Her room and mine are so different. Her bookshelves are nearly empty of books but full of trophies from her years of playing basketball. And softball and soccer. There are pictures taped up on her walls of her friends at parties or on the bus after games. And there's a framed photo of her and Mom on her dresser. Cordie's six or seven in it, so it's not long before Mom died. Her hair was already short from the first round of chemo she went through.

"Hey," I say. "Are you going out?"

Cordie unwinds her hair from the wand, leaving a perfect brunette spiral behind.

"Yeah, there's a party at Steve Axelrod's house," she says. He's a senior who plays on the varsity basketball team. Cordie looks at my damp hair and red face. "What are you doing? Is Carter staying for dinner?"

I suddenly don't want to tell her about what happened between me and Carter. I haven't seen her most of the week so she doesn't know I've been running with Adriana instead.

"No," I say. "I'm probably just gonna get some work done. Maybe do some research for the podcast."

"On a Friday night?" she says incredulously.

I wait for her to invite me to the party, but she just continues wrapping her hair around the wand.

"Yeah," I say. "Okay, well, have fun."

"Thanks," she says, sounding preoccupied. "You too."

I leave my sweaty clothes in a pile on the bathroom floor and climb into the shower. I manage not to cry, which makes me pretty proud of myself, but when I get out, Cordie is gone. Dad is gone too, out with Hannah for the night. And I'm alone in the house with no distractions.

I consider spending another night with Britt Monaghan and Minding Her Business, but instead, I search for Adriana's podcast. She's got almost a dozen episodes already, even though she only started about six months ago. Impressive.

I find the episode about past lives and press play.

"Welcome to *Unexplainable*," says Adriana. The sound is pretty good, much better than on my podcast. It doesn't quite sound professional, but it's close. "On this episode, we'll dive into the possibility of reincarnation and past lives. Starting with the story of a small boy named Ryan from Oklahoma who insisted to his family that he had lived before, in Hollywood with a big house and a pool. He once even tried to tip his mother for cleaning his room."

I can't help laughing, but as Adriana unrolls Ryan's story, as well as the stories of several other children with past-life memories, I can't help but wonder if maybe it's not so unexplainable after all.

——————➤

Mrs. Rodriguez opens the door the next afternoon and immediately pulls me in for a hug.

"How are you?" she asks as she kisses both of my cheeks.

I'm almost too surprised to reply. The Naglers aren't huggers, as a general rule. Dad isn't even likely to answer the door at our house, much less hug one of my friends. I wonder briefly if Mom would have.

"I'm fine," I say stiffly. Awkwardly. "Looking forward to hearing Adriana's interview."

I catch a brief wince as she releases me, but then Mrs. Rodriguez is smiling again.

"Yes, the podcast. Adriana does not stop talking about it. She tells me you have one too?"

I start to nod but then say, "I used to. I haven't kept up with it since my best friend passed away."

Mrs. Rodriguez looks like she wants to pull me in for another hug, but she refrains. "Adriana told me about your friend. I'm so sorry for your loss," she says.

I never know how to respond when someone says that. "Thank you" doesn't really feel appropriate, but I can't say nothing.

"I'm sorry about Adriana's grandmother too. Was that your mother?"

Mrs. Rodriguez swallows and looks away. "Yes. She had a brain aneurysm. It was very sudden."

"I lost my mother too," I say, "when I was little. Breast cancer."

Mrs. Rodriguez takes my hand, squeezing it between

both of hers. "I'm sorry," she says. "You've had too much loss for someone so young."

I try to shrug but can't quite manage it. "There's never a good time," I say.

"No," she says, patting my hand. "You're right."

I turn toward the hall. "Is Adriana in her room?" I ask, hoping for an escape.

"Yes, she is. You go ahead. I'll bring you girls a snack in a few minutes." Mrs. Rodriguez dabs at her eyes with a tissue as she heads to the kitchen.

I swipe a finger below both eyes before I get to Adriana's room.

"Hey," I say as I knock on the open door. "I hope I'm not too early."

Adriana is typing something on her laptop, but she sets it down when she sees me. "No, not at all. I was just making some notes."

"So, I listened to your episode on past lives last night," I say as I wheel the chair out from her closet and sit down beside the bed. "It's hard to believe the detail some of those kids remembered."

Adriana beams. "Isn't it? I mean, how could they possibly have known that much about a person who lived decades before they were even born?"

"It was really amazing," I say. "And I think you're really good at this. I'm excited for this interview."

She shyly ducks her head. "Thank you," she says. "That means a lot coming from you."

I don't really know what she means. "Why? I only recorded, like, eight episodes and then quit."

"I know, but you did them so well. I just . . ." Her voice trails off.

"What?" I prod.

"I wouldn't have thought of doing a podcast if you hadn't done yours, and it's meant a lot to me to have this outlet. I feel like I owe you so much."

I feel myself blushing. "Thank you for saying that. Jules kind of hated my podcast, so I've always felt a little self-conscious about it."

Adriana's brows lean toward each other. "Why would she hate it?"

I shrug. I don't want to speak negatively about Jules, but it actually really hurt that she didn't support me.

"She just didn't understand my interest in the cold cases," I say. "She felt like it was morbid and weird, and she said my podcast wasn't helping; it was just rehashing old news and capitalizing on other people's pain and misery."

Adriana doesn't seem to know how to respond. Her mouth is slightly open and the crease between her brows has deepened.

"I think Jules was a little sensitive to other people's business being discussed in a public way," I say. "Given the fact that her whole life was on display for other people to comment on, I guess I can't really blame her."

"Yeah, but . . ." Adriana pauses. "You were trying to help solve murders. I don't think that compares to her situation with her mom."

I wish I'd never brought up this topic. One of the things Jules accused me of before she died was using her to try to promote my podcast.

"Maybe not," I say. "So tell me about the person you're interviewing."

Adriana catches on and shifts topics, telling me about the medium and the research she's done on spiritualism and the afterlife.

I try to listen to Adriana, but I can't stop thinking about Jules and our argument the night before she died. She was so angry at me. And I was angry at her. And we both said so many things we couldn't take back. And now I'll never get the chance to apologize.

———

Twenty minutes later, Adriana has connected with the medium, Willow, via video chat and, after a couple minutes of small talk, starts recording their interview. I sit off to the side, out of frame but where I can see the screen.

Willow isn't what I expected from a medium, especially one with that name. She looks like a suburban housewife. She's in her fifties, probably, and wears a loose magenta cardigan over a white T-shirt. Her hair looks like she didn't even look in the mirror. She doesn't wear makeup, but she does have on a delicate gold chain with a jagged black stone dangling at her collarbone.

"Can you tell us a little about what it's like to speak to a spirit that's passed on?" Adriana asks.

"Sure," Willow says. "It's a little different for every

medium, but in my case, it's not a conscious choice I'm making. The spirits are there whether I ask them to be or not. I can't control when they come and go, but if they want to speak to the person I'm doing a reading for, they will make their presence known. I can sense that they're there before they try to communicate."

"Is it scary?" Adriana asks.

"No, no," Willow says. "It's not even necessarily like having a real conversation. I can feel their presence, but I can't really physically see them. It's almost like they project images to me to work with, and often it's something from my own life to help me understand. Like, if a grandfather wants to show me that he only knew someone as a baby, he might show me a picture of my dad with my son. He died before my son was even a year old."

"That's interesting," Adriana says. "What other sorts of messages do you receive?"

"Well, a lot of the process of a reading is usually proving to the person I'm reading for that their loved one is really there. So I try to give as much detail as I'm able to about how they died or what they were like in life."

Adriana nods, then remembers to say, "Sure, that makes sense. Lots of skeptics out there."

Willow chuckles. "They usually don't leave as a skeptic once they've heard what I have to say."

My palms are suddenly sweating. I want so badly to ask her if Jules is here. I have so many things to say to her. But this isn't about me, I remind myself.

But Willow seems to get the sense that Adriana is feeling the same way I am.

"Actually, there's someone who's been with me since last night, waiting to talk to you," she says. "I believe she's your grandmother because I'm seeing my grandma, who died when I was a teenager. But she's holding her head. Did your grandmother die of something sudden, something in her brain? Did she hit her head or have an aneurysm?"

Adriana's eyes widen. "Yes," she whispers. She blinks and tears cascade down her cheeks. "She's here?"

Willow nods, then says, "She's always with you. She visits your mom sometimes, but she's mostly with you."

Adriana stifles a sob.

"She wants you to know that her passing wasn't traumatic," Willow adds. "She knows it was for you, and she's so sorry that you were the one who found her. But she passed quickly and was welcomed by her loved ones on the other side."

My chest tightens painfully as tears build in my eyes. I want so much for that to be true of Jules too.

"Thank you," Adriana whispers.

"You're welcome," Willow says. "And I want to say, to you and to your listeners, that you can talk to the people you love. I know it feels a little silly at first, but they are listening. You don't have to do anything special. You don't have to be a medium to communicate. You just have to talk."

Adriana nods. "I talk to my grandma all the time."

Willow winks. "I know," she says. "And she loves it."

I feel guilty that I don't talk to Jules, except for the times when I visit her grave. And even then, I've never believed she was actually listening.

But before I can spiral too deeply into my guilt, Willow continues. "There's someone else here too. Do you know . . ." She pauses. "Oh, no. Oh, this is so sad. Do you know someone who took their own life?"

Adriana's eyes dart to mine as my mouth drops open. "Yes, I do. Sort of."

Willow's gaze is focused off camera. "She doesn't seem to be here for you, actually. Is someone else there?"

Adriana nods. "Yes, I have a friend here."

My heart is racing. I feel like I might throw up.

"Does the name of the person who passed begin with a J?" Willow asks. I nearly fall out of my chair.

"Yes," Adriana breathes.

Willow sounds a little choked up when she speaks. "She'd like your friend to know that she's happy now. But she hates how much pain her death has caused. Was there some unfinished business between them?"

Adriana glances at me and I nod, wrapping a hand over my mouth to keep from sobbing. I want to hear every word Willow says.

"She's full of regret," she says. "But she doesn't want your friend to feel the same way. She wants them to know that it's okay to move forward. And that she knows that in order to do that, your friend has to let go of her a little. And that's okay too."

Tears pour from my eyes, but I manage a nod.

Adriana motions for me to join her on camera so Willow can see me, but I can't move. I'm frozen in place.

"Thank you," Adriana says for me. "I think she needed to hear that."

---

As I leave Adriana's, I feel lighter. Full of a relief that I didn't expect. Whether Willow was channeling Jules or not, she's right: I do need to let go of Jules some. I do need to move forward.

And I need to start by letting go of my anger toward Britt. I can't keep living in the past, digging up all of Jules's old pain and embarrassment. She hated my podcast for the same reason she'd hate what I was doing now. No matter how satisfying it might feel to expose Britt as a liar and a fraud, it wouldn't feel good to rehash Jules's misery.

And I finally understand now that I care more about honoring Jules's memory than I do about exposing Britt.

So when I get home, I unfollow Britt on Instagram and Facebook. I delete my bookmarks for the blog and the *Herald*. And I move all my notes into the trash folder on my laptop.

When I'm done with the purge, I wish I could call Carter and tell him about everything that's happened. I don't know how he'd react to hearing that I received a message from Jules from beyond the grave, but I also don't really care whether he believes or not. It just feels wrong not to tell him.

But when I picture his face after he kissed me, I feel sick to my stomach. He looked so ashamed and disgusted. And I don't want to see that ever again.

# CHAPTER
## 19

When I walk into school on Monday, the energy is frenetic. Prom is coming up in two weeks and suddenly it's all anyone can talk about.

Jules and I had planned to skip it and watch movies with Carter instead. Jules never liked going to school dances, and neither did I, especially since I never had a date. We figured we'd reassess senior year, but most likely, we'd skip prom then too.

So when I sit down at the team's lunch table next to Adriana and everyone is talking about it, I nearly stand up and walk away. But it's too late; they're all looking at me.

"Who are you going with, Nat?" Louise asks.

I try not to snort or scoff. I school my face into neutrality. "I'm not going," I say.

The girls look mostly confused. As if it hadn't occurred to them that not going was an option.

"I mean, I don't have a date, and it's a little late to find one now, right?" I add, as if that's the real reason.

Adriana jumps in. "Well, that's what we were all just talking about. I don't either, and neither do Lindley and Nia. Louise is going with Harry, and Casey and Mala are going together, of course."

Casey and Mala look a little embarrassed to be the only ones on the team who are going together, but then they start talking about what they're wearing and where they're eating beforehand and the limo they've rented, so I'm able to just eat in silence for a few minutes, at least.

"The four of you should just go together," Louise says, as though it's the most obvious thing in the world. "It's not like having a date is the only reason to go."

Adriana and I exchange a wary look. "What are the other reasons?" she asks skeptically.

"You get to dress up, and get your hair and makeup done, and ride in a limo, and dance with all of your friends!" Louise stands, grabbing her lunch bag. "I went stag last year and it was still super fun."

Casey and Mala stand up too. "Just come, folks," Mala says. "We'll all end up hanging out together anyway, right?"

Once they're gone, the four of us look around at each other expectantly.

"So . . . should we just go together?" Adriana asks.

If Lindley or Nia had asked, I'd have said no. I don't know them that well and I don't feel like I owe them anything. But Adriana's been nothing but kind to me and if she wants to go, I'll be her date. So I nod.

"Sure," I say.

Adriana covers her smile. "Cool," she says. I can tell she's aiming for nonchalant, but she looks a little giddy.

"Cool," I echo, sounding less enthused.

I've never been to a school dance before, or even a wedding, so I've never shopped for a fancy dress. I don't even remember the last time I wore a dress. I've also never gotten my hair or makeup done. I don't really even do my own makeup.

I might need to start thinking of excuses to get myself out of this.

———————

On my way to Spanish that afternoon, I'm rounding a corner when I run into a wall of abs.

"Ow! God!" I say angrily, pushing my hair from my face. I look up into Carter's hazel eyes blinking with surprise behind his glasses.

"I'm so sorry," he says. He puts up both hands as if he's surrendering to me.

I open my mouth, but nothing comes out. I had just let down my guard after avoiding him all last week. I had finally stopped peering around corners and hiding between classes until just before the bell rang. But I wasn't expecting to bump into him almost immediately.

"Are you okay?" he asks with an adorable head tilt. Until I realize it's because it's been at least ten seconds and I still haven't spoken.

"Oh, um, yeah, no, I'm fine," I finally manage. Super convincing.

He doesn't say anything but continues to peer at me with concern.

"Listen, I'm sorry about, um, what happened. At the camping trip," I spit out. "Can we just forget about it?"

Carter's forehead wrinkles. "Yeah, but I mean, you don't have to apologize. That was all on me. I just kind of panicked." He's flushed from the tips of his ears to his collarbone. "Let's definitely just forget about it."

My stomach sinks even though that was literally an echo of what I just said. But I say, "Yeah, of course. We were just drunk. It's no big deal."

He nods slowly. "Right, yeah." He reaches out as if he's going to put his hand on my shoulder, but then drops it. "I gotta get to class," he says. "See you later?"

I nod, but he's already walking away.

---

I canceled therapy today because I'm not ready to face Lisa after yelling at her last week. But after that conversation with Carter, I'm kind of regretting that choice. I need to do something with all this guilt and anger or I'm going to lose it.

So I ask Adriana to meet me halfway between our houses at four to go running.

"So, Lindley and Nia want to get dinner before the prom together," she says as we stretch. "Would you want to do that?"

I pause, bent over with my head near my knee so I don't have to look her in the eye.

"I don't know," I say. "Can I let you know later?"

"Sure," Adriana says, but I can feel her disappointment.

I stand up. "It's just weird to do this without Jules. She and I had plans to skip prom and hang out with Carter, and now he and I aren't really even talking and I'm doing things without her . . ." The rest of my words get stuck in my throat.

Adriana looks up at me. "Would she have wanted to do all of this?" she asks.

I snort. "God, no. She'd think I was wasting my time. Running, camping, going to prom—she hated all of that."

"But . . ." Adriana pauses. "But what do you think about them?"

I shrug, but it's half-hearted. "I kind of like it. But it feels like a betrayal of our friendship. And I've already betrayed her so many times."

She tilts her head up to look at me. "Betrayed her how?"

But I can't tell her.

"You mean with Carter?" she asks.

I didn't, but I nod anyway.

Adriana puts her arm around me and squeezes. "You're a good friend, Natalie. And kissing Carter isn't really all that bad on a scale of one to Judas."

Then why do I feel like I ate bad seafood?

"He doesn't seem to think so," I say quietly. "He couldn't get away from me fast enough today."

Her eyes widen. "You saw him? Tell me everything."

We start off down the sidewalk and I tell her all about Carter's and my literal run-in. But when I'm done, I can't help wondering what Carter meant by our kiss being "all on him." I'm sure he feels as guilty as I do, but I still don't want him to regret kissing me.

At this point, I just want my friend back. If I can't have Jules, it feels especially wrong to not have Carter in my life either.

We're silent for a few minutes aside from our heavy breaths.

"So what did you think of Willow?" Adriana finally says. I can tell she's been wanting to ask. We didn't get much of a chance to talk after the interview on Saturday because she had to go to a family birthday party.

"Honestly?" I pause. "I'm firmly a believer. I know some of the things she said were pretty general. Telling a grieving person they can move on isn't novel. But she knew about Jules's suicide. She knew the first letter of her name. The things she said . . . made sense. They felt like Jules. I have to believe that message was real."

Adriana grins, which is impressive since we're just breaking into our second mile and my head feels like it might explode if I keep talking.

"I'm so relieved," she says. "I was worried you might think she was a kook. Or that I am."

"If you are, I am," I say, panting.

She smiles again and then pulls out her phone. "Want to just listen to something the rest of the way?"

I nod. "But also, can you send me Willow's contact information? I'm sort of curious if I can connect with my mom."

She doesn't ask questions. She solemnly nods and immediately texts it to me.

"Thanks," I say, putting in my earbuds and starting up a podcast.

---

When I get home, Dad is just emerging from his bedroom.

"Hey, Bug," he says. "How was your day?"

I shrug. Too many things have happened lately that he doesn't know about. It's just easier to say, "Fine."

It's not like he and I were super tight before, but since he started dating Hannah, I feel like I barely see him. Or maybe it started after Jules died.

I follow him into the kitchen. "So how are things with Hannah?" I ask.

His cheeks flush. "They're fine too. I'm seeing her tonight."

It's my night to cook dinner and I'm actually a little hurt that he didn't tell me sooner. "But I was going to make tuna noodle casserole. With potato chips on top, no less."

I shouldn't care. There's nothing in tuna noodle casserole that will spoil. Not for at least three years. But it's the principle. It's basic manners to tell someone when you're going to stand them up for dinner.

"Aw, Bug, I'm sorry," he says. He goes in for a hug, but I cross my arms over my chest. "You know how much I love your tuna noodle casserole. Will you make it anyway so I can have it for lunch? And leave some potato chips for me to sprinkle on top so it's crunchy? Because you're the best daughter I've ever had except for Cordie because you're tied for first place?"

I slump against him so he doesn't see my smile. It's hard to be mad at him.

"Fine," I say. "But I can't promise Cordie and I won't eat all of it."

He releases me and pretends to punch me in the arm. "You wouldn't do that to your old dad," he says.

I roll my eyes even though he's right.

Cordie walks into the kitchen then. "What's happening in here?"

"Dad is abandoning us for his girlfriend. Again," I say. I try to sound like I'm just giving him a hard time, but it's masking the fact that I'm actually a little hurt. I've barely seen him the last few weeks.

But when I look at Cordie, she's grimacing. "Actually, I'm not going to be here for dinner either. I'm sorry, Nat."

I don't even try to conceal my disappointment. "Really? You're ditching me again too?"

She tries to hug me, but I step away.

"Don't be mad," she says. "I have a group project due on Wednesday, so I'm going to a friend's house to work on it."

"They could come here?" I offer. "You can eat the casserole while you work."

Cordie's grimace is back. "I don't think the rest of my

group would be as excited about tuna noodle casserole as Dad is, especially when we already agreed to order pizza."

I don't know why I'm pushing so hard. It's not like I can blame them. Tuna noodle casserole isn't exactly a gourmet meal. If Jules were cooking, neither of them would have been able to say no. But my cooking doesn't entice anyone to cancel their plans, not even me.

"It's fine," I lie. "I'll make it anyway."

"Maybe Carter would want to come over?" Cordie offers.

I feel my expression darken. "Yeah," I say, already walking out of the kitchen. "Maybe."

———————→

About an hour later, my phone rings while I'm breaking up potato chips into tiny pieces to sprinkle on top of the casserole. My hands are covered in chip crumbs and grease, so I ignore it, assuming it's probably spam. No one ever actually calls me.

But when I check to see who it was after washing my hands, my heart seizes. It was Britt. She left a voicemail, so I press play.

"Hey, Natalie," her familiar voice says. I hate that voice. "A calendar reminder popped up today that the prom is in two weeks. I was going to surprise Jules by taking her shopping for a dress."

Classic Britt. Offering to take Jules shopping—an activity she hated—for a dress she wouldn't want to wear to a dance she didn't even want to go to. Incredible.

"I miss you, sweetie," she continues. "And I wanted to know if maybe we could go shopping together instead? And if you don't want to do that, maybe we could get coffee? I just . . . Well, call me or text me or whatever. I love you."

Seriously?

I'm relieved I didn't answer because even though I don't know what I'd have said, it wouldn't have been friendly or pleasant. I want to call her back just so I can hang up on her. I want to march over to the house and tell her she's a terrible mother who destroyed Jules's life. I want to tell her there's no way I'd ever want to spend even five minutes with her.

But I also can't help but wonder why she'd even want to see me. She must know how angry I am. I haven't contacted her since Jules died.

And then it dawns on me: she probably wants to talk to me to get material for the book.

I push the casserole into the oven and slam the door closed.

I pick up my phone and stare at it, then listen to Britt's message again. It makes me even angrier the second time.

But it also makes me sad. I suddenly wish my mom were around to take me shopping for my prom dress. I don't even feel like I can ask Cordie to go with me. She's been so busy lately that I doubt she'd be able to find time. I haven't even had the chance to tell her I've decided to go.

I set the timer and retreat to my bedroom, pulling up Adriana's text with Willow's information along the way. On my laptop, I find her website. The testimonials from past clients are glowing, praising Willow for connecting them with their loved ones who have passed.

The small hole in my chest that I've been ignoring for more than ten years suddenly widens into a chasm. A sob unexpectedly bursts from my lips. I barely remember my mom, but I miss the idea of her. I miss the idea of a mom who'd be there when I got home from school every day. Who'd take me shopping for a prom dress. Who'd make me tuna noodle casserole instead of me making it for an empty house.

I used to get jealous of Jules all the time. Britt may be a pain in the ass who violated Jules's privacy and used it for her own financial gain, but she was there, present, a part of her life every day. She even put reminders in her calendar to take Jules shopping. Probably so she could write a column about it, but still.

I don't feel sorry for myself very often, but I can't stop the pity party this time. Especially when I see Willow's rates. I definitely don't have a couple hundred dollars to spend on a private session.

But Willow did say that I could just talk to Jules or Mom. It's not the same as having someone there to tell me what they're saying back, or what they want me to know, but it's something.

So I close my eyes.

"Hi, Mom," I say. "I don't know if you can hear me. I don't know if you're around all the time, or if you have, like, things to do on the other side. Maybe you have a job or friends or, I don't know, a cat. But I hope you're listening."

Oh boy, this is not starting off well. What the hell am I even talking about?

"Sorry for being so awkward," I continue. "I wonder if I was like this when you knew me? Maybe this isn't unexpected for you. If you've been watching me for the last ten years, you must know how weird I can be."

And somehow, it's getting worse. I scrub my hands down my face.

"Um, so, I'm sorry I haven't talked to you much before now. It's not that I don't think about you; I just never really believed in an afterlife. But then my best friend died. You never met Jules—"

The words get stuck in my throat. For some reason, it makes me indescribably sad that my mom never got to meet the person who meant the most to me in all the world.

"Maybe now you have," I whisper as tears slide down my cheeks. "She could use a good mom. She deserves to have someone wrap their arms around her and tell her how amazing and kind and beautiful she is. And I know I don't remember a lot about you, but I remember your hugs. I remember feeling safe in your arms."

And now I'm sobbing. Thank God no one is home. I pick up the stone that Adriana gave me and rub my thumb against its rough black surface.

"I hate everything right now," I admit. "I want my old life back."

And that's the truth of it. I want my mom, yes, but I also hate this new reality that I'm stuck in. I miss my old routines with Jules. I miss hanging out with her while she cooked in the kitchen, eating our weight in pasta and cake, and then falling asleep on the couch with our legs tangled together. I miss spending lunch together, usually quietly. We'd eat leftovers of whatever she made, and she'd look for new recipes while I listened to a podcast or did research for mine. Sometimes Carter would eat with us, and he and I would rank our favorite episodes of *Law & Order* and *Criminal Minds* while Jules rolled her eyes.

It was so normal—it never occurred to me that it could disappear.

It's not that I didn't know Jules was depressed or that she had suicidal thoughts. Almost every time she was sad, she'd say that she wished she were dead. But because of that, after a while, it stopped feeling like a threat. I mostly stopped worrying that she meant it. And as far as I knew, she didn't attempt suicide again after that night freshman year.

But I didn't ask.

I didn't ask if she was serious about killing herself, I just told her how much I needed her to be here. I didn't ask if her depression was getting worse, I told her how good it was when she occasionally seemed happy. I didn't ask if she needed me, I told her I would be there when she did.

I should have asked. I should have pushed. I shouldn't have waited for her to tell me she needed me.

"Do you think I could have saved Jules?" I ask my mom. But it's like asking the wind, because there's no answer. There will never be an answer.

There's just the question I'll live with for the rest of my life.

The next night, when I get home from my run with Adriana, Dad is in the kitchen making dinner. He's singing a Huey Lewis and the News song while he pours spaghetti sauce into a pan with several sizzling Italian sausages.

"Are you home tonight?" I ask him.

He nods. "Yep. Just me, you, and the sausage."

"Where's Cordie?" I ask.

He smiles. "She hasn't said anything, but I'm pretty sure she's dating someone. She's been doing a lot of 'group projects' lately."

Cordie has been out for a couple of years, but as far as I know, she's never dated anyone. My heart simultaneously feels full of joy for her and full of jealousy that I'm officially now the only single Nagler left. For years we were a trio, but now I'm just the fifth wheel.

"Do you think we'll ever get to meet her?" Dad asks.

I shrug. "Don't ask me. I didn't even know Cordie had a girlfriend." I sound more bitter than I intended, but it's an honest response.

Dad can clearly hear the hurt behind the bitterness, though, because he looks up at me with a tight smile. "I think she probably didn't want to flaunt her happiness when you were struggling."

"Is that why you waited to tell me about Hannah?"

He breathes out heavily, but I don't think it's a sigh. More like he's been holding his breath, avoiding mentioning her, and now I've hit the release valve.

"Yeah, Bug. It's only been a few months since Jules died. And I know you're doing better, but grief is like the ocean. Sometimes it's just lapping quietly at your toes and ankles while you walk along, but other times, a huge wave will come out of nowhere and pull you under."

He turns the heat down on the stove when a bubble of tomato sauce spits over the side of the pan.

"Anyway," he continues, "you've been dealing with enough stuff, and I didn't want to pile on. But I also didn't want you to think I was hiding her from you. So it seemed like a good idea to at least mention that I was seeing someone."

I nod. I do understand. And I don't have a problem with Dad dating, really. But haven't I lost enough? Now I also have to compete for time with the two people left in the world who love me? It just doesn't seem fair.

So I do the typical Nagler thing and ignore it.

"I've decided to go to prom," I say instead.

Dad raises his eyebrows, but I'm not sure if his surprise is about prom or about the change in topic.

"I thought you should know so that you don't panic when I stay out late next Saturday night."

Instead of responding, he takes the lid off the spaghetti pot and drops in the pasta. He's silent while he pushes the spaghetti under the boiling water with his wooden spoon. Then he turns back to me.

"I think that's great," he says finally. "It'll be good to do something with your friends."

I realize what he's working up to.

"I don't have a date," I say quickly. "So you don't have to worry about me getting a hotel room to lose my virginity or anything."

The blatant relief on his face almost makes me laugh.

"Glad to hear it," he says. "But why do I get the feeling that was a tactic to make me feel relieved when you change the topic to how much this is going to cost me?"

It's my turn to be surprised.

"You realize this isn't my first time parenting a daughter?" he says with a grin.

I shake my head. "I should have compared notes with Cordie before coming to you."

"Yeah, well, you'd have to track her down first," he says as he gives the pasta a stir and turns off the burner under the frying pan. "So listen, here's the deal I came up with for Cordie last year: I'll give you two hundred bucks and you can spend it however you want. On the dress, on dinner, on a limo, whatever. But that's it. And next year, you're on your own."

I nod. "That's more than fair."

He points the dripping pasta spoon at me. "And no using your college fund either. You'll have plenty of time to get a job and save up for prom next year if you want."

It's not that we're struggling for money, exactly. We're not rich, but we make do. But Dad likes to "help" us appreciate the value of money by making sure we understand how much things cost. And according to him, the best way to do that is to spend your *own* money. So Cordie and I don't get an allowance; we get paid for doing chores. And then when we want something like new clothes or a phone, we're expected to pay for it ourselves.

Our college funds, however, are accounts in our own names into which he puts money every month. Neither of us has enough money for more than a year at a state school, but it's a start. And for Cordie, who has a full scholarship to UNC, it's going to help pay for all the things she needs, like books and a new laptop. The pressure is on now for me to get a scholarship too, but I'm not even half as good at field hockey as she is at basketball. I have a better hope of getting an academic scholarship.

As Dad fixes us each a plate of spaghetti and sausage, he casually asks, "So have you thought any more about meeting Hannah?"

I'm glad he can't see the face I make. But I guess I take too long to answer because he raises his eyebrow when he hands me my plate. We sit across from each other at the table.

"I was just thinking maybe you'd need help picking out a dress. She'd be pretty good at that." His gaze is focused on his noodles, but I know this is important to him.

So I lie. "Oh, um, Britt Monaghan actually offered to take me," I say. "And I already said yes."

Dad pretends along with me. "Okay, no big deal. We'll find another time."

I nod. "Yeah, definitely."

We fall into silence while I chew on the lie I just told. I don't even know why I said it. But it's too late now. I guess I'm going prom dress shopping with Britt.

# CHAPTER
## 20

I text Britt the next morning on the way to school.

*Thanks for offering to take me dress shopping*, I write. *I don't have a lot of money to spend, so maybe you know where to find a dress for $100? If you do, I'll meet you there on Saturday.*

Britt texts back almost immediately.

*I know you'll try to say no, but the dress is on me. Meet me at Nordstrom at Tyson's Corner at noon on Saturday.*

I knew she'd try to buy my dress for me. It's not worth arguing with Britt, but I haven't decided whether I'll let her pay or not. If I want to call her out on being a terrible mother and try to destroy her career, it seems a little wrong to also take her money.

I just send back a thumbs-up and tuck my phone into my bag. When I look up, Cordie's eyes meet mine.

"What's up?" she asks.

But I don't want to get into it with her. She'd just give me grief about being a hypocrite after all the time I've spent hating Britt. And all of her time I've wasted talking about it.

"I should be asking you that," I say.

I try to raise one eyebrow, but I can feel how ridiculous the face I make is instead. Cordie bursts out laughing.

"Stop!" I protest. "I'm trying to make you feel like you're under investigation!"

She laughs even harder. "I don't think that's what intimidation is supposed to look like," she wheezes.

I can't help but laugh along with her.

"I'm not joking!" I insist, trying to force my face into seriousness. "Dad says he thinks you're dating someone. Do you have something to tell me?"

Cordie's porcelain skin suddenly has a pink tinge. Her cheeks and the tips of her ears turn practically neon.

"Oh my God, you *are* dating someone!" I squeal. "Why didn't you tell me?"

Her smile drops briefly and when it returns, it doesn't look quite as wide.

"I didn't want to rub it in," she says. "I'm sorry, Bug."

I wish people would stop holding back their joy around me. I don't want them to feel like they can't be happy just because I'm miserable. That just makes me more miserable.

But I push my lips into a smile. "So are you going to tell me about her?"

She gives a happy little sigh as she pulls up to a red light.

"It's Kayla," she says. Her best friend for the last five years. Cordie's version of Jules.

My chest constricts painfully, but I manage to keep smiling.

I'm happy that Cordie is happy. I love Kayla, and I love the idea of them together. But that doesn't stop it from hurting that she gets to fall in love with her best friend while mine is gone forever.

But almost more painful is knowing that Cordie felt like she couldn't share her happiness with me.

I take her hand and squeeze it three times.

———————>

I text Carter as I walk to my locker. He's the only person I know who'll understand.

*Hey. Do you feel like people don't want to be happy around you anymore?*

I hold my breath. When I see the dots that mean he's replying, I nearly burst into tears.

*All the time*, he texts back a minute later.

*It makes me feel bad*, I reply. *Do they think we want everyone else to be sad too?*

*No*, he says. *They just don't know that we can be happy for them and sad for us simultaneously.*

*Maybe we should tell them*, I say. *What do you think? Sandwich boards? Billboard? Skywriter?*

When I look up from my phone, I see that he's standing next to my locker, smiling at his phone screen. His wavy blond hair is just long enough to get in his eyes. He's been growing it out since Jules died. Or maybe he's just too sad to get a haircut.

I feel that way too. I don't want to change things because

Jules will never know. I won't watch movies or TV shows that we said we'd watch together. I haven't even gotten rid of the last of the brownies that she made for me a couple of weeks before she died, even though I'm likely to break a tooth if I try to eat them.

"I think we can be a little subtler," he says when I stop in front of him. "Maybe YouTube ads?"

His relieved grin when I laugh tells me he's as happy to be talking again as I am. Regardless of whether I want to kiss Carter, I just really missed talking to him. He's been my best friend since Jules died, and even though I have Adriana and the field hockey team now too, I still need him.

"It's good to see you," I tell him.

His smile tightens, but he says, "You too."

He puts out his hands for my backpack and holds it while I fill it with the books I need.

I try to sound casual when I ask him if he has plans to go to prom. I can barely look at him. But I see the surprised sneer.

"Definitely not," he says. "Wait. Why? Are you?"

I nod and I can feel the heat rising in my cheeks. "The field hockey girls who don't have dates are all going together," I explain.

He still looks surprised. And a little disappointed that I'm not following through on my plans with Jules to not go.

"Oh," he says. "I sort of hoped maybe . . ."

I pause my packing and look up at him. Did he think we were going to hang out on prom night like Jules and I had planned? "What?"

But he shakes his head. "Nothing. So, have you been running?" he says, changing the subject.

I appreciate the diversion. I'm sorry I even brought up the prom. "Yep. Adriana and I are up to three and a half miles, thank you very much."

He smiles. "I'm so proud. Maybe I could join you guys one afternoon?"

The bell rings then, so I take my bag from him. "Anytime," I say. "You know where to find me."

I sound much more laidback than I feel. But at least it's a step closer to normal.

———————————➤

That afternoon, instead of running, Adriana and I head to her house to work on our *Hamlet* project.

Mrs. Barrett is pretty open-minded about what she wants from us. The instructions are simply to "find a creative way to explain one important aspect of the play." We can act out a scene, stage a debate, write an alternative ending, or probably even embroider a quote on a pillow. Mostly, I think she just wants to be sure we understood the play. Or at least read it.

Adriana and I have spent the last week trying to figure out what we're going to do, but neither of us came up with anything that felt right. Until today.

A new podcast came out today about the Night Stalker, a serial killer who terrorized California in the mid-eighties. Richard Ramirez murdered and assaulted dozens of adults and children over the span of a year in the Los Angeles and San Francisco areas. He was also a Satanist.

And as I was listening, I couldn't help thinking of *Hamlet* and how often the paranormal is tied into murder. The play starts with the ghost of Prince Hamlet's father demanding that Hamlet seek justice for his murder. And by the end, pretty much everyone is dead.

"So what do you think of doing an episode of a true crime podcast covering the murders?" I explain to Adriana as we ride the bus to her house after school.

Her eyes widen and she grins. "That's an amazing idea!" she says. "We can start working on the script today!"

I'm relieved by her enthusiasm. I don't think Jules would have agreed to this plan. She'd have wanted to create an Elizabethan feast or something.

Adriana and I spend the afternoon on the porch, passing my laptop back and forth and taking notes on the plot of the play. Mrs. Rodriguez brings us snacks and drinks while we work. I catch her pausing at the door to look back at Adriana. When she smiles, I get the feeling that she hasn't seen Adriana smile this much since her grandmother died.

Around six, I start packing up my things to head home. Dad is out tonight, but Cordie promised to be home to eat leftover casserole with me and tell me more about how she and Kayla got together.

But I can tell that Adriana has something she wants to say. She keeps looking up at me and then away as soon as I meet her eye.

"Is everything okay?" I ask as I hoist my backpack onto my shoulders. "You wanna walk me halfway home?"

Adriana nods, then pops her head in the front door to tell her mom she'll be back soon.

"So, I've been thinking," Adriana starts as we walk together down the sidewalk toward my house. "I love my podcast, and I love yours, but I think maybe we should consider doing one together."

Goose bumps sprout on my arms. "Oh my God, that's such a perfect idea!" I say.

Adriana's relieved grin tells me she's been thinking about this for a while. "Really?" she says.

I nod enthusiastically. "Yes! I haven't had the energy to get back into doing mine since Jules died, but I miss it. And when I listen to yours, I get really jealous."

Adriana ducks her head in embarrassment. "Why are you jealous?" she asks.

"You're so passionate about it," I say. "I miss that feeling."

She slips her arm around my waist and squeezes. "I know what you mean," she says. "But we'll get it back."

And I believe her. Because without even discussing what our show will be about or how we'll do it or when, I know that she'll be an amazing partner. I know that we'll have fun together. And I know that she'll support me no matter what.

On Saturday, I take the bus to the mall to meet Britt. My stomach is in knots the whole way, which I don't recommend as an ideal way to ride.

I can't even focus on the podcast I'm listening to about the Atlanta child murders from the late seventies and early eighties.

Adriana and I haven't yet figured out what our podcast will be about, but we've got a lot of ideas, ranging from a hunt for the Woodbooger to a series on the mysterious deaths of three young women in DC who were all interns on Capitol Hill prior to their murders.

I'm excited for the first time in a long time. It helps temper the cocktail of emotions I feel about seeing Britt. At least a little bit.

As I cross the marble floor of Nordstrom, I can see Britt waiting by the front doors. I would have expected her to be on her phone, scrolling through Instagram or responding to comments, but she's just staring through the glass at the parking lot.

She looks smaller. Maybe it's because she's wearing flats instead of heels, or because her hair is pulled back into a low ponytail instead of left free in her usual cascading, voluminous waves. She's wearing black jeans and a white boatneck shirt that makes her look both younger and older somehow. Normally, she wears a lot of florals or pink or teal or yellow. I've never seen a blond look good in yellow, but Britt somehow pulled it off.

As I get closer, I can also see how tired she looks. Her

makeup can't hide the puffiness of her eyes or the deep creases in her forehead. I can't judge though. I look that tired too.

When Britt sees me, she smiles, but it doesn't reach her eyes. She was always a good actress, smiling and posing for photos when someone recognized her. But that seems to have faded too.

"Hey, honey," she says when I reach her. She holds out her arms for a hug.

I hesitate, but as I lean into it, the hug feels surprisingly comforting. Even though Britt is smaller than me, I can't help but recognize her motherly embrace: the soft scrape of her fingernails as she rubs my back, the smell of her expensive perfume, the way she kisses my cheek before she lets me pull away.

"Goodness, I've missed you," she says, capturing both of my hands in hers.

And I find myself saying, "Me too."

Her face relaxes a fraction, but I can still feel her nerves. I've never known Britt to be anything but confident. Or annoyed. Sometimes angry. But never nervous. It makes me feel anxious too.

"Do you want to get lunch first?" she asks.

I grimace. "I don't think I want to try on dresses on a full stomach," I say.

She nods. "Smart."

We head toward the dress section of the juniors' department. It's a sea of pastel and sequins that makes my palms sweat. My eyes can't seem to settle on one thing, so I hardly know where to start. None of these dresses look like anything I'd wear.

But Britt doesn't even pause to assess. She immediately dismisses the first six racks of dresses we pass without even looking twice. Then she works methodically through the next few racks, pausing momentarily to touch some fabric or pull a dress out to see its length. I mostly watch her rather than looking at the dresses. But everything she's dismissed is something I'd have ignored too.

Finally, she deems a dress acceptable: a long, navy satin, strapless but with a sturdy-looking built-in corset. It's simple, but elegant. She holds it up against me.

"You're lucky to be average height," she says. "I've always had to get my dresses altered. And poor Jules always looked like she was waiting for a flood."

The comment burns through me like lightning. "No wonder she never wanted to go shopping with you," I grumble as I take the dress from Britt and drape it over my arm.

Britt blinks in surprise, but doesn't snap back at me. She just moves on to another rack of dresses.

"You're right," she says after a minute. "She'd have hated this."

There were times when I didn't understand why Jules hated her mom so much. This is not one of them.

After years of body shaming from her mom, Jules couldn't see herself the way I did. She may not have been thin, but she was stunning. And though it didn't happen often, she never looked as beautiful as when she laughed at something that she really thought was funny. Her eyes would be so squinted that she couldn't see, which would make her laugh harder, and her whole face would light up.

I almost want to ask Britt if she ever saw that Jules. But she has approved another dress and is holding it up to me. It's a soft blue tulle with a full skirt and a corset back, and the bodice is covered in small appliqué flowers that cascade down just past the waist. It's beautiful.

As I drape the dress over my arm, I push down the guilt that's rising in my throat like bile. Britt is clearly trying to make amends, but even if my natural inclination is to want to forgive, I can't forget her role in taking Jules away from me. From the world.

As we browse in silence, Britt finds a few more dresses that she likes. She doesn't even ask if I like them, but she doesn't have to. They're all ones I'd have chosen for myself. Somehow she just knows this, like she knows my size or that I'll want to wear my hair up because I hate how hot I get with it on my neck. I guess that's partly because she's known me for years, but it's also part of who she is. I mean, Dad wouldn't have any idea what size dress to buy me. I don't think he even knows what size shoe I wear. But Britt has always been an observer. She's always seen things that other people didn't. And though Jules hated the scrutiny, even she had to admit that her mom paid attention to things that many other parents didn't.

When my arms can't hold any more dresses, Britt and I head to the dressing rooms. She sits in a chair near the entrance to wait.

"Do you want me to come out in all of them?" I ask nervously. The times Cordie and I have gone shopping together, we just shared a dressing room. It was easier and neither of us cared about changing in front of each other.

Britt nods and smiles encouragingly. "Unless you really hate it and don't want to be seen in it," she says. "But if you need help zipping or anything, just shout."

I strip out of my clothes and try on the first dress. It doesn't zip, and I can tell it won't even with help. But I can also tell immediately that the color isn't good on me. So I don't bother going out.

The next one I like okay, but it bunches in awkward places. I open the door to let Britt see and she immediately shakes her head. "You're beautiful, but that dress isn't doing you justice," she says. "Next!"

I try on the navy strapless dress and it's gorgeous, but the corset is so tight that I can't imagine being able to sit in it. And the high slit up my thigh makes me feel like I'm exposing myself every time I take a step. When I open the door to the dressing room, Britt's face lights up.

"Now that's a dress!" she says. "Your dad would probably kill me for letting you wear it, but I kind of don't care. What do you think?"

I smile as I run my hands down the soft satin. "I like it, but it's not exactly comfortable."

Britt shakes her head. "Sometimes discomfort is worth it, like in a wedding dress, but you have to be able to dance at prom. And you also have to be able to sit."

The next few are also nice, and they fit well, so Britt and I designate them as "maybes." But I've saved the last one till the end for a reason.

It's emerald satin, long and fitted through the hips. It has a high neck with a soft satin collar, so I wouldn't have to wear a necklace, but is otherwise strapless and will show my whole back.

I step into the satin and fasten the button at the back of the neck. The dress fits my body as though it were made for me. It's not so tight that it shows every curve, but it's tight enough to show that I do have some after all.

I've spent most of my life in jeans or mesh shorts and T-shirts, covering my body with fabric. I'm not ashamed of it; I just never felt like there was anything to show off about it. I'm athletically built, wide shouldered with small boobs and narrow hips. Not the body I'd like to have, but also not one that stands out in a crowd.

But in this dress, I feel special.

And I can't help thinking that I wish Carter were going to see me in it.

I step out of the dressing room, and Britt's face breaks into a brilliant smile. Not the smile she shows on Instagram, but her proud mom smile. It warms me from the inside.

"You look stunning!" Britt says, opening her arms wide.

She motions for me to turn so she can zip it up. When I turn back around, she says, "This is the dress."

I didn't even look at the price, but as I run my fingers

across the cool satin, I know it won't be cheap. But Britt can afford it.

"I don't want to take it off," I admit, letting a genuine smile slide onto my lips.

Britt nods knowingly. "That's how you know it's the right one," she says. "But once you take it off, we get to go to lunch. I'll even let you pick where we eat."

With images of a food court feast in my head, I head back to the dressing room and take off the perfect dress. I only let myself sigh once with regret that Carter isn't coming to prom.

And then I shake it off and leave the dressing room as my old self.

———————

Britt isn't as horrified by my food court smorgasbord as I expected her to be. But I guess since it was Jules's invention, she just isn't surprised by it. She follows me as I pick out spring rolls and lo mein from Panda Express, a pretzel from Auntie Anne's, and a cheeseburger and fries from Five Guys.

Britt peels off a piece of the pretzel and takes a bite. "I've missed mall pretzels," she says.

I had no idea she'd ever eaten a mall pretzel. She's so tiny, and I almost never see her eat anything at all. But I guess Britt had a life before I knew her.

"Jules loved Auntie Anne's pretzels," I say before I can stop myself.

And Britt surprises me again when her eyes fill with tears. She grabs a napkin from the stack on the table and dabs at her eyes. She's wearing a lot less makeup than I'm used to, but I guess she still has to worry about her mascara running.

That's enough to make something snap inside me. "Do the tears mean you miss her?" I ask.

Britt looks up from her napkin, her brow wrinkled in a way her esthetician probably wouldn't like.

"Of *course* I do!" she says. "Do you really think I wouldn't? We may not have gotten along, but Jules was still my daughter."

I feel a little sheepish. "I'm sorry," I say. But then a bolt of anger shoots through me. Anger at her, yes, but also at myself for apologizing. Because I'm not sorry. "The thing is, Britt, I've spent a lot of the last four months blaming you for what happened. And I'm not totally convinced yet that it isn't your fault that she's dead."

Despite the fact that I've dreamed of saying those words to her, that I've fantasized about how it would feel to finally call her out for everything she did to make Jules miserable, it's still hard to say it to her face. I idolized Britt in a lot of ways, but I counted on her too. She was my mom when I needed one. And it hasn't been easy to cut away the love I have for her and to only keep the anger.

Britt dabs at her eyes again, lips pursed. She doesn't seem surprised by my words, or even angry; she just looks sad. Then she takes a long, deep breath in and out, and then does it again. That's a trick Lisa taught me. I wonder if Britt's in therapy too.

"Honestly, Natalie, I'm not sure that it's not my fault either," she says finally.

Her words have a "poor me" tone that bugs me, but she seems genuine. There's some satisfaction in that.

"I've relived that day hundreds of times in my mind," Britt says. She stares down at the table, crushing her napkin in one hand. "And I don't know what it was that pushed her to that point where she felt she had no other option, but I do know it didn't help that I . . ." She stops and takes another long breath. "I did a lot of things wrong."

My ribs feel tight, squeezing my lungs. "I still don't know whether I should have told you about Jules's previous suicide attempt," I admit quietly. "She was so angry at me for that."

Britt's head snaps up. "You absolutely should have," she says. "You should have told me the minute it happened." Her eyes are narrowed, her voice quiet but sharp. I can picture her speaking to Jules in the same way. She never yelled, but her words landed like acid.

I'm ready to bolt from the table when her shoulders slump.

"But I understand why you didn't," she says, not meeting my eye. "Your loyalty to Jules was honorable, even if it wasn't always the right thing."

Her tears spill over again. Our feast sits forgotten between us.

"I know how hard it must have been to come to me," she says, reaching for my hand. "Jules wasn't always easy when she was sad. And I know that I didn't make it easy for her either."

"That's an understatement," I say, pulling my hand away from hers. "But also, don't blame Jules for 'not being easy.' She was seriously, clinically depressed, and you acted like she was a nuisance. Like just any other snotty teenager."

"I did try to help her though," Britt says. She's defensive, but she also sounds like she's trying to convince herself as much as she is me. "Jules was on antidepressants for years, and in therapy for even longer. Chris and I even talked about getting her treatment at an in-patient facility. The day she died, I was on the phone with her psychiatrist talking about that, figuring out what we'd need to make it happen, when she came downstairs, furious, demanding that I hang up. She was convinced that I was talking to my editor at the *Herald*, pitching a story about her mental health struggles."

My eyebrows shoot up. "But you weren't?"

Britt slowly shakes her head. "The fact that you even have to ask that just makes it clear how little Jules trusted me."

I don't respond, but my silence says enough.

"I know I screwed up," Britt says quietly. "I didn't truly understand how Jules felt about me and the blog—and everything—until after she was gone." She takes a shaky breath. "I didn't try to understand. Not until it was too late."

"Why?" It's the only thing I can think to say.

Britt hugs her arms around her tiny frame as a tear slides down her cheek. She doesn't even bother to wipe this one away.

"When I started writing about being a mom, I wasn't even a mom yet," she says. "I wasn't anything. I didn't know what I wanted to do with my life, and Chris was flying most of the time, so I was alone a lot. We were trying to get pregnant and failing, over and over again. Everything I did made me feel like a failure."

She sniffs. "When we started IVF, I found a community online who'd been through the same experiences I was going through. Some of them were chronicling their journeys on blogs, and I thought at least if I did that, I'd have an outlet for all of my emotions. And I'd be able to share my story with other people who were struggling, so we wouldn't feel so alone."

I knew that Jules was conceived via IVF because Britt mentioned it sometimes in her columns or captions. But I hadn't ever really considered how she got started blogging, or why. I never went back that far in the archives, I guess.

"I built some of my closest friendships online, with women who'd experienced the same things I had," Britt says. "And hundreds more found my blog and started commenting about how much it helped them to know that others were struggling the same way they were. So when Jules was born with the hole in her heart, I wanted to keep writing, to share all the new difficulties I was dealing with."

I guess I can't fault her for wanting that feeling of

community support. Parenting seems like a pretty thankless job, even without a sick kid.

Britt sighs. "The first six months of Jules's life were some of the darkest, most difficult days I've ever lived through. But blogging brought the world back to me. Or I guess I should say that it brought me back to the world."

I can almost see those words neatly typed up in her book, or as a quote spoken in an interview. A sound bite to explain away her exploitation of Jules. It turns my stomach.

But then she adds, "And then it distorted my reality."

# CHAPTER
## 21

I stare at Britt across the slowly cooling food on the table in front of us.

"So now you're going to distort reality even further by writing a memoir? So you can exploit Jules one last time?" I ask. There's so much adrenaline running through me that I feel like I'm vibrating. "Or are you just going to keep going back to the dead daughter well until people are tired of hearing about it?"

I expect Britt to snap back at me, because that was really cruel. Even I'm surprised by it. But instead, she hangs her head.

"I know that's what it looks like," she says. "It's certainly what many people have accused me of since I announced the book. Even Chris."

I feel my eyebrows lift, but Britt doesn't see. Her eyes are still on the table.

"What did he say?" I ask.

She slumps miserably. "He wants a divorce."

I can't stop my sharp intake of breath. Jules always said she was surprised they were still together, but I could see how much Chris loved his wife. He liked every photo she posted, commented on every blog, shared every column. He spent their vacations together taking pictures of her for her feed, filling both of their phones with her face. The way he looked at her when she walked into a room, the way he kissed her goodbye before he left for a trip—it all made me believe in a love that lasts.

Britt tries to shrug it off, but I can see how much it's hurting her. Losing your marriage after losing your only child is a harsh punishment. But then she suddenly sits up straight, pushing her shoulders back and wiping away the mascara under her eyes.

"It's nothing more than I deserve," she says. "I see that now. Losing Jules after all I went through to become a mom felt like a cruel joke at first, but it was a wake-up call. I see now how Jules felt exploited and ignored at the same time. And that's because she was."

"So then why are you writing the book?" I ask.

"It's a mea culpa," she says. "And an apology. And, as I've always done, it's a way to share my pain with others who may be experiencing the same thing. To make amends, if that's possible. But mostly, it's to help other parents whose children are struggling."

A knife slices through my heart. Because her story is now that she's a mother of a child who died by suicide. And other parents who have lost their child may need to hear that story, or maybe some will recognize the signs in their own child before it's too late.

"Oh," I manage to say before the tears block my throat.

Britt's hand covers mine now. And when I look up, her eyes are earnest.

"I know that you're angry with me," she says. "And I don't blame you. But I want you to know how sorry I am. I know it doesn't change anything or fix anything, but I needed to say it."

I don't know how to respond. My mind feels like it's been in a blender, and I'm not sure how I feel anymore.

There's a lot more to this than I realized. I never really even stopped to wonder about Britt's past and how she got to be who she was by the time I met her. I never thought about her side of the story. I never even knew all of Jules's story.

But at the same time, why should I care? Does knowing Britt's past change anything? No. Jules is still dead. And it is still Britt's fault.

She must sense my mind racing because she squeezes my hand, making me look at her.

"Before you judge the book, will you please read it?" she asks. "I want you to see that I'm not exploiting Jules's death. But mostly, I want your opinion. You knew her better than anyone in the world. Better than Carter, better than Chris, better than me, obviously. And I want your blessing before it goes to my editor."

I nod again because I don't have words.

I don't know how I feel about this book, or even about Britt, anymore. But maybe I can reserve my judgment until I've actually read it.

———————➤

Britt drops me off at home so I don't have to carry my dress on the bus. She makes me promise to send a photo of myself on prom night, but she doesn't mention that it's because I blocked her on Instagram.

When I open the front door, Cordie is on the couch with her feet in Kayla's lap watching a movie. They both raise their eyebrows when they see my garment bag.

"Natalie Eleanor Nagler, did you buy a prom dress?" Cordie asks. She's already walking toward me with her arms outstretched, reaching for the bag.

I try to hold it away from her, but Cordie's arms are longer than mine and the gesture is futile. So I let her unzip it.

Kayla wolf whistles when she sees the emerald satin. Cordie immediately reaches for the tag.

"How can you afford this?" she asks. Her eyes dart between me and the tag suspiciously.

"Britt," I say, trying to sound natural. "She offered to take me shopping."

Cordie's eyebrow shoots toward her hairline. "The same Britt who you've been talking shit about for years? Who you accused of wanting her daughter dead?"

"Yes."

I carefully zip the dress back into its bag so I don't have to look at her. When I finally get the nerve, she and Kayla are exchanging an unreadable look.

"I'm going to put this in my room," I say, so they can continue their silent conversation without me.

But Kayla shouts, "No! You have to try it on! First rule of prom dress shopping, you have to try it on again at home to make sure it's still the right one."

I can't tell if she's joking or not, so I just stand there blinking at her.

"Cordie, go with her in case she needs help," Kayla says, shooing us both down the hall toward my room.

Cordie looks as confused as I am by this development, but she doesn't argue. She just closes my bedroom door behind her.

As I hang the dress and start stripping off my clothes, Cordie sits in my desk chair, looking down at the keyboard. The silence is unbearable. And uncomfortable.

"Are you mad or something?" I ask. I start to step into the dress, hopping on one foot, when I hear the chair squeak as Cordie stands. And then her hands are holding the dress open so I can step inside with a little bit of grace.

She fastens the buttons at the neck and zips up the back. And then she tells me to turn around.

"Wow," she says, holding one hand to her mouth. "That is some dress."

I look down shyly, spreading my fingers like a starfish against the deep green fabric. "It is, isn't it?"

She slides her hand down my arm to link her fingers with mine. "You look beautiful."

"Thanks," I whisper. I'm not used to feeling pretty or even good about the way I look. But I believe her.

Cordie squeezes my hand three times, tugging me to look at her. "Why didn't you tell me you were going to prom?" she asks. "I'd have taken you dress shopping."

I sigh. "I don't know. I don't like to make a big deal out of things."

She's quiet for a moment. "But . . . you told Britt?" she says finally.

"Yeah, well, she kind of insisted. And I wanted to talk to her about the book anyway." I tell her what Britt told me about the memoir being an apology. "So, two birds. And hey, free dress!"

I sound more flippant than I feel. Seeing Britt was one of the hardest things I've had to do since losing Jules. I hadn't seen her since the funeral, and with so many people there that day, I almost avoided her entirely.

But Cordie sees through my casual air. "I'm serious, Bug," she says. "I wish you'd told me."

I nod, swallowing my guilt. "I know you're not going to want to hear this, but I sort of feel lately like you've already moved away. I barely see you except on the way to school in the morning. And that doesn't count. Half the time Kayla's there too."

I could go on. I could tell her how much it's hurt to not have her and Dad around when I've already lost Jules. And Mom. And Carter too, in a way. But I don't want to be melodramatic. I just want to keep pretending I'm fine. Maybe eventually I will be.

Kayla knocks on the door. "So what's the verdict?" she calls out. "Is it a keeper? Can I see?"

I open the door, grateful for the interruption. She squeals and puts her hands to her lips. "Oh my goodness," she says. "It's amazing!"

I can't help smiling. "Thanks, Kayla. So tell me what you guys are wearing."

It's a perfect distraction, though I can feel Cordie's eyes on me while I try to focus on what Kayla is saying. Until she remembers they both have their dresses in Cordie's room. So while I change out of my dress, she and Cordie go to her room to put on theirs.

And with the spotlight off me, and with my sister's happy laugh echoing down the hall, I start to feel a little more at ease.

---

"Want to go for a run this afternoon?" Adriana asks as I slide into the desk next to her in English on Monday morning.

My stomach sinks. I have therapy this afternoon. Which means I have to face Lisa again after yelling at her.

"I can't today," I say vaguely. "Tomorrow? And afterward we can work on the script for our *Hamlet* podcast?"

Adriana nods, but I can tell she wants to ask what I'm doing this afternoon without her. It's strange how much of a fixture she's become in my life after such a short time. And while I'm not embarrassed to be in therapy, I don't feel like talking about it within earshot of a dozen other people.

"What's your next episode of *Unexplainable* going to be about?" I ask, shifting subjects.

Her expression lightens. "It's about out-of-body experiences," she says. "Have you ever heard about them?"

She grins when I shake my head.

I love how excited she gets about her show. Her enthusiasm for strange phenomena reminds me of Jules's passion for cooking.

"Well, during an OBE, people have reported feeling like they're hovering over their bodies while they're unconscious," Adriana explains. "Usually it happens when they're in a hospital; sometimes their hearts have stopped beating or they're experiencing a trauma, and they can see what's happening in the room. Patients have reported knowing what type of instruments doctors used on them or what the doctors and nurses said to each other, which is later confirmed."

My eyebrows lift slightly. I don't want to seem skeptical, but there has to be some sort of explanation. Anesthesia that's too light, maybe. But Adriana continues.

"Sometimes people report visiting an otherworldly realm where they're greeted by people they either know who have died or who they don't know but feel comforted to see," she says. And I feel my eyebrows raise even higher. "But eventually they're told that it's not their time and they have to go back. Most report feeling sad that they have to return to their bodies because of the peace they experienced in that other realm."

"So, it's like heaven?" I ask.

She shrugs. "I don't know. I was raised Catholic, so I believe in heaven, but I think that's just a word for a place we can't understand. The human brain isn't complex enough to fully grasp what happens to our consciousness after we die."

I have the sudden urge to hug her. Tightly.

I never thought about heaven or hell or anything else about the afterlife until Jules died. But now I want desperately to believe that somewhere, Jules is watching over me. But more than that, I want to believe that she's living, happily, however unlikely it seems. Maybe it only seems unlikely because my simple human brain just can't understand the truth.

———————➤

I open the door to Lisa's office that afternoon with my chest as tight as a fist. I know she's a professional and she won't hold my outburst against me, but that doesn't make it okay.

When Lisa sees me, her expression doesn't change, but she pushes herself up out of her chair. And then she opens her arms. I rush to hug her.

"I'm sorry," I say into her shoulder. She just squeezes me harder.

Lisa is about my mom's age, or the age my mom would be had she lived. She doesn't look or sound like my mom—she's Black and British, to start with—and I've only known her a few months, but she is about as close to a mom as I've had since Jules died and I stopped seeing Britt. Even so, I bet she doesn't hug many of her clients. I appreciate that she made this exception.

"How are you?" she asks as she releases me.

I settle into the armchair across from hers and tuck my feet beneath me.

"Better," I say. "I saw Britt this weekend."

"Really?" she asks. She can't hide her concern. "Last time we spoke, you wanted to call her out for her role in Jules's death. Did you do that?"

I shake my head. "Sort of," I say. "But as usual, you were right."

"About what?" She knows, but she's going to make me say it. Typical.

"There's more to the story, and it's a little easier to understand now that I know it," I admit. "I'm still not happy about it, but she says the book isn't the exposé I was worried it might be."

She looks relieved. "That's good," she says. "For you and for Jules."

I nod. "She even told me I could read the book before she sends it to her editor. She wants my blessing."

Lisa's eyebrows rise. "Really? Do you think you'll give it to her?"

I shrug. "I don't know. It depends on what's in it, I guess."

"So you are going to read it, then?" she asks.

I pause. Because I haven't actually decided that yet.

"Maybe," I say finally. "I'm not sure if I can stand to spend that much time inside Britt Monaghan's brain."

"That seems fair," Lisa says with a sympathetic smile. "I'm proud of you. You seem to be doing better."

I think she's probably giving me too much credit. I don't know yet how I'll react when I actually read the book.

"I guess so," I say. "But things with Carter are still awkward. We mostly just avoid each other."

Lisa doesn't say anything for a few seconds. "Have you thought about dating someone else?"

I can't stop the laugh that bursts from my chest. Lisa seems a little taken aback.

"Sorry," I say, catching my breath. "It's just that . . . no, there's no one else who's interested in dating me."

Although when I think about it, the truth is that I've never been interested in anyone else at school. At least not seriously. Jules used to try to get me to go out with some of Carter's friends, and while a few of them are cute, I just couldn't see myself with any of them. I was happy just being the third wheel with Jules and Carter, even if I did get jealous of their relationship.

Lisa just looks at me. Her eyes narrow.

Finally, I sigh. "What?"

"How long have you really had this crush on Carter?" she asks. Right to the point, as usual.

My stomach churns with guilt. "Since he moved here," I admit. "I'd see him on the soccer field while I was playing field hockey. But once he and Jules met, I knew I had no chance. So then it was a safe crush because I knew nothing could ever come of it."

Lisa looks a little smug. "Until now."

I nod. Until now. And now it's not safe anymore. Because now I know the truth: he doesn't even want me when he's single.

"It's so unfair that everyone else seems to be finding love," I whine. "My dad has Hannah, Cordie just started dating her best friend . . ."

"That is hard," she says. "Have you met Hannah yet?"

I shake my head. "No, but I told Dad I would. Eventually."

She smiles. "That's good! I'm glad you're willing to do that."

"Yeah, I guess," I say.

"You don't want to meet Hannah?"

I cross my arms over my chest. "I don't know. I guess I just don't know how I'll feel about seeing my dad with someone."

"Someone who's not your mom?" she asks.

I frown. "No, just anyone. He's never dated anyone, as far as I know. He didn't even really have friends for a long time. Not until he started playing basketball again."

"It sounds like he's needed this for a while," Lisa says.

I nod. "He does. I know it's good for him. I wonder why he waited so long to date? I mean, aside from having two kids to raise."

"People move on at difference paces," she says. "Because every relationship is different. Some people move on quickly because they want the distraction from their grief. Some date because they need proof that they can find love again. Some move on slowly because they think they don't deserve to be happy. Some feel they'll never be able to replace their late spouse. It just depends on the person. And the situation."

I can't help but wonder at what pace Carter is moving. It hasn't been that long since Jules died—a little more than four months now. Sometimes it feels like it was yesterday. Sometimes it feels like it's been a year.

But it only takes a moment to remember how it felt to hear that she was gone. And I know that pain will linger forever.

# CHAPTER
## 22

Dad is in the kitchen when I walk through the door. He's cooking something in a big pot on the stove, and he's singing along to the Joe Crocker song that's playing on the wireless speaker he hung over the sink. Most of the time, he listens to a sports podcast or has his iPad propped up so he can watch a game while he cooks. But on the good nights, he sings.

He didn't hear me come in, so I stand in the doorway and watch him for a minute. I hadn't noticed how much he's changed recently. He looks lighter, and not just because he's skinnier. He lost the weight before he met Hannah, but it isn't until now that I can see he looks comfortable in his skin.

As he does a shuffle dance and a spin, he finally sees me and clutches his hands to his chest with a yell. Then he bursts out laughing.

"You shouldn't sneak up on an old man!" he says as

he hits pause. "I could have a heart attack!" But he's still laughing.

I want to meet the woman who's made him this happy, I decide.

"Don't stop on my account," I say. As I move toward the stove so I can peer into the pot, he blocks my path. I narrow my eyes with suspicion. "What are you making?"

But as I breathe in the smell of chicken and tomatoes, I know. He's making Jules's chicken Provençal.

My eyes fill with tears. "Oh, Daddy, thank you," I say, hugging him.

He kisses the top of my head. "I miss her too, Bug."

I nod. "I know. And you know I miss Mom too, right?"

He pulls back so he can look at me. "Of course. Why would you ask that?"

I shrug, swallowing my tears. "Because you're not the only one who avoids talking about her. I don't talk about her either, but I think about her all the time. And I just want you to know you're not alone."

He reels me back in for another hug before releasing me. "Thanks for saying that," he says, turning back to the pot. I notice him wipe his eyes with the dish towel he has draped over one shoulder.

"And I want to meet Hannah," I say. "Maybe next weekend?"

He smiles at me over his shoulder. "Sounds great," he says.

And then he presses play and starts singing into the handle of his wooden spoon.

———————➤

I'm relieved that Adriana and I have our *Hamlet* project due on Friday to distract us from the fact that prom is on Saturday, because everyone else seems to have entered some sort of fugue state.

All I hear in the halls as I walk to class on Thursday is conversations about dresses and limos and dinner and corsages.

I can't help being jealous of the people who get to go to prom with their boyfriends or girlfriends. Or even more, of the people who are going with someone they have a crush on.

Though I haven't admitted it, I keep hoping that Carter will come around to the idea of prom. Even if we aren't going together, I'd like to at least see him there. He still hasn't even followed up about joining me and Adriana on a run. In fact, I haven't seen him for more than a quick "hello" since last week.

But I can't dwell on it. It just makes me too sad. And I'm already too full of sad at the moment.

After school, Adriana and I take the bus to her house, where we head to her room. We've been working on the podcast script all week and I'm excited to finally record. We even turn down Mrs. Rodriguez's offer of snacks.

Adriana pulls a second chair into the closet where we

set up my microphone and headset that I brought from home. Sometimes in the background of my podcasts you can hear Dad's treadmill whirring or Cordie singing in her room. But the closet is silent when Adriana shuts the door.

"Welcome to *Ghosts of Elsinore*," Adriana says in her radio voice. "I'm your host Adriana Rodriguez and this is my co-host, Natalie Nagler."

"Good morrow," I say in my best British accent.

Adriana laughs. "I'm sorry, I'll edit that out. But that was a terrible accent!"

I laugh too. "Well, let's hear yours, then!"

She shakes her head. "No way. I have many strengths, but accents are not one of them."

I laugh again. "Okay, fine, no accents, then."

"Good!"

She starts her introduction again and this time I just say "hello" in my normal voice. But it still makes her laugh.

"What?" I say. "I did it normally that time!"

"I'm sorry," Adriana says breathlessly. "I was just remembering the last time. Okay, here we go for real."

This time we make it through the introduction.

"Our story starts on a misty night in Denmark, at Elsinore Castle," Adriana says.

"And it has everything you could ask for in a murder mystery," I say. "Like, a ghost!"

"An avenging prince!" Adriana adds. "And a usurper of the throne!"

254

"A misunderstanding!"

"A fight to the death!"

I laugh, but this time it's allowed. "Okay, maybe it sounds a little far-fetched, but it only gets more bizarre. So buckle up for the story of *Hamlet*."

———————————

I have an email from Britt when I get home that night:

*Hi sweetie,*

*Thanks again for letting me take you shopping. It made my week. My month. Maybe my year. I appreciate you. And I appreciate you reading the book too. I know it won't be easy, but I hope it helps explain my side. And helps you see the changes I'm making too.*

*Love,*

*Britt*

I download the file on my laptop, but my heart is racing. I don't trust Britt, but I want to believe that she's trying to do the right thing. It's easier than believing that she's a monster who murdered her daughter.

So I start reading. I read through the night, ignoring my homework and my phone. I turn down Cordie when she invites me to watch a show with her and Kayla. I tell Dad I'm not hungry when he says dinner is ready, so he brings a plate of leftover chicken Provençal to my room.

Britt's book is moving and devastating and incredible and disgusting all at once. It's as if she reached into my mind and sifted through all the terrible things I've thought about her over the years and then turned them into essays.

Halfway through, I retrieve my notes—my dissection of Britt's blog and Instagram account—from the trash. I read through them, looking at the difference in how Britt told a story on her blog versus how she now tells it in the book. And in how I remember it happening, or how Jules told me it happened. And then I compile more notes.

Britt writes about trying to get pregnant and the miracle it felt like when Jules was born. She writes about finding a community of people online who listened when she talked and how strange that felt after feeling directionless for so long. She explains why Chris encouraged her, even though he could see what it was doing to Jules. She admits that she was addicted to the fame.

And she admits that she's responsible for Jules's death.

Not in the way that I originally thought she might be—she's not a murderer—but in the thousands of ways that she made Jules feel as though she wasn't good enough. And all the warning signs that she ignored. She even gives solid advice on how to recognize those signs of depression and what to do about it.

When I finish reading, I don't feel better. I feel nauseated, and my eyes burn from wiping away tears. But as I click back to my document of proof of how she screwed up as a parent, I'm tempted to delete the whole thing again. It doesn't really feel useful or relevant anymore. And I can't help being a little grateful for that.

## Excerpt from *Minding Her Business: A Mother's Tale of Love, Overexposure, and Grief* by Britt Monaghan

When Jules was born, she had a hole in her heart. A very small hole, an atrial septal defect, and the doctors believed it would close on its own with time. But we had waited for this baby for what felt like forever. We'd done multiple rounds of hormone therapy. I'd had three miscarriages and two rounds of failed IVF before I got pregnant with Jules, and I remember each of those babies. They have names. I mourn the loss of each of them every single day. So the thought of losing Jules so soon after meeting her felt like a hole was being ripped in my own heart.

Every night, I would tell myself that watching her wouldn't keep her alive. But I didn't sleep anyway. Those first few months of her life are a hazy blur of anxiety and exhaustion. I have pictures and blog posts about that time, but I have no real memories of anything but crying.

My husband, Chris, came with me to Jules's six-month checkup. Tears streamed down my face as the nurse gave her the vaccinations. Jules cried less than I did. Chris had mentioned to the doctor that I'd been feeling a little blue, but after that display, he insisted that the doctor come back and prescribe something for me.

I began taking antidepressants and was given a mild sedative to help me sleep. I used a sedative every night for the next sixteen years.

I stayed on the antidepressants until Jules went to preschool. The hole in her heart closed up, just as the doctors said it would, and my anxiety lessened slightly. But I suddenly had all this free time while Jules was gone during the day.

I'd been blogging since before Jules was born about our fertility problems, and I had leaned on that community hard the first few years of Jules's life. But I needed something more creative. Having been a visual arts major in college, I felt the need to flex my creative muscles.

I'd always taken pictures of Jules for my blog posts, but I decided to take a class on digital photography and photo editing. And when I started sharing my pictures of our house and of Jules, and our travels together, there was so much support from a whole new community of mothers. They liked it when I was open about my struggles with having a toddler while my husband, who was a pilot, was gone half the week. And they also loved the way I'd redecorated Jules's playroom, when Chris couldn't care less.

I was excited about blogging again for the first time in years. And it was bringing in money too. Money that we needed, at first; and later, money that I could spend on the things I wanted instead of having to ask Chris for it.

I was independent for the first time since college. And then suddenly, I was famous. And so was Jules.

# CHAPTER
## 23

The next morning when I wake up, I can barely open my eyes. They're as swollen as they were the morning after I found out Jules was gone. My throat is raw, my nose is sore from blowing it, and my head throbs like I've been listening to EDM on full blast all night.

And I have the *Hamlet* presentation in two hours. Luckily, the podcast does most of the talking for us, but I'm going to have to stand up in front of the class looking like I've been up all night crying. Because I was.

I should have saved the book to read later, but I couldn't stop myself. And now I just have to deal with it.

Cordie picks up Kayla on the way to school, and I let her sit shotgun so I can close my eyes in the back. I was hoping they'd talk and ignore me, but they seem to know that something is different because they just listen to music quietly while I doze.

When we get out of the car, Cordie tells Kayla to go

ahead. She gives us a worried glance but heads inside while we hang back in the parking lot.

"Are you okay, Bug?" Cordie asks.

I think about lying just so I don't have to talk about it, but there's no point.

"Not really," I say. "I just . . . I miss my old life. I want it back. And I'm just so angry all the time."

She nods, reaching out to take my hand. "What are you angry about?" she asks gently.

I breathe a heavy sigh. "Too many things to list. I'm angry that Jules is gone. I'm angry that Britt's book is as well written as I expected it to be. I'm angry that she gets to tell her side of the story, and that it's sympathetic and it's going to win a lot of people over." I sigh again. "I'm angry that Mom is gone and that I know almost nothing about her. I'm angry that things between me and Carter are weird. I'm just angry. At everything."

She squeezes my hand three times before letting go.

"I'm sorry," she says. "Those are all valid reasons. And there's nothing I can do about any of them. But I am here for you. If you want to talk about Carter or Jules or Britt. And if you ever want to talk about Mom, you can just ask."

"Thanks," I say. But I let my shoulders slump. Because I don't feel better. I didn't really expect to. "We should get to class."

Cordie looks like a puppy dog left in a crate.

I turn to walk away but pause, looking back at her. "Hey," I say. "Why do we do that hand squeeze thing?"

Her eyes widen. "You don't know?"

I shake my head, but I feel a murky memory swimming to the surface of my mind. Mom in a hospital bed, holding my hand. Squeezing three times.

"Was it Mom?" I ask. "Did she used to do that?"

Cordie's chin trembles as she nods. "Yes," she whispers. "When she couldn't talk anymore, at the end. It was her way to say 'I love you.'"

Now my eyes are filling with tears too. That's not going to help the puffiness.

Cordie pulls me in for a hug, ignoring the stares of the people around us. "I forget sometimes how little you were. That you don't remember the same things I do."

"You were little too," I say into her shoulder.

I feel her take a deep breath before she lets me go. "I know," she says, "but not like you were. I'll try to write down some of my memories of her for you, okay?"

I nod, wiping the tears from my face. "Thanks," I say.

"Good luck," she says. "You're going to do great on this presentation."

I shrug, but Cordie doesn't move.

"No, listen to me," she says. "You're so smart, and talented, and you're an incredible storyteller. I know you never believe in yourself, but I do. So go be amazing."

I reach out and squeeze her hand three times.

"I love you too," she says.

———————

As soon as she sees me, Mrs. Barrett offers to let us do our presentation on Monday. That's when I know just how bad I really look. Jules was in this class, so Mrs. Barrett must also know why I look so awful.

But I shake my head. "No," I say, "but thanks." Then I turn to Adriana. "But can I say something to the class before we start?"

Her brow creases in confusion, but she nods. "Of course," she says. "Whatever you need."

We're up first, so as soon as everyone is settled at their desks, we step in front of the class. There are a few whispers and murmured comments, but I just dive right in.

"Adriana and I have chosen to do our project as though the story of *Hamlet* were being told on a true crime podcast," I say.

People raise their eyebrows in surprise or smile, which is encouraging.

"But I wanted to talk for a second about true crime and the way that our society, including myself, is obsessed with the salacious details of other peoples' lives and deaths," I continue. "We binge true crime podcasts and TV shows as if they were Hollywood stories, forgetting the real people behind them. We follow strangers online and crave their lives, emulating them instead of finding out who we are."

I pause, swallowing past the dryness in my throat.

"But there is always more than one side to every story," I add. "And you can never know the truth of what someone is really feeling or thinking." I pause again, but this time for dramatic effect. "Sometimes those misunderstandings even lead to death. In the case of *Hamlet*, the death of pretty much everyone."

The class laughs.

"But the one that haunts me the most is the death of Ophelia. She spent her life being manipulated by the people around her. People who believed they knew what was best for her. But they were wrong. And ultimately, her death was the only thing she could control."

No one is laughing now. No one even moves. They all know what I'm alluding to.

I clear my throat. My chest is fizzy with nerves. "So, you may notice that I look like I've been crying and like I didn't sleep last night," I say. "Or for, like, months. And you're right. Because that's exactly what's been happening. My best friend died by suicide four months ago, and I feel haunted by memories and questions."

I see Adriana's small, encouraging nod out of the corner of my eye.

"Just like Hamlet sees the ghost of his father, I can't escape the ghost of Jules," I say. "Like Hamlet, I feel crazed by the grief. And I want to hold someone responsible for what happened to her." I take a breath. "And that's why I think we love true crime stories. Or at least, that's why I'm fascinated by them. Because most of us can't fathom the idea of killing another person, or of manipulating someone until they take their own life. We want to understand what would drive someone to commit such horrible acts. And we want it dissected, preferably over several episodes."

This makes people laugh again and lightens the mood in the room.

"But when a true crime story is told to us on a podcast, or a TV show, or a documentary, we get to know the motivation behind a murder. We know the ending, most of the time, and we know that the bad guy has been caught. Justice has been served. And I think we need that reassurance that evil doesn't win in the end."

I glance at Adriana to see if there's anything she wants to say, but she smiles at me and tells me to keep going.

"So with that, I give you *Ghosts of Elsinore*," I say. "It's only one episode, but I hope you enjoy our dissection of the motivation behind all the murders. And I hope it makes you think more deeply about the tragic loss of life and the real person behind the story next time you watch a true crime show or listen to a podcast."

And then I press play.

———————

When the bell rings for lunch, Carter is waiting for me at my locker. I'm tempted to try to smooth my hair or duck into the bathroom, but I just can't care right now.

I'm exhausted and exhilarated. I even extend my arms and pull Carter into a hug when I reach him.

He stiffens for a moment with surprise, but then he melts into it, wrapping his arms around my waist. He breathes into my hair, and I shiver.

"I've missed you," he says softly.

My insides feel as wobbly as Jules's flan.

"Me too," I say.

I don't know how he means it—whether he missed my friendship or if absence made his heart grow fonder—but I almost don't care. I'm too happy to be hugging him.

When we finally pull apart, I feel like something is missing. But hugs can only last so long before it gets awkward.

"I heard about your English presentation," Carter says. He gestures for me to hand him my backpack.

"You did?" I say as I hand it to him.

"Yeah, people are impressed, but apparently, you also made the rest of the class's presentations look half-assed."

I can't help grinning. "Yeah, we kinda did," I say. "Adriana and I got a standing ovation. A couple people even said we should do podcasts on other books or plays. Adriana and I are considering it, but I think we're done with Shakespeare for a while. The tragedies are just too . . . tragic."

He laughs. "I'm proud of you," he says. But then his smile slips. "I also heard you talked about Jules."

The familiar tightness in my chest returns. "Yeah," I say. "It was hard, but I think it made an impression. And even if it doesn't make a difference to anyone else, I feel better that I got to say some of the things I've been holding onto."

Carter smiles, but it's really more of a grimace. "I can imagine," he says. "It would probably feel good to finally say all the things I've been keeping inside."

I don't know if that's an invitation to ask him, but something else is weighing on me.

"I have to tell you something," I say.

He tilts his head curiously.

"I read Britt's book last night."

His eyebrows shoot up. "How?"

"She sent it to me," I say. "She wanted my opinion."

He almost seems reluctant when he asks, "And? How was it?"

I sigh to show my annoyance. "It was really good," I say. I put my books in my bag and take it back from him. "I can send it to you, if you want?"

He nods, swallowing hard. "Yeah," he croaks. "I want to read it."

"I'll send it tonight," I say. "So are you doing okay?"

"I guess so," he says. "It's starting to feel more normal that she's not here."

I nod. "I know. It makes me feel guilty."

"Me too." He leans against the locker next to mine.

"Sometimes I don't feel completely sad," I admit. "Sometimes I even feel happy. Like now."

His lips tilt into a small smile. "Me too," he says again.

"And when I'm running," I say, waiting for his smile to grow. My stomach tightens when his dimple makes an appearance.

"You have no idea how happy that makes me," he says. "I love that I've turned you into a runner."

I hold up both hands. "Whoa, let's not get crazy now. I'm only up to four miles."

He hoots. "That's great! And that still makes you a

runner. You don't have to be a long-distance runner. Four miles is awesome."

"Thanks," I say, ducking my head shyly.

"Do you want to maybe go for a run this afternoon?" he asks.

I really, really do, but I promised Adriana we'd talk about our podcast.

"I can't," I say. "And tomorrow is prom, but maybe Sunday?"

He flinches a little when I say "prom," but he recovers nicely. "Yeah, let's do that. I'll text you in the morning. And hey, have fun at prom."

I give him a tight smile. I wish he were going. "Thanks," I say.

He nods, but he's already walking away.

## Excerpt from *Minding Her Business:*
## *A Mother's Tale of Love, Overexposure, and Grief*
## by Britt Monaghan

Two days before Jules died, I made the biggest mistake of my life. I wrote a column about how I reacted when I found out that she was having sex with her boyfriend. The ironic thing is that when I wrote it, I was feeling so smug and superior about how I'd handled it. I was bragging when I wrote the column.

I thought I had everything figured out.

And then Jules took her life.

It's no secret that Jules and I had a difficult relationship, but it was more troubled than I let on.

Jules hated me.

She made it very clear a long time ago that she neither appreciated nor respected what I'd chosen to do for a living. The life I'd chosen for her.

It made me so angry. How dare she hate me for the thing that makes me happiest in the world? How dare she not appreciate the work that I put into my role as a writer and influencer? And how dare she not appreciate the success and fame that I worked so hard to create for us?

But now I know that it wasn't the writing that made me happy. It wasn't sharing my story with others so that they could benefit from my experience or feel comforted that they weren't alone. It wasn't the time I spent with Jules while I forced her to pose for photos. It wasn't even the free vacations I took or the home I spent years designing.

It was the fame.

I hate even admitting that to myself. I hate that my daughter is dead because my ego needed stroking twenty-four hours a day. But I made her life fodder for my work. I bribed her and, when that didn't work, bullied her into posing for photos. I created a persona, a mold of what I needed her to be, that she could never fit into.

Because Jules was bigger than the life I tried to force on her. She was more than the image I tried to create. She was bold and opinionated and beautiful and brave. She was a brilliant chef with a creative artist's spirit.

And she saw right through me.

Sometimes I hated her for it. And she saw that too.

# CHAPTER
## 24

I throw my mascara into the trash can next to my desk with such force that it bounces back out. It's at least a year old and smelled sour when I pulled out the wand. No way am I putting that near my eyes.

I can't believe I didn't even bother to check my makeup stash until now. It's three hours before I'm supposed to meet Adriana at her house to go to dinner with the other girls and my hair is wet, my makeup is expired, and my dress is wrinkled. And I have no idea what to do about any of it.

Tears build in my eyes as I carry my dress to the bathroom and turn the water on at full heat, but as I look around our tiny bathroom, I realize there's nowhere to hang my dress near the steam where it won't get wet.

Dad walks by just as I'm about to throw my dress out the door. He pauses, his eyes widening. With the steam billowing around me and my hair frizzing, I must look a little terrifying.

"Everything okay in here?" he asks, gently prying the hanger from my hands. He hangs the dress from the doorframe.

I collapse onto the toilet lid, putting my head in my hands. "Not really," I say to the tile floor. "I forgot that I don't really know how to be a girl."

I hear his soft sigh as he leans against the counter. "I guess that's kind of my fault?"

"No," I say, still not looking at him. "I just always let Jules handle these types of things. She had all the makeup and the hair products and stuff, because of Britt. I never had to."

He's quiet for a few seconds. "Do you want me to call Britt?"

Now I look up at him, surprised that he'd even offer. "Not really," I say. I'm still figuring out my response to her book and I'm not ready to talk about it with her.

"Your sister is with Kayla?" he asks.

"Yeah, but I don't want to bother her with this," I say. "It's her senior prom."

He purses his lips. "It's your prom too. And she's your sister," he says.

But I shake my head. A tear dislodges and drips onto the floor with a soft plop.

"What if I called Hannah?" he asks. His eyes are hopeful. He really wants to help. And I want to let him.

So I nod. "Tell her we have frizzy hair, no makeup, and wrinkled satin."

He nods gravely as he pulls out his phone. "Hey," he

says, turning to walk down the hall. His voice is gentle and a little giddy. "Listen, we could use some prom prep help here at the Nagler residence." He's quiet for a second. "Yeah, it's Nat."

He's far enough away by then that I can't hear the rest of the conversation, but when he returns, he nods at me. "She'll be here in fifteen minutes."

I turn off the shower, feeling a little sheepish for freaking out. "Thanks, Dad."

He steps into the bathroom and puts his hands on my shoulders, like a coach bucking up their star player at halftime.

"We're gonna take care of this," he says. "I don't know how, but Hannah will."

I manage a small smile. "Thanks for asking her for help."

He pulls me into a hug. "Thanks for letting me."

I know I don't ask for help, or accept it, very often. And it's not in my nature to share how I'm feeling. But maybe I'm getting better at it.

———————

Exactly fifteen minutes later, there's a knock on the door. I let Dad open it.

Behind the screen door stands a woman who is somehow not what I was expecting but exactly what I'd pictured for Dad. She's tall and solid, in a broad-shouldered Xena the Warrior Princess way. But she has long, dark hair that falls in soft waves around her shoulders and gray eyes, lined lightly in black. She has on natural makeup and is wearing straight-legged jeans and a simple black T-shirt, with cute flats that are a shimmery rose gold. Her jewelry matches.

She's holding two tote bags, which she sets down next to the door before walking toward me.

"You must be Nat," she says, holding out her hand.

I shake it, noticing that she doesn't have a manicure but her nails are clean and short. Her hands are a little rough, calloused on the palm, and I wonder what could have caused that.

But Hannah has already started sizing me up. I can feel her eyes on my wild hair and bare, zit-marked skin.

She clasps her hands together in front of her. "Okay, first things first: show me the dress."

I can't help smiling as I lead her to the bathroom. I love this dress. I wish there were more occasions to wear it. It doesn't seem fair that something so beautiful, and expensive, should only be worn once.

I like Hannah even more when I hear her gasp as she sees it. She reaches out a hand to gently stroke the emerald satin.

"Wow," she says. Her eyebrows are raised as she turns to me. "You have extraordinary taste."

I flush with pride. "Thanks," I say. "I would never have been able to afford it without Britt, though."

But Hannah is shaking her head. "Just because someone else paid for it doesn't mean you shouldn't get credit for picking it out."

She rummages in one of her tote bags for a second, then pulls out a handheld steamer.

"Nick?" she calls out the doorway. Dad appears a second later. "While I start on Natalie's hair, can you please fill this with water and steam the wrinkles out of the dress?"

He starts to step into the bathroom, but Hannah places a firm hand against his chest. "Maybe in the kitchen?" she says pointedly.

The bathroom is small for even two people, so a third would have really been pushing it. But I think she mostly wants to give us a little privacy. To talk about him.

Dad nods. "Yes, ma'am," he says. He leans in to give her a quick kiss before backing out of the bathroom. I want to be grossed out, but it's actually kind of cute. I like that he's happy.

When he's gone, Hannah digs around in her bag again before pulling out a hair dryer.

"Did your dad tell you I used to be a hair stylist?" she asks.

I shake my head. "No, but . . . I sort of haven't asked him much about you," I admit.

She smiles softly. "I know this must be hard for you," she says. "The first girlfriend since your mom died."

I try not to let her see my surprise at the word "girlfriend." It probably shouldn't have surprised me though.

Hannah points to the closed toilet lid, telling me to sit. "So what do you want your hair to look like?" she asks.

I shrug. "I don't know," I say. "I know most girls usually

want an updo for prom, but I pretty much always have my hair up in a bun. So wearing it down would be the bigger change."

She squints at me for a second, considering.

"What do you think would look best with the dress?" I ask.

"With the high neck?" she says with a smile. "I'd go with it up."

I nod once. "Up it is," I say.

Hannah pulls a few more tools out of her tote bag, including clips, a spray bottle, several different types of products, and a round brush.

"So what do you and my dad do?" I ask as she sprays my frizz down with water. My cheeks warm when I realize the implication. "I mean, when you go out on dates. Does he, like, take you to the batting cages? Basketball games?"

Those are literally the only activities I can picture Dad doing, even on a date.

She laughs. "Yes and yes. We even play basketball sometimes. But we also go out to dinner. He took me to a concert out at Wolf Trap last weekend."

I raise my eyebrows. Dad's got game. I'm impressed.

"I know, right?" Hannah says. "We have a lot of fun together."

I like how happy she looks, but I can't help also feeling a little jealous of the fun she has with my dad, when all I get from him is conversations held over the monitor of his computer. But I'm also jealous because I miss having my best friend around to have fun with. I really wish Jules were here with me getting ready. Maybe part of the reason I didn't give any thought to my hair and makeup is because I couldn't work up the enthusiasm to do all of this without her. Maybe I wanted an excuse not to go at all.

I blink back tears, glad that Hannah hasn't done my makeup yet. But she hasn't missed that I'm getting emotional. She hands me a tissue and then resumes sectioning my hair, clipping it in little buns around my head.

I dab at my eyes. "Thanks," I say. "This, um, this isn't about you and my dad." I gesture to the tissue. "I'm glad that you make each other happy. And it's long past time for him to have started dating again."

Hannah doesn't say anything, but her relief is pretty clear.

"I assume my dad told you about my best friend?" I watch her nod in the mirror.

"He did," she says. "And I'm so sorry."

"Thanks," I say softly. "I just miss her a lot tonight, that's all."

Hannah squeezes my shoulders. "I understand."

I like that she doesn't feel like she has to ask a bunch of questions about Jules, and that she's not morbidly curious about what happened.

"One thing your dad and I have in common is that I lost my partner too," she says. "My fiancé died three years ago in a car accident, a month before our wedding."

I gasp, then cover my mouth with my hand. "I'm sorry,"

I say. My stomach clenches just thinking about how much pain she must have been in.

She nods but doesn't meet my eye in the mirror. "The pain of losing someone you love never goes away entirely," she says. "But over time it becomes part of the landscape of your life. That stab in the gut when you think about that person, when you miss them after something good or bad happens, it dulls a little but never truly goes away."

She rests a hand on my shoulder.

"A friend told me once that grief is the cost of love," she says. "It's a pretty steep price, but it's worth paying. Because the love doesn't go away either."

I reach back and squeeze her hand. "Thanks," I say. "For sharing that with me. It helps when people get it."

Hannah squeezes back. "It does," she says. "Did you know your dad and I met at a grief group? For people who have lost their partners?"

I shake my head, trying not to let my mouth drop open. "I didn't even know he went to one."

"Yeah," she says with a small smile. "He started coming about four months ago. Seeing the pain you were going through after losing Jules made him realize he hadn't dealt with much of his own grief about losing your mom."

I didn't know that either.

She picks up the hair dryer, but before she can turn it on, I ask, "Do you ever feel guilty for moving on with someone else?"

She nods slowly. "I do," she says. "But just because I fall

in love with someone else, it doesn't diminish the love I had for Jason. I'll always love him, but he'd want me to find happiness, even if it's without him."

I think Jules would want that too. She may not have been happy, but she never wanted me or Carter to be miserable alongside her.

Hannah meets my eye in the mirror, checking to see if I want to keep talking.

"I think so too," I say. "And I'm really glad you and Dad found each other."

She blushes. "Well, it's still early."

I shrug. "Maybe. But it's obvious that you make him happy. So thank you."

She's smiling as she turns on the hair dryer and starts blowing out my long hair. And I can't help smiling with her. I may not have Jules with me tonight, or Carter, but Adriana and I have a really great time together. And I think I might actually enjoy this night after all.

———————————➤

Two hours later, I stand in front of the mirror, hair done, makeup applied, and dress wrinkle-free.

My hair is in a low bun with a few loose tendrils around my face. And I'm wearing more makeup than I ever have, but I still look like myself. Just fancier. Smoother.

Hannah is kind of a badass. I can see why Dad likes her so much.

I grab the gold clutch Hannah pulled out of one of

her magical Mary Poppins totes and at the last second, I tuck the little black stone Adriana gave me inside. I have the feeling I might need some emotional support tonight.

Hannah and Dad are waiting in the living room. I feel silly and awkward as I walk down the hall toward them in my kitten heels, but there's something comforting about seeing them waiting for me, beaming like proud parents. Hannah's even snapping pictures like a paparazzo.

I pose for her. "So? Will I stop traffic?"

Hannah nods. "Definitely. You look incredible."

"Let the record show that I think you look beautiful in pajamas with bed head," Dad says, "but you look stunning in that dress, Bug."

I might even have caught a glint of a tear in his eye, but he blinks and it's gone.

I want to hug them, but I'm afraid of wrinkling the dress, so I just grin.

"Hannah, I can't thank you enough for your help," I say, turning to give myself another glance in the mirror by the front door. "You're a miracle worker."

Hannah walks up behind me and tucks a stray hair back into my bun. "You're gorgeous," she says. "It was easy."

The doorbell rings, so Dad opens the door for Adriana. She's wearing a short red dress with super high heels that have ribbons that tie around her ankles. Her hair is down, with soft curls that brush her shoulders. She's also wearing a gold chain holding a raw amethyst that hangs between her collarbones.

We spend a minute telling each other how great we look

and admiring our dresses, then I introduce her to Dad and Hannah. They insist on taking pictures of us in front of the house, so we act like we're each other's dates. I even make Adriana take a photo in the classic arms-around-the-waist pose with me behind her.

"I'll send you these pictures," Hannah promises as we get into Adriana's car. Then she hands me a travel-size spray bottle of wrinkle remover. "Before you go into the dance, just spray this on and smooth it with your hands to get some of the wrinkles out from sitting."

I thank her as I tuck it into the clutch. She also tucks in some spare bobby pins, breath mints, and the lipstick she used on my lips.

"Have fun!" Dad and Hannah call from the driveway as we pull away.

I can't help but watch them in the rearview mirror. Dad pulls Hannah against him and kisses her, then they stand there smiling goofily at each other for a few seconds.

"They're super cute," Adriana says.

I smile. "Aren't they?" I say. "I feel bad I put off meeting her for so long."

She grins back. "Yeah, but I have the feeling you'll be seeing a lot more of her."

Adriana and I meet Lindley and Nia at Olive Garden. None of them really knew Jules, but I've been making an effort to talk about her more around them. I want them to feel like they knew her. I want her to be remembered by more than just me and Carter.

Once we've ordered and are filling up on breadsticks and salad, I raise my glass of soda.

"A toast," I say, "to the best prom dates I could have hoped for."

They clink their glasses against mine.

"Thank you for coming to Olive Garden," I continue. "I know it's not exactly the dream pre-prom dinner location, but it means a lot to me to be here tonight. Jules would have loved it."

"To Jules," Adriana says, raising her glass again. Lindley and Nia echo her.

"I just want people to remember her for more than a scandal, or a suicide, or her mom's Instagram," I add. "I want her to be more than just a tragic story."

The three of them are quiet as they sip their drinks.

"I know you said you didn't want to do a podcast about her," Adriana says finally. "And that is completely reasonable. But what if it was a podcast about remembering people who have died too young? We can call it *Before Their Time*. We can tell stories about people who were killed or died by suicide or in an accident, and we can interview their loved ones about what they were like in life, rather than making it all about their deaths."

I can't respond because my throat is suddenly too tight. So I nod, then dab at my eyes with my napkin. Thankfully Hannah used waterproof mascara.

"I would listen to that," Nia offers.

"Me too," Lindley says.

I blink back my tears. "I think even Jules would have listened to something like that," I say. "We could even interview experts about dealing with depression or suicidal thoughts, or dealing with grief. And there are so many murders that get ignored and go unsolved because they're not sensational enough, or because there isn't enough attention drawn to them. Maybe if we make people care about the victims, people will put pressure on the police to look deeper into the cases. Or maybe someone will come forward with information."

Adriana offers a small smile. "That would be amazing. But even if we don't end up solving crimes, I think we could be really good at this," she says. "I think people need this."

"Me too," I say. I know I do.

Nia and Lindley look back and forth between us.

"Where do you think you'll start?" Nia asks. "I mean, do you have anyone in mind?"

I take a sip of my soda. "Actually, I think I want to start with Jules."

Adriana raises her eyebrows. "You do?"

I nod. "Someone will want to cover her case on a podcast eventually," I say. "Or they'll want to write about her, or make a TV movie or something. And I want the truth about who she really was, the Jules that I loved, to be out there. Not just in Britt's book and some sordid *Dateline* episode."

Adriana holds up her glass again. "We can start tomorrow," she says.

Now I just have to break the news to Britt and Carter.

───────────

Adriana, Nia, Lindley, and I walk into the hotel ballroom. Shoulder to shoulder, we strut into the dark space, into the blaring music, into the crowd. The three of them immediately head for the dance floor.

I pause at the edge while they all break into dance. I've never danced in public. Like, never took a dance class, never went to a school dance, never even celebrated with an end zone–style touchdown dance after scoring a goal. No one aside from Jules has ever seen my "moves." Because really, no one should.

But Adriana doesn't let me stand there for more than a few seconds before she pulls me into their circle and spins me around. And then Harry and Louise are there too, right in the middle of the circle, and everyone's eyes are on them instead of me. So it doesn't feel so awkward to move with the rest of them.

Trey shows up too with his date, and he kind of stands there bobbing his head and shifting up and down. No one could look more awkward than him.

Louise pushes Harry toward Nia and shimmies over to me.

"You look beautiful!" she says. Or shouts, really. "I'm so glad you came!"

She drapes an arm around my waist, and then pulls Adriana against her other side. And the three of us dance together.

Suddenly, I'm laughing and crying at the same time. Because I miss Jules, and because I wish she were here even though she would have hated this. But in this new life, in this new normal, with my friends who are dancing and laughing and loving each other, I can lean into the cheesiness and the frivolity and the fun. And I can love it too.

A slow song starts then and the dance floor turns into a sea of couples with their heads bent close together. Nia and Lindley dance together, but Adriana and I use it as an excuse to get some water.

As we reach the edge of the dance floor, Adriana elbows me.

"Ow," I say, rubbing my ribs. But then I follow her eyes to the door.

Carter stands there, his eyes searching the room. He looks like he's wearing his dad's tuxedo. It's a little big in the shoulders and fabric is gathered at his ankles, but it's still adorable.

"Go talk to him!" Adriana says, giving me a small push.

Carter's eyes land on me. His eyebrows lift as he mouths "Wow." Or maybe he said it aloud. I'll never know.

As he walks toward me, I see that he's holding a clear plastic box with a corsage in it. When he reaches me, he holds it out.

"I had a dream last night," he says. He has to lean in so

I can hear him. "I know it sounds kind of nuts, but Jules was holding this corsage and she told me it was for you."

My eyes widen.

"I know, it's weird," he says with a shrug. "And I know it's also a weird pick-up line to use, but well, I think my dead girlfriend wants you to have this?"

He opens the box and takes out the blush pink rose corsage, holding it out to me. I notice it has a small succulent too.

"The guy at the flower shop said you can plant the succulent tomorrow," Carter says. "Jules seemed to find that part very important."

I'm trying really hard not to cry, and failing. Because Jules and I used to joke that giving someone flowers was dumb because they're basically already dead, so we said we'd much rather get a succulent because we could at least keep that alive.

"Is this okay?" he asks as he slides it onto my wrist.

I nod, swallowing my tears. "It's perfect."

Carter grins, and we just stand there awkwardly staring at each other for a second. Then he asks, "Do you want to dance?"

And I nod. I take his hand and lead him onto the edge of the dance floor.

"Why are you here?" I ask as he slides his hands onto my waist.

His cheeks redden. "Well, Jules told me to."

I look up at him. "Is that really why?"

He shakes his head. "No. I just . . . I guess I didn't want you to be here without me. And I didn't want to miss out on seeing you in your prom dress." He pauses. "And I missed you."

I'm glad for the dim lighting as blood rushes to my cheeks. "I missed you too," I say.

I smile, but he's still got a serious look on his face.

"There's something you don't know," he says softly. I have to lean in to hear him.

"What?" I ask.

"Jules broke up with me before she died."

My mouth drops open. "What?"

He nods. "I had a feeling she didn't tell you," he says.

"But . . . why?" I ask.

He shrugs, but I can see on his face that it still hurts to not really know. "She said she was too broken. And that I couldn't understand how she felt after her mom published her column." He breathes a heavy sigh. "She was angry that I wasn't more embarrassed, I guess."

I don't know what to say. All this time, I thought he was grieving the lost love of his life. But he was also grieving from the breakup.

But Carter isn't finished. His face looks pained as he continues.

"The thing is, when she broke up with me, I was . . ." He pauses, gazing over my shoulder, maybe gathering courage. Then he blinks and looks into my eyes. "I felt a little bit relieved."

My stomach squeezes. I want to be shocked, but I'm not.

I understand. But I don't have time to say that because he starts explaining in a rush of words.

"I loved her so much and I would have done anything to make her happy," he says. "I would have tried forever. But it's like I was always waiting for her to flinch. To pull away. Or to get angry. It was exhausting sometimes."

I pull him against me, hugging him close. His hands are trembling on my waist. "I know," I say into his ear.

He nods against my cheek. "I know you do," he says. He leans back so he can look at me. "You're the only one who does."

I give him a sad smile. "It's hard to feel responsible for someone else's happiness," I say. "I always felt like I was letting her down when I couldn't snap her out of her depression."

His eyebrows raise. "Me too," he says. "And I've felt guilty for months because I made her angry enough to break up with me. I made things worse instead of better. And I'll never know if that's what made her kill herself."

I'm shaking my head before he's even done talking.

"My therapist likes to say 'Don't add guilt to an already full plate,'" I say. "You weren't responsible for what happened, just like you weren't responsible for her happiness. Jules was always going to do whatever she wanted. You know that. She always did."

He laughs a little, but it's a sad laugh. "That's very true," he says. "Despite hating herself most of the time, she was never afraid to have strong opinions."

I smile. "I loved that about her."

"Me too."

I swallow hard, knowing I have an admission to make too.

"She was mad at me that night too," I say. "Because I'd told her mom about her previous suicide attempt. I told Britt that I was scared Jules was going to do something to herself, and Jules punished me for it." I blink back tears. "So I said terrible things to her that I can never take back."

I take a deep breath. I will not cry and ruin my makeup. "But the other thing my therapist reminds me of regularly is that Jules was pushing us away so that it would be easier to leave us."

Carter's eyes widen. "That makes sense."

I smile. "Yep. Thank God for therapy, right?"

A fast song starts then, and when I drop my hands to my sides, Carter reaches out and takes one in his.

"Can we go outside for a minute?" he asks. He looks pained by the loud music. Or maybe it's nerves.

"Yeah, sure," I say.

I follow him out the glass doors onto the balcony. The warm spring air feels light after the oppressive smells of sweat and body odor from the dance floor. There are a few other people out here—a couple making out against a wall, two girls talking in the corner, and a lone guy who is very obviously drunk—but Carter pulls me to the railing, still holding my hand. He clears his throat, nervously shuffling his feet. But he doesn't speak.

I squeeze his fingers. "What's going on?" I ask gently.

He breathes heavily, then meets my eye. "When I kissed

you that night in the woods, I was happy for the first time in months," he says.

My heart lifts. "Me too," I say. "But then . . ."

He nods. "Then I screwed it all up. It was too soon, I think. And maybe it still is. But when I started having feelings for you, I was worried that maybe I was subconsciously trying to get revenge on Jules."

And then my heart plummets to my feet. "Do you think you were?" I ask.

His eyes lock on mine. "No," he says firmly. "I don't."

"How do you know?" I ask.

"Because," he says, "I don't need revenge. Jules was just hurting when she broke up with me. And she may have been pushing me away, but she wasn't doing it to be cruel. I didn't do anything wrong then, and I'm not doing anything wrong now."

My heart is racing like Carter and I just finished a run. "So what now?" I ask.

He takes my other hand in his, wrapping my arms around his waist. "Now I kiss you?" he asks.

I've barely nodded before his lips are on mine.

When he pulls away, I grab his lapels and pull him back to me.

"I'm not done yet," I whisper.

He laughs. "Don't worry," he whispers, his lips brushing against mine. "I'm not going anywhere."

## Excerpt from *Minding Her Business:*
## *A Mother's Tale of Love, Overexposure, and Grief*
## by Britt Monaghan

Jules didn't know she was famous for a while. But by the time she was seven or eight, we couldn't go out in public without being recognized. Fans always wanted a photo with us. I was fine with that, of course, but Jules wasn't. She'd recoil when people touched her, always without permission, and shrink back behind me in fear. She didn't understand who these people were and why they felt like they knew her.

I taught her how to be gracious while also not giving in. She could offer to take the photo of me and the fan, for instance, or offer a high five or fist bump if the person tried to hug her. So she did those things, and sometimes they worked. Sometimes people hugged her anyway, or took a picture of her while we were walking by.

But I still posted her photos on my Instagram and blog. She still let me take her picture when she was playing or cooking, or even to pose in some of the clothes designers sent over. Even after I explained where I used them and showed her my Instagram. She liked spending time with me. She liked making me happy.

She bent to my will even though I never tried to bend the other way for her.

Meanwhile, Chris never criticized my blog or Instagram. In fact, he was so supportive that it was almost sycophantic.

When we went out as a family, Chris happily posed for

photos or took them for fans if they didn't want him in it. He never told me to stop showing Jules's face or stop writing about her. He even suggested column topics sometimes.

But after the Texas pool photo incident, when Jules started asking me not to post about her anymore, he immediately took her side.

I was angry at first. It wasn't fair for her to ask me to stop writing about her. But when I asked Chris why he agreed with Jules, his answer broke my heart.

"It's hurting her," he said. "She doesn't let anyone touch her or even take a picture of her, not even family. She doesn't sleep. She has circles under her eyes that rival mine after a flight. She begs me not to leave sometimes. I hear her crying as I walk out the door."

I asked him why he never said anything about this. And he said he was afraid of what I'd say. He thought I'd leave him if he stood up to me. I didn't need his money anymore. I didn't need him to travel. He thought I didn't need him at all.

He was wrong.

Chris and I met when I was twenty-five. I was waiting tables at a restaurant not far from where he lived, and he'd come in a couple of times a week for dinner. He was usually in his captain's uniform because he'd come straight from the airport after getting off a flight. He always came alone, and it was usually late enough that my other tables were either finishing up or had already been cleared, so we'd talk. Usually about his flights or where I wanted to travel once I'd saved enough money.

When he finally asked me out, he wouldn't tell me where we were going. He picked me up and drove straight to the airport. I gave him some serious side-eye, but he promised we'd be back by midnight, so I let him take me through security and walk me onto a shuttle to New York.

No man had ever taken me out of state, especially not just for dinner. I'd only ever been on a plane twice before. My family wasn't wealthy, and I have two brothers and a sister, so any vacations were within driving distance.

But my parents also weren't exactly warm. Dad was mostly absent, either at work or at the bar, and Mom was angry. She seemed to think she deserved more out of life, and having four children in a tiny house in rural Pennsylvania wasn't it. If we were too loud or if we got in trouble, she'd take it out on us with a wooden hairbrush. It left welts on our calves and thighs, across our backsides, and up our backs. Wherever she could reach before we got away.

Before I met Chris, I dated men like my father: heavy drinkers who disappeared for days at a time with no explanation. But Chris was like the sunshine, highlighting all the things he loved about me. He made me feel like I was worthy of love in a way that I didn't know was possible.

I just wasn't great at reciprocating. I hadn't been taught how to love. Only how to hunger for more.

Chris is the one who found Jules that terrible night. Then he yelled at me that I'd done this to her.

And I couldn't argue. Because he was right.

Chris handled everything. He called the funeral home

and our family and friends. He called her best friend. He wrote a statement for the press, and he called the police when reporters so much as stepped foot on our lawn.

He barely looked at me.

The day after the funeral, he packed his bags and left.

I never asked him to stay. I knew he wouldn't. Couldn't. I could barely look at myself in the mirror, so I didn't blame him.

Our friends took his side, of course. His family didn't speak to me. Mine barely did.

After they ran the obituary, my editor at the *Washington Herald* called and told me that they were going to suspend my column. Which made sense because it was a parenting column, and I was no longer a parent.

In the end, I had nothing left but a million Instagram followers.

# CHAPTER
## 25

The next morning, I send Britt a text with a photo of me in my dress, asking if I can come over. She immediately responds, *yes!*

I borrow Dad's car and drive across town. I haven't done this drive for months, but it's still so familiar. I know every curve and turn that used to bring me closer to Jules. It was always such a comfort to pull up to her big white house and climb the two stories to her bedroom. I'd find her in bed or on the floor, watching cooking shows and making notes about recipes.

The best days were the ones when her face brightened when I walked in. When she'd leap up and hug me, and ask what adventure we were going to have.

So when I pull up to the house and see the For Sale sign in the front yard, I feel like it's been stuck through my chest.

I march up to the front door and hammer at it with my fist.

"You're selling the house?" I say as soon as Britt opens the door. My voice is trembling. My hands are shaking. I feel weak.

Britt's eyes fill with tears as she nods. "Yes," she says. "Believe me, this wasn't an easy decision. But there are just too many memories here. So Chris and I are going to sell and split the equity. And I'm going to move to a smaller place."

As much as it hurts, I understand why they'd want to do that.

I notice how dark the circles are under her eyes as she reaches for my hands. She's in leggings and a sweatshirt, and her hair is in a high ponytail. She's not even wearing makeup.

"I was going to ask for your help going through Jules's things," she says. "I don't know where to start."

I nod. It'll be hard, but I'd much rather I do it than Britt. She'd probably get rid of the things that were important to Jules without even knowing it.

"Of course," I say. "That's sort of why I asked to come over. I missed her a lot last night, and I wanted to be in a place where I could feel like she was with me."

Britt doesn't seem to think that's weird. She just leads me up the stairs.

The door to Jules's room is closed, and Britt pauses with her hand on the doorknob. "I haven't been in here since the night after she died."

I take a deep breath as she pushes the door open. I wasn't expecting to be saying goodbye to the place where I spent most of my time with Jules, the place that feels like she could walk in at any moment.

"It still smells like her," I say, choking on the words. It smells like vanilla and lavender. And just . . . Jules.

We stand in the doorway, peering into the space that held Jules's life. Her big personality and her hopes and fears. There are pictures on the walls of me and Carter, her dad, even one of her and Britt. Menus from her favorite restaurants are pinned to the corkboard behind her desk, which is stacked with cookbooks.

The white Christmas lights she hung above her bed are still lit. The bathroom door is open, as if she might just be in there. Her bed isn't made. Her laundry is still overflowing.

Time stood still in here for the last four months.

"Do you want me to give you some time?" Britt asks. "We don't have to go through her things today, but if there's anything you want to keep, feel free."

I nod. "Okay," I say. "Thanks."

Britt closes the door behind her. I sit down on the unmade bed, running my hands across the lumps in the comforter.

"Hey, Jules," I say. "I miss you."

I can almost hear her in my head saying "But I'm right here!"

"I went to prom last night," I tell her. "I know, we said we weren't going to, but it was actually really fun. Though not as much fun as staying home and eating snacks on the couch with you ever was."

I'm beating around the bush.

"I also kissed Carter," I admit. "Though maybe you already know about that."

I kick off my shoes and lie back against her pillows, then pull the comforter up to my chin. When I slept over, we shared this bed and I'd often wake up to Jules being the big spoon to my little. One of her legs would be thrown over mine, her arm squeezing my middle like I was a body pillow. I'd have to untangle myself just to get up and use the bathroom. And somehow that never woke her. I'd come back and find her exactly where I left her.

I snuggle deeper under the covers, inhaling her familiar smell.

"I guess I'm asking your permission," I say into the comforter. "Not about Carter. I think you'd give us your blessing. I hope you would . . ."

I really do think she would. She loved us both. And we're both the same kind of broken now. Maybe we can help heal each other.

"But about this podcast Adriana and I want to make," I say. "I don't want you to feel like I'm exploiting you. I just want to talk about how amazing you were. And maybe share a recipe of yours. Probably the one for chicken Provençal."

I pause, as though she'll start telling me how much she loves olives. If she were here, she would.

"I don't know if this is what you'd want, but I think I need to do it," I tell her. "I need this record of who you were. Not who you were as Britt Monaghan's creation, not through her lens, but as my best friend and Carter's girl-friend and your dad's child. And Britt's too."

I hope I'll listen to the podcast when I'm missing her and feeling sad and I will remember all the things we loved about her. All the things that made Jules who she was.

I roll onto my stomach and bury my face in her pillow.

"I'm sorry we fought," I say, my voice cracking and muffled. My tears soak her pillowcase, but I don't care. "I'm so sorry."

There's no magical moment when I feel like Jules is there, or that she's forgiven me. But after a few minutes, I roll back onto my side and stare out into the room. My eyes land on her desk again. The photo of us that her mom took when we were at field hockey camp is sticking out from the pages of one of her cookbooks.

I swing my legs over the bed and walk over, then open it up to the recipe she was marking. It's a recipe for enchi-ladas made with pulled pork and pineapple, with green chile sauce. And in pencil next to it, she'd written, "Nat's bday?"

My birthday is next month. She'd been planning to be alive for it. She was going to cook. And she was going to make a recipe that she knew I'd love but that she probably wouldn't.

I stack the book, with the photo, back on the desk. Then I pull out my phone and start taking pictures of everything in the room. I want to remember it just how Jules left it. Dirty laundry and all.

———

"Hey, Britt?" I call as I walk down the stairs a half hour later.

She meets me in the front hallway. "What's up?" she asks.

I show her the things I'm planning to take—just a few cookbooks and some photos, for now—and tell her I'll come back the next weekend to help her go through the rest.

"I also wanted to ask you something," I say. "I'm starting a new podcast with my friend, and it's going to be about people who died too young. I want the first episode to be about Jules."

Britt brings her fingers to her open mouth. "Oh, honey, that's really sweet," she says.

"I wanted you to know, and I thought maybe you could do an interview with us for the podcast. I'd like to ask Chris too."

She gives me a tight smile. "I'm sure he'd love to talk about Jules," she says. Then she pauses, looking away. "Did you read my book, by any chance?"

I nod. "I did. I finished it the night you sent it to me, and I keep trying to figure out what to say about it, but all I've come up with is 'wow.' "

Britt's shoulders shake as she starts to cry.

"Thank you," she says after a minute, drying her eyes on the sleeve of her sweatshirt. "I really needed to hear that."

"I'd like to send you an email with some notes though, if that's okay?" I say. "Just a few things that I remember differently. It might help to have a different perspective. Something closer to Jules's."

Britt nods. "That would be great," she says. "I could definitely use some perspective."

---

I save my tears until I'm back in the car. But these aren't the sobbing, heaving, snotty kind of tears. It's more of a gentle release. Because it was good to feel near Jules again. And because it was hard, but not as hard as I expected.

I know there's never going to be anything that makes Jules's death feel okay. No religion, no relationship, no amount of mediums or meditation will help. Not even pastries, as Jules would have said. It will always hurt. But sometimes, it hurts less. And sometimes, it even feels bearable.

For now, that's the best I can hope for.

From: NatNagler@gmail.com

To: Britt@mindingherbusiness.com

Subject: Your Book

Hi Britt,

As I told you, I loved the book. I actually think Jules would too.

But there are a couple of things that you missed the mark on, and I made notes when I thought you were letting yourself off too easy. I even included my own memories of certain events you wrote about in your old columns or on Instagram that I think you owe to Jules to revisit. But I know this must have been an incredibly hard book to write. You laid yourself bare and threw yourself on the mercy of the internet. You were raw and honest, painfully so sometimes, and I know admitting all of those things— even to yourself—must have hurt.

I do think Jules would be proud of you. And she didn't hate you. At least not always. She wanted nothing more than for you to love her. The real Jules, not the Jules you imagined she could be or should be. She was never going to be that Jules.

I know that you know that now.

I don't know if I can ever truly forgive you, if I'm being honest. I will always blame you for Jules's death. But I'll always blame myself too. And Carter. And Chris. We all played a role.

But it's important for us to understand that none of us is truly to blame. I know now, as do you, that mental illness isn't a problem that can be solved with one solution. Jules was in pain, more so than she ever let on, and she did the only thing she could think of to make the pain stop.

But I believe that she's still with us, and I believe she's forgiven us. And I believe we will forgive her. And that I will see her again. And so will you.

In the meantime, please keep in touch. I lost one mom already and as angry as you made me sometimes, I still loved having you as a surrogate. So I'd like to keep you in my life, if you're open to it.

With love,
Nat

Attachment: Minding Her Business book.doc

# MENTAL HEALTH RESOURCES

If you're struggling with your mental health and need someone to talk to, you are not alone. I know it may feel that way. I know life may feel impossible sometimes. But you will not always feel this way and there is help in the meantime. Tell someone about how you're feeling if you feel safe doing so, find a therapist and/or psychiatrist who you can talk to regularly, or call or text one of the resources below.

**National Suicide Prevention Line:** text or call 988, 988lifeline.org

**Crisis Text Line:** text HOME to 741741, crisistextline.org

**The Jed Foundation:** to learn how to talk about your mental health, visit jedfoundation.org

**Teen Line:** call 800-852-8336 (from 6 p.m. to 10 p.m. PST) or text TEEN to 839-863, teenline.org

**National Eating Disorder Association:** call 800-931-2237, nationaleatingdisorders.org

**The Trevor Project (for LGBTQ Youth):** call 866-488-7386, or text START to 678-678, thetrevorproject.org

And if you're worried about someone who's struggling, let them know that you are a person they can talk to, but also ask how they're doing. And then keep asking.

# ACKNOWLEDGMENTS

When my husband Karl died two months into the pandemic, my world fell silent. He had this deep, booming voice that fascinated babies and frightened the elderly, and I couldn't imagine never hearing it again.

I desperately needed something to keep my brain occupied. I was spending an unhealthy amount of time crying on the floor of my apartment and I had no motivation to get up. I needed to write about grief, but I couldn't yet write about Karl. So at the depths of my sadness, I returned to the wispy threads of this book that I'd begun almost a year earlier. And as I dove into Natalie's grief with her, I sprinkled pieces of my shattered heart throughout her story. I grieved for Jules alongside her. I cried her every tear.

I used to apologize to Karl for being broken. I've spent a lifetime hating myself, just like Jules. I have major depressive disorder and I've been a self-harmer. I've had suicidal ideations since I was a teenager. And sometimes I feel even more broken now than I ever did when Karl was alive. But I've also learned that I'm not as fragile as I thought. I didn't shut down or kill myself, even when I wanted to. Even when I got dangerously close. Instead, I kept getting out of bed (or off the floor). I talked to my friends and family about how I was feeling. I talked to my therapist and worked with my psychiatrist to change my medications. And I poured my grief into this novel.

This book broke me and put me back together, stitched up my broken heart and tore it back open. But it was a healing experience when I needed it most.

But I didn't do any of this alone.

I owe each of my friends and family a pile of snuggly puppies, but instead, they get their name in this book. It's not really a fair trade.

Mom, thank you for teaching me how to write and making me feel safe to embrace my weirdness by embracing yours. You are the opposite of Britt, I promise. And Dad, thank you for being the best editor, storyteller, and taste test organizer. You deserve that Ferrari.

To my sister, Anna, thank you for always making me laugh when I'm crying, even when I'm being unreasonable. You deserve a Ferrari too. And Steven, thanks for always calling when I don't even know I need to talk. You're the brother I never knew I wanted.

Aunt T, Aunt Jane, Uncle Maury, Della, Andrew, Rob, and Robyn—thank you for loving me and for being so easy to love back. If I wrote all the amazing things that I think about you, this would be the length of another book.

Betty and Al, there aren't enough words to say how happy I am to have you in my life. Karl may have brought us together, but we're family now, so you're stuck with me.

To Jamie Pacton, Ksenia Winnicki, Meredith Bracco, Kara O'Donnell, Erin Hogan, Alex Bracken, Susan Dennard, Liza Weimer, Lily McCrea, Sean McCrea, Jill Bendonis, Jeff Bradford, Justin Asher, Nicole Jefferson Asher, and Matt Mendez: thank you for being amazing friends who support me even when I'm maybe the worst communicator in history. Thank you for continuing to reach out, for holding my hand (even if virtually), and for loving me. I would be a puddle without you.

To my agent Stephen Barbara, as always, thank you for helping me tell my sad stories. I couldn't do any of this without you.

To Sarah Shumway: thank you for believing in this book, for loving my sad girls, and for seeing this story in a way that I couldn't. To the team at Bloomsbury: Kei Nakatsuka, Hannah Rivera, Oona Patrick, Elizabeth Degenhard, Katharine Wiencke, Laura Phillips, Jeanette Levy, Donna Mark, Nicholas Church, Lex Higbee, Ariana Abad, Erica Barmash, Lily Yengle, Beth Eller, Kathleen Morandini, Alona Fryman, Erica Chan, Jo Forshaw, and Chelsea Graham, thank you for all the hard work you do. As you know, I understand exactly what it takes to make a book, so to have this one in your hands means the world to me.

And thank you, reader. I know this book wasn't easy, but I'm so grateful that you read Jules's and Nat's story. If you, like Jules, are hurting more than you can bear, I beg you to seek help. If you are having suicidal thoughts, tell someone you trust. This sadness, this heartbreak, this loneliness, this anger—it does not last forever. There is so much more you have left to do and the world needs you in it.